The Changes Cascade

Evans took a deep breath. "Senior Tech McHugh is missing. I made sure to investigate before I brought this to you, ma'am."

"You're forgetting the geo-sensor." Sue tapped the tiny bump hidden in the hair above her right ear. "Mr. McHugh would not simply disappear, even if he *could*."

"The tracking screen was the first thing I checked. Pull it up if you could, please, and we'll make sure."

"One missing," she whispered. "Even if he were dead..."

She switched over to the report on McHugh, and a deeper chill ran through her. The yellow of Invalid flashed behind his name.

Not one other person showed that impossible status.

Restricted Species

"The freighters won't bring any food with them," Jim said. "Even if we warn them, they can't detour to another supply planet."

Rob's face was pale. "There aren't any close by."

"Not that they could re-route to." Jim scrubbed his face. "We won't actually starve to death. At least I don't think so. But with a year or more before we get a good harvest, we'll have a planet full of miserable cadets and furious miners on our hands."

He knew all too well how shortages and hardships they weren't prepared for could turn a difficult situation into a nasty one.

The Becalmed

"II don't think it's trauma," Luis said, "or disease. I don't believe this is contagious at all. What do you think is going on?"

Tears stood in Willis's eyes. "Some of us are afraid it's some kind of poison we're passing along to our children."

"I can't rule anything out yet," Luis said. "But your medical center here has tested for everything we know of, and off-world facilities have too. Nothing seems out of line with your bodies. Nothing seems to accumulate or get depleted over time."

"Except our kids' feelings," Myrtle said. She didn't look sad. She looked furious. "That's depleting, more and more every year."

To Walker

A fellow Science, Science Fiction, and Space Opera Fan
And my favorite Star Wars date

DISPATCHES FROM THE GALAXY

A SPACE OPERA NOVELLA TRIO

KARI KILGORE

SPIRAL PUBLISHING, LTD.

CONTENTS

A CHILDHOOD MADE FOR SPACE OPERA

Like many people who grew up in the 1970s and 80s, my childhood was steeped in Science Fiction.

I'm not sure how old I was when I first encountered a rerun of *Lost in Space* on television at a friend's house. I know it was long enough ago that adjusting the spindly metal antenna on top of the set was still an option. I couldn't tell you what season the episode was part of, even though season one was the only one filmed in black and white.

I was young enough that the television *itself* may have been a black and white model.

Star Trek entered my consciousness before I started first grade. My signpost for that is I remember seeing the cartoon during its first run, and it ended in 1975. I watched the cartoon because I already loved the series.

From that point on, the 1970s provided a feast for kids who were thrilled by the idea of getting *out there* or contemplating what the future might bring. *Space: 1999* also came along in 1975, and I clearly remember seeing *Logan's Run* from the balcony of a theater in 1976. I enjoyed the later TV series as a kid, but I somehow doubt it would hold up as well as the movie does for me.

Of course 1977 looms large in the minds of many Science

Fiction fans because of the summer of *Star Wars*. I'm grateful to remember exactly how it felt to see it on the big screen for the first time along with millions of others.

But almost as large in my memory is getting to go on an exclusive mommy/daughter date to see *Close Encounters of the Third Kind* that same winter. A story much closer to home that promised a grand adventure for the imagination.

The brief run of *Battlestar Galactica* starting in 1978 delighted me so much that I taught my Merlin to play the theme song. If you're younger than Generation X, you may quite reasonably have no idea what a Merlin was.

They were incredibly cool. Trust me.

The last big Science Fiction event of the decade for me was *Buck Rogers in the 25th Century*, which my whole family saw at the drive-in, then continued to watch when it made the move to television.

(Alas, I was a bit too young to see *Alien* in first run despite seeing quite a few movies before my time. And while I saw *Flash Gordon* several times in the theater and love its campy joy to this day, it doesn't quite fit in with the Science Fiction I'm talking about.)

Watching as a family was one of the best things about Science Fiction in my childhood. We watched these movies and shows together most of the time. In case you're quite a bit younger than I am, that was more important than you might realize.

Many homes way back then only had one television, and odds were high any secondary sets were tiny and often black and white.

Watching these movies and shows as a family also kept me from developing any sense of it being strange or odd that I so loved to escape the bounds of Earth and our solar system.

Carl Sagan's wonderful *Cosmos: A Personal Voyage* series in 1980 got me focused on the science side while giving me a strong foundation to branch out into writing fiction.

Add in the fact that my parents let me stay up late to watch incredible video footage from Mars, Jupiter, and Saturn, and I was hooked on science and Science Fiction for life.

I was an avid reader of Science Fiction and science writing at the same time, into the 1980s, and still today. But that's a much larger discussion for another day.

While there are many subgenres of Science Fiction (and they change frequently), my favorite is the subject of this collection.

Space Opera.

Some compare Space Opera to highly dramatic stage operas or long-running daytime soap operas, and that's fine by me. I'm the last person you'd see get into any sort of genre argument. Primarily because I mix and match and cross and smash genres with complete delight and abandon.

My own definition of Space Opera is it must indeed be set in space, whether on a ship or on another planet, and it's definitely not Hard Science Fiction. You won't find long, technical discussions of a ship's drive systems or the detailed development of hypersleep pods in these stories. Perhaps in other stories someday, but not these.

I do at least pay attention to the major laws of physics and such, though I might then proceed to bend or break them.

What I hope you'll find in my Space Opera is a sense of adventure. Of reaching beyond our current limitations of Earth and even our solar system.

Hopefully beyond some of the other limitations that plague humanity.

In *The Changes Cascade*, we join one of the initial forays into the galaxy. All onboard the remarkable feat of engineering that is *Expedition Mission Bellagos* goes smoothly several years into their generational journey.

Until an all too familiar problem from our current high-tech lives throws everything into chaos.

Restricted Species visits Mossera 4, a thriving colony planet established to provide food and recreation for a vital mining operation on a nearby planet. A peaceful, calm existence, even with groups of inexperienced, green cadets arriving to learn the fine art and science of farming so far from Earth.

Then the failure of the dependable pollinator drones threatens not only the miners, but everyone who works to keep them fed and happy.

And finally, *The Becalmed* joins a years-long mission to Bitanthra: the most important planet in the galaxy. Without the vital Bitan that makes faster-than-light communications possible, the sprawling network of human colonies would face isolation and possible collapse.

Solving a mysterious problem with the human colony on Bitanthra is their only chance of survival.

I didn't write these stories to be connected parts of the same fictional story universe, but I definitely see how they could be. Each and every one is brimming with ideas I hope to explore in future fictional adventures.

And even more, I see how the seed of each of these stories took root during those heady years of my 1970s childhood.

That little girl who so happily enjoyed escaping into the future and into space would have enjoyed every one.

I hope you do, too.

KARI KILGORE

THE CHANGES CASCADE

*To all of my fellow IT folks,
past, present, and recovering.*

*The world changes,
but IT challenges remain the same.*

Chapter 1

Systems and Security Chief Sue Warrell watched the main security console, endless alerts and questions and worries running across the screen and through her mind. The command pod was small, only five paces across with dark gray curved walls and ceiling, but she loved the secure, comfortable feel of the space.

The chilly temperatures required for the thousands of comps that kept the ship running were a bonus to what she called her high metabolism.

Here more than anywhere else in the vast, interconnected series of living pods, production pods, and mechanical pods that made up *Expedition Mission Bellagos*, Sue felt at peace.

But today her normally calm and sedate console flashed orange and yellow rather than her beloved green. She was surprised and strangely irritated that not a single one of them advanced into the red of a confirmed failure.

The problem, the worst one in her long career in interstellar security, wasn't anything as dramatic as a debris strike, onboard systems failure, or a careless adjustment by one of the thousands of crewmembers.

Sue had been through more variations of those disasters than she cared to count, if she had the spare brainpower for counting. She was an expert at pinpointing, solving, and figuring out how to prevent bad choices and bad reactions, or she never would have beaten out thousands of other applicants for this multi-generational mission.

Nothing in her training or experience or her vivid imagination had prepared her for a nightmare straight out of the infancy of the digital age, one only Sue's youthful obsession with tech history gave her the means to recognize.

A corrupted systems upgrade from Earth HQ had infested the vessel's operations, interrupting one function after another before anyone realized what was happening. Since a neuro-alarm jarred her out of the hectic routine of getting ready for the supposedly routine update three days ago, Sue and nearly everyone else on board had been on emergency response status.

The nearly two-day-cycle message transit time between *Bellagos* and Earth HQ wasn't helping. Sue had sent the alert immediately, but she had no control over sheer distance and time. And she didn't know the massive software packages nearly as well as she knew the systems that depended on them

Rolling everything back without knowing more—and without assistance from HQ—could make bad enough trouble even worse.

She leaned back, the chair adjusting to her new posture with a faint sigh, and clenched her hands into fists to relieve the stress of hours of non-stop motion over the touch screens. Bio-engineers had perfected the nutrients and stimulants for sleepless days many years ago, ushering in a new age of technological advancement along with chronic overwork. The stims were safe enough if you didn't push past more than a week with no sleep, though Sue had never gotten used to the bitter, metallic taste and low ringing in her ears that went along with them.

She'd hacked the override on the audible alarms that made the ringing worse years ago, and she blessed that bit of rule breaking if no other.

Unfortunately all the hydro-showers in the galaxy wouldn't keep the oily stink of stress sweat from building up again. Not until she got some real sleep.

Stims aside, her body reacted to the strain of hours of tapping each orange alert into Investigate status, dispatching someone to the affected sector, and shifting the alert into the yellow of Invalid. Sometimes multiple times on the same blasted alert, and still no reds of confirmed trouble. Noting the fakes on her touch tablet slowed her down too much.

For the last several hours, she'd been relying on her brain's built-in ability to notice details and understand patterns.

Sue leaned forward, stretching her fingers against her thighs as the chair shifted her into a new angle. She was moving to tap eleven alerts into Invalid status when a piercing alarm broke through her silence hacks. The bass entrance request bong for the door behind her sounded at the same time. Her skull and all of her bones echoed the wretched noise.

"Blast these damn overrides!"

Sue pivoted to the right to slap the door status to Unlocked, then slid all ten fingers upward on the touchscreen to bring up the virtual keyboard. Before she could start typing, the door hissed open.

"What is it?" Sue said, not turning around. "I ordered Emergency Response Status hours ago, meaning no interruption. It better be good."

"Ma'am, I am so sorry to intrude," a low voice said.

Sue continued to type, growing more desperate to silence that screeching alarm by the millisecond.

Younger. Male. Odd musical accent, likely the southeastern sector of United North America.

Respectful, but brave enough to face her temper during a mess like this.

"What is it, Mr. Evans?"

The alarm stopped, and Sue let out a breath and shifted her knotted shoulders. She turned to face Security Tech Brandon Evans. He was tall enough to have to hunch a bit to keep more than his thick brown hair from brushing the ceiling, and he was wringing his hands. She'd never known Evans to be the nervous type.

That's when unease started gnawing around the stress in Sue's belly.

"We've had a problem, ma'am, one I can't leave to anyone else but you."

"It can't possibly be more of a problem than this." Sue waved an aching hand at the console as another eight lights shifted from green to orange.

"Well, I'm sorry, Chief, but it is." Evans took a deep breath. "Senior Tech McHugh is missing."

"What the hell do you mean, missing? In case you've forgotten, this is a deep space vessel, Evans. No one can get in or out."

The gnawing warmed up, much like the lumbar stress relief protocols of her chair kneading against her lower back.

"I understand, ma'am. I made sure to investigate before I brought this to you. Just like you taught us."

"I also taught you about the geo-sensor, didn't I?" Sue tapped the tiny bump hidden in the hair above her right ear even as the gnawing in her belly picked up speed. "Mr. McHugh is an experienced member of our crew. He would not simply disappear, even if he *could*."

"Yes, ma'am, the tracking screen was the first thing I checked after his son reported him missing. Pull it up if you could, please, and we'll make sure."

Sue pushed off with her foot, the numbness spreading through her body keeping her from using the right amount of force. The chair compensated and brought her in front of the ship status console. After three shaky tries, she brought up the tracking screen.

Her eyes darted to the crew count, and her whole body flashed hot, then cold and clammy.

"Eight thousand seven hundred fifty-three," she whispered. "That can't be right. Even if he were dead…"

She switched over to the specific report on McHugh, and a deeper chill ran through her.

The yellow of Invalid flashed behind his name.

Not the normal green that every single other person showed, or the sad black of the deceased that Sue hadn't yet had to deal with on *Bellagos*.

Not one other crewmember showed that impossible status.

"No one has seen him for more than twelve hours," Evans said, wringing his hands again. "I knew you'd want me to check with you first, Chief."

Sue stared at the screen, re-reading that impossible number. She didn't have to count to know one-third of the systems were now in Invalid, with another quarter still in Alert and under investigation.

She also didn't need any procedures training to realize she could not possibly deal with one more emergency.

The raging fire in her gut told her that, impossible or not, another had landed in her lap.

"I tried to replay his location for the last day cycle," Evans said. "Observation recordings, too. Neither system is online."

"Along with half the systems in this slow-motion disaster." A quick glance confirmed the whole recording suite was locked in Invalid mode. "Non-essential systems my ass. The data should still be there, but we can't get at it until I clear everything else."

"Are we any closer to bringing everything offline for a reset, ma'am?"

"Not until we hear back from Earth HQ and the Great Update Disaster stops knocking things offline at random. Can't take the chance of missing a real alarm or making everything worse trying to fix it."

Sue groaned, rubbing her face. "Okay, Evans, you did the right thing. You're taking lead on this since you obviously know how easily a panic can spread with everyone on edge. Let me see if I can get ahead of this. Bring his son in for a talk. Quietly."

Chapter 2

By the time Evans made it back an hour later, Sue and her over-worked crew had wrangled all the remaining false alarms down to Invalid status. Nothing new had tripped over for half an hour. As long as she ignored the maddening clumps of yellow across all sectors of her console, she could tell herself things were under control.

A hearty swallow of a ginger-laced calming infusion she and everyone else involved in this update disaster carried constantly had settled her belly to a reasonable level of discomfort.

At least this time, Evans had the decency—or self-preservation instinct—to use a text alert to get her to open the door rather than the skull-splitting alarm.

Sue blinked, ignoring what felt like grit in her eyes, when she saw McHugh's son huddled behind the lanky Evans. The boy was years younger than she'd thought, probably not yet out of his first decade. His rumpled dark green pants and tunic showed no signs of rank or assignment, only his name on his chest just under his left shoulder. He had McHugh's wavy brown hair and bright blue eyes, but he was barely waist-high to Evans.

Eyes obviously red and swollen from crying, not from being awake for days like Sue's.

"This is Liam McHugh." Evans stepped to the side, but he didn't push the boy forward. "He reported his father missing."

Sue resisted a strong urge to bark orders at Evans, or maybe to get up and storm out herself.

Anything to avoid focusing on the kid's frightened and hopeful face.

"Thank you for letting us know, Liam." She leaned forward, deciding not to unfold herself from the chair just yet. Liam looked like he'd bolt at one sharp noise. After hours of sitting, she'd grunt loud enough to scare him *and* Evans. "You were born on board *Bellagos?*"

Liam stepped forward, both fists clenched against his skinny thighs. He took a couple of shaky breaths before he met Sue's gaze.

"Yes ma'am, I was."

"So you know how the ship works," Sue said. "Your father can't have gone far, and he has to be on board somewhere. We'll get this figured out. Is your mother off shift yet?"

Too late, Sue noticed Evans's wide eyes and shake of his head.

"My birth-mother lives in another pod, ma'am." Liam's face turned red, but he didn't look away from Sue. "They weren't bonded. Only assigned to each other until I was born."

Sue had heard of such arrangements, one of many ways humans dealt with generations spent on board a massive, sprawling ship in deep space.

In love or not, the species had to continue.

She wondered sometimes if assigned mating wasn't easier than trying to manage a bonded relationship long enough to have children, much less raise them.

Most of the time, she was thankful to be years past such concerns.

"Don't worry, Liam, we'll find you somewhere to stay for now. Or someone to stay with you. Did your father say anything about where he'd be? What he was going to be doing today?"

Liam kicked his soft boots against the gray carpeted floor.

"It's his leisure day. Or at least it was." Liam held his breath for a second, then went on in a rush. "But he never did come home last night, ma'am. I thought he was just working late, so I went to sleep. He wasn't there this morning, either. He goes out after his shift to get supplies sometimes, so he doesn't have to leave our pod early on his leisure day. Then today we were going to...I don't know. Whatever I came up with."

Sue tried not to scowl, but she knew she sucked at keeping her feelings to herself. Especially when she was this strung out.

Of course McHugh was on a leisure day. Even during an emergency, the crew took their regulation time off if they possibly could. At least they were supposed to, not following Sue's rotten example. McHugh had missed enough of his leisure days that this one was mandatory, no matter how many lights flashed orange and yellow and thankfully not red under Sue's fingers.

If McHugh had been on duty, she would have had him racing around with everyone else verifying these damn false alarms. She hadn't seen him all day.

And if McHugh had been on duty, missing his much-needed leisure day or not, this frightened boy would know where his father was.

"Good, we can start with that." Sue couldn't stop herself from glancing at the console. Steady for the moment. "Evans, why don't the two of you figure out what supplies McHugh might have been after? What he and Liam were due in the food rotation. We can go from there. Do you need anything right now, Liam? Anything we can get you?"

Liam pressed his lips together until they turned white, but that didn't stop his chin from trembling.

"We were...we always get frozen chocolate, ma'am. On my dad's leisure days. It's his favorite."

"I'll make sure there's some waiting, then," Sue said. "For when he's back with you."

Evans nodded, and she knew he hadn't missed the first clue. The tropical pod on the far edge of *Bellagos*, where the high humidity, temperature, and light wouldn't disturb any other growing pod or lifepod.

The only source for real chocolate on board.

The surrounding pods grew the best ingredients for frozen confections, a staple of human diets even light years away from Earth. Herbs and spices, roots and nuts for smooth, sweet flavors. Every kind of fruit they could manage to bring along did double duty.

Feeding the colonists on the way to seeding the colony.

Sue's overheated brain brought the pathetic contents of her own food stores forward, the lack of any kind of stress-relieving high-calorie treat flashing as bright as her consoles. When she thought back to the last time she'd remembered to eat, she realized that might account for part of her unruly belly.

"Know what?" she said. "If you can hang on for a few minutes, I'll call in my second-in-command. I'm long overdue for a break, and I'm out of just about everything that's fun to eat myself. How about if we talk while we walk over there together?"

Chapter 3

Tima Chou, Sue's second, had been all too happy to step in for as long as she was needed despite her own ongoing efforts to quiet the emergency. Unlike Sue, Tima's short black hair was gleaming and perfectly styled against her head, her uniform clean and unwrinkled. Her second-in-command had shown up so fast Sue wondered if she'd been hovering, waiting for this chance to prove herself in a difficult situation.

Much like Sue had been decades ago when she'd first started getting these opportunities for herself.

Sue did her best to hide her watering eyes from Evans and Liam as they stepped into the bright transit corridors. The curving walls and ceilings were wide enough to let several people walk by in different directions, with the source of that light invisible to anyone who hadn't engineered it.

Same with the source of fresh, almost sweet-smelling air, as if a cleansing rainstorm had recently passed through *Bellagos* unnoticed.

Right now the corridors were awash in the warm yellow of the Earth sun in the early morning hours, the cycle still matching the planet they were leaving farther behind with each passing second. People even picked up a healthy amount of Vitamin D from exposure, something Sue suspected she was lacking, as usual.

As *Bellagos* reached the halfway point on the decades-long journey from Earth to Junos 7, the light cycle would begin the shift to the longer, dimmer day on their new home.

Another lack made itself known in her stiff legs and back. She managed not to walk hunched over, forcing herself into a relatively normal healthy stride to keep up with Evans and Liam. Still, every step, even on the soft, resilient brown surface of the corridor, highlighted how much she'd been working over the past few days.

Well, Sue could be honest with herself even if she ignored both her human and electronic physical monitors' scolding. She'd underworked her body as badly as she'd overworked her mind, fighting that damn corrupted update from Earth HQ with no end in sight.

She hoped her optimism in leaving wouldn't turn out to be misplaced. The slowdown in systems tripping into Alert still held steady, so walking away for a bit shouldn't be a problem. Sue fought to keep her mind off how many of Invalids would await her attention when they returned.

This little boy needed his father, who most certainly should not be in Invalid status.

And Sue desperately did *not* need a mystery disappearance onboard.

She kept half an ear on Evans talking to Liam, the tech's slow, musical drawl only occasionally interrupted by the boy's higher voice. She knew without asking that Evans was recording the conversation like *Bellagos* normally tracked all crew movements, and making mental notes to himself about who else they could assign to search for the missing Mr. McHugh.

A fragment of conversation drifted back to her, mainly because both Liam and then Evans glanced over their shoulders at her. "…short cut, but not right now."

Evans grinned at Sue with a brief shake of his head. She snorted.

If anyone on her security crew could calm Liam down enough to get him to help the investigation, her bet was on Evans.

The thought of a shortcut was anything but calming. *Bellagos* was confusing enough to navigate through official pathways with lighting and signs.

As far as Sue was concerned, getting off the normal paths and into the sections rarely used for anything but maintenance was a fool's game.

A handful of people joined them in the corridor, with only a few jogging in the center lane reserved for them. Not nearly the crowd that would surge out of the various pods at the end of the typical duty cycle for an evening stroll.

Even when given total flexibility in their waking, sleeping, and working hours, a remarkable number of humans went for the standard.

Liam's voice, raised in childlike excitement, caught all of Sue's attention.

"The forest pods are my favorite. They smell like *everything*, and the breeze is a lot stronger. My dad said…" He paused, taking a deep breath. "They say some places on Earth still have forests big enough you can walk across them for days."

"I've seen it myself," Evans said. "Back in the Georgia Zone where I was born. Used to be more city than forest, but they've fixed it all back up now that so many humans are moving off-planet. You could walk for days until you get clear to the ocean."

"The ocean," Liam whispered. "I just can't imagine all that water."

Sue nodded. "That's where I was born. Not in the Georgia Zone, but farther north in the Commonwealth Zone. The water goes on forever it seems, so far you can't see the end of it. Has waves in it, too."

"Like the ones I make when I get to go to the swimming pool?"

"Sure, kind of like that," Evans said, smiling at Sue. "But these move all by themselves without a person or a machine making them. Tides, they're called. The Moon makes them when it goes around and around the Earth."

Liam sighed. "I wish I could have seen the Moon. With my own eyes, on Earth, I mean. Video isn't like the real thing."

"No, it's not." Sue wondered, not for the first time, if it wouldn't be better for these kids to be born once they reached Junos 7. Even if it did make crew numbers pretty much impossible to maintain. "But Junos 7 has three moons, and you'll see those."

The boy shrugged. Sue turned her head so he wouldn't see her pursing her lips. Liam might see those moons as an old man. Neither she nor the much younger Evans would. McHugh wouldn't have either.

No, McHugh *wouldn't*.

Sue refused to let herself slip into past tense, even in her mind, and even when thinking of their eventual deaths in deep space. Not exactly the conversation to have with a scared little boy who simply wanted his father.

Thankfully Evans rescued her.

"Smell that, Liam? I think that's the tropical pod, don't you?"

Sue lifted her nose when the other two did, and the change itself made her feel better. More alert. Instead of clean but recycled air of the corridors on the huge ship, she smelled green and growing things. Sweet and spicy flowers, pungent soil and fertilizer.

The air felt different as they walked closer, too. Warmer, definitely more humid. Full of life in a way she knew she didn't have the words for, but her nose and body recognized.

As they walked through the next curve, Liam's face lit up in a huge grin.

There were surprisingly few signs in the corridors since everyone alive on most of the ship had seen or helped build and connect each new pod.

But the supply pods were different.

To the right, a bold, black-lettered sign in several primary languages and stylized pictograms declared they would find Tropics and Warm Exotics. To the left, Cold and Frozen Supplies. The two opposite pods might appear to be side by side, but past these few meters of corridor, the pods were separated by the void of deep space.

"Frozen chocolate?" Sue said. "That's your dad's favorite?"

Liam's smile faded, but didn't disappear. "Yeah, it's what he always gets on his leisure day. He says we can't keep it around all the time or he'll eat too much of it."

"I'm the same way with anything cherry flavored," Evans said. "I think I'll get some right now, though."

They stepped inside the open portal door that was wide enough to let the three of them walk through together. No one waited inside the white-walled room except three bored attendants. The walls were livened up by larger-than-life display models of everything in stock, along with Earth photos of winter or the frozen Polar Zones. A row of boxy white chairs lined both walls, ready for the much busier strolling hour this evening.

Thank goodness this room was only a couple of degrees cooler than the rest of *Bellagos* instead of the painful cold of the storage areas.

A young woman with a bouncy brunette ponytail, wearing the pale blue uniform of this zone, brightened when she saw the three of them. Sue thought it was just typical sales behavior—no different here than back on Earth—until the woman focused on the boy.

"Hey there, Liam! Haven't seen you in ages. Where's your dad?"

Chapter 4

Sᴜᴇ ᴅɪᴅɴ'ᴛ ʜᴀᴠᴇ to look to know Evans was making his wide-eyed caution gestures, but he was too late. Liam tried to be brave again, smiling with his chin quivering. He finally leaned forward, holding his belly against the sobs.

"It's okay," Sue said when she saw the woman's stricken face. "You didn't know and we didn't get a chance to warn you."

When Evans touched Liam's shoulder, Liam charged forward for a hug so fast that Evans staggered backward a step. The two of them barely made it to the chairs.

"What happened?" the woman said. Sue finally had a chance to look at her name on the uniform. *Cassie* said. "I didn't mean to upset the poor kid."

Sue shook her head. "*You* didn't upset him. When did you last see Liam and his father?"

The two other attendants wandered over, another young woman and a young man. Cassie turned to them, but they both shook their heads.

"On his last leisure day," she said, frowning. "Seems like that was a long time ago, though. Did he miss some of them?"

Sue closed her eyes, surprised at how hard that guilt hit. She'd never thought twice about forcing McHugh, Evans, or anyone else to miss their leisure days. Probably because it never crossed her mind to worry about missing her own.

"We've been pretty busy in Systems and Security lately. McHugh was fine just over twelve hours ago. Liam wanted some frozen chocolate, and we needed to ask around. Seemed like a good reason to get a bit of exercise."

Cassie glanced at the other two attendants before stepping closer to Sue.

"Is something going on with the ship, Chief? We've been having trouble with our systems here, and suppliers coming in are saying the same thing. Most people are afraid to ask what's wrong. Is *Bellagos* in trouble?"

Sue took a deep breath, wishing she could get a full sleep cycle before she answered Cassie's questions. It would have been tough enough to explain how a crew member could go missing on a ship in deep space. Sue had been too busy and buried in her systems nightmare to realize people onboard outside of Security knew what was happening.

"We're adjusting from a new systems update from Earth HQ," she said, knowing it wouldn't be enough. "A few hiccups, nothing to worry about."

Cassie stared at Sue for a few seconds, then shook her head.

"Nothing to worry about. Sure. Our monitors are glitchy and unreliable, something happened to this poor kid's father, and our suppliers are fighting every bit as hard to keep conditions in their pods stable as we are. Okay then."

She closed her eyes and lowered her head for a few seconds. When she looked back up and smiled—so fast her ponytail bounced again—Sue would have sworn Cassie had rebooted her own internal system.

"What can we get for you? I bet Liam wants frozen chocolate. How about for you and your friend?"

Sue blinked, trying to get her sluggish and yet anxious mind to function. What kind of frozen treat *did* she like?

"Evans likes cherry," she finally managed. "I'm not sure what... can you just mix them? Cherry and chocolate?"

Cassie smiled, and Sue was surprised to see it looked genuine.

"That's my favorite way to do it. Three double scoops, coming right up, Chief."

Sue waited for a second, but all three of the attendants vanished through the door to the freezer compartment. Probably to get away from the crying little boy and the grumpy security chief.

She sat beside Liam, who was now down to sniffing and trying to catch his breath.

"I'm sorry about that," she said. "You okay, Liam?"

He nodded before he spoke.

"I'm okay, ma'am. I just miss my dad. I wish he was here."

Sue sighed, staring at the blue carpet rather than at the little boy. She wished McHugh were here, too.

"Where else do you usually go on leisure days?" she said, turning back to Liam. His eyes were red, but he looked calmer. "Is there anyone who your dad knows that you think we should talk to? Or some kind of supplies you were supposed to go get, after your treat?"

A buzz from her wrist comm had Sue back on her feet in an instant.

Tima, her second, reporting another crew member missing, from a couple of hours after McHugh had disappeared. Flipped over to that disturbing Invalid status.

Crew numbers down to eight thousand seven hundred fifty-two.

She looked up to tell Evans to look for connections—well, to bark orders at him, to be honest—but the words died when she saw the horrified, wide-eyed look on Evans's face.

And the frightened look on Liam's.

"I'm sorry," she said. "Wrist comm startled me."

She forced herself to sit again, but the trembling from a jolt of over-stimulated and under-slept bodily systems had already set in. Sue knotted her fingers together in her lap and concentrated on Liam.

He swallowed hard. The obvious movement in his slender neck might have been funny if Sue hadn't been feeling so guilty.

"We were low on protein," he said in a quiet voice. "The meat kind, not the bean kind. I like the meat kind better."

Sue nodded. "I do, too. I'm probably low on that myself. Maybe we can head over after we finish our treats if you're feeling up to it."

She was thankful Evans didn't get the chance to jump in with one of his Old Earth history tidbits about where meat protein used to come from. Cassie walked out then carrying a platform with three transparent cups, gleaming metal spoons standing straight up in the middle of each. One was full of dark brown frozen chocolate, another with dark red cherry. The third held a striped mixture of red and brown.

Cassie still had her bright customer service smile, but Sue thought her eyes were strained and overly bright.

"Here you go! This should get you fixed right up until you find your dad, Liam."

Sue took her bowl, hoping her smile looked at least a little natural. The surface was the same temperature as the room, not cold like she expected. She held it up to the light. Two layers, with a tiny space for air in between.

"Does everything look okay?" Cassie said, a furrow on her smooth brow.

"It looks great," Sue said. "I was just thinking I'd love to have some of these bowls for my place. Do they work for hot things, too?"

"They work fine for hot," Cassie said. "But there are better designs for that. You're better off picking them up at the supply pods. Ours all have tracking units embedded in them."

Liam nodded, taking a few seconds to finish his huge spoonful.

"Yeah, I know all about that. I accidentally walked out with mine, a long time ago when I was little. Big loud alarms went off."

"That's right," Cassie said. "I remember when that happened. Good thing we're all too old for things like that now."

She smiled again, then turned fast enough that her ponytail whipped out behind her.

Sue finally got a spoonful of her own concoction. Rich dark chocolate and sweet-tart cherry, perfectly balanced. She closed her eyes and sighed, ship and personnel troubles forgotten for one blissful second.

"Good, isn't it?" Evans said. He'd already eaten most of his, and his words sounded like his tongue was half-frozen. It and his lips were dark red. "Everything grown or produced here on *Bellagos*. Nothing dried or frozen from Earth at all now."

"Don't worry about the bowls." Liam's tongue and lips were chocolate brown. "You just leave them on the counter and you won't get in any trouble."

Sue took another huge mouthful. This was nice and all, but she really should check in. Another missing crewmember, no sign of McHugh, and who knows how many more problems from that Earth update.

She abruptly stood and walked toward the exit.

"Chief?" Evans called. "You okay?"

Sue ignored him, pausing for a second before she stepped across the threshold. She didn't realize how much she'd tensed up for Liam's big loud alarms.

Nothing happened.

She took several steps just to be sure, but still.

Silence.

Her mind was weary and overstressed, but Sue saw the row of orange and yellow alerts back in her command pod clearly before she even pulled out her comm. Not one of them was for the tracking systems on board.

Those were green all across, or they had been when she left Tima in command.

Evans stood at the edge of the pod, managing to look puzzled and worried at the same time. Liam waited behind him, eyes wide.

"Go on," Sue said. "Try it. Make sure there's not some fluke with mine, or interference from my comm or me."

Evans shrugged and stepped over, and Sue saw his shoulders relax when everything stayed silent. They both turned and waved Liam forward.

The boy stuck his toe over, then slowly held the bowl out. At the continued lack of big loud alarms, he grinned and scooted over to Sue and Evans.

"It's turned off," Liam said, scraping the bottom of his bowl. "We could take all kinds of things with us!"

Sue raised one eyebrow and met Evans's gaze.

"No alarms on the tracking sensors," she said. "They show all green."

"But something's wrong," he said. "Might be time for that reboot."

"And switch out to the old systems if we can force the rollback. Looks like we're about to get in trouble, alarms or not."

They all turned to see Cassie and the other two workers staring at them, arms crossed and nearly identical frowns on their faces.

"We better take these back in," Liam whispered, but he was still smiling. "Or they might not serve us next time."

Chapter 5

A closer read of Tima's message about the new missing crewmember alert had Sue detouring them all away from her command center and back toward the protein pods after all.

"You're sure?" Evans said, trying to keep his voice too low for Liam to hear. "The missing woman was going to the same place McHugh was?"

Sue nodded, smiling when Liam glanced back at them.

"Last time she checked in with her partner, that's where she was headed. Restock on protein. The meat kind."

"And we still can't check video."

"Nope. Not until Earth HQ says I can roll back that update and get us onto a reliable systems suite. Nothing new has gone orange for what, an hour now? We should be able to roll back the second I get the all clear in a few hours."

The protein pods were only one corridor away from the frozen pods, or else Sue would have passed this off to someone else. At least that's what she told herself.

The truth was she felt certain this would turn out to be important. Too important to leave to anyone else, no matter how itchy she got about the botched update and waiting for Earth HQ.

The entrance looked similar to the one they'd just left, with the two protein pods splitting off the main corridor. In this case, the signs showed that the growing pod off to the left held soybeans, peanuts, and even a few species of tree nuts that had been modified to thrive when kept short and compact.

The pod off to the right was just as interesting in the opposite way.

That one was row after row of vats, most of them too regulated and carefully controlled to allow for visitors. A few were maintained out front for educational purposes, so youngsters like Liam could see where their protein came from.

And older crewmembers could be reassured that it no longer came from living creatures somehow confined and hidden away onboard *Bellagos*.

Only the cellular descendants from the original tissue samples taken over a century ago from some of the last farmed cattle, chicken, fish, and other creatures had made this trip.

The pod looked similar to the frozen treat one they'd just left, with bright white walls and photographs of what was available for residents of *Bellagos*. Images of prepared dishes rather than the source of the protein, of course. A row of the educational, smaller versions of the grow tanks lined one wall, their green walls contrasting with the vivid reds, pinks, and whites of the growing protein. The attendants even wore similar cheerful uniforms and friendly smiles.

But Sue saw even more strain and worry behind those smiles than she had with Cassie.

One of them who wasn't smiling stepped forward, a stone-faced gray-haired man about Sue's age. She had her protein and most other supplies delivered when she remembered to get food at all, so she only vaguely recognized him.

Quite handsome, really, if in a mildly intimidating way.

"Chief Warrell. We've been expecting you. Dan Greenwell."

He didn't offer his hand, only stood with his arms crossed.

"Expecting me, huh? Evans, why don't you and Liam go take a look at those tanks?" Sue waited for Evans to nod and for him and

Liam to walk to the farthest tank. "Exactly why were you expecting me?"

Greenwell shrugged, shaking his head.

"Our first contact today was with the young woman's partner, wondering if she'd been here. She hadn't. This was after we've been fighting with our systems and tanks for three solid days. The only way anyone could disappear from *Bellagos* would be some kind of systems error. Thus, we were expecting you."

"Fair enough. Are you familiar with Senior Tech Andy McHugh, or his son Liam?" She jerked her chin at the boy.

"Sure, I know Liam," Greenwell said, nodding. "Haven't seen Andy in here for a while now."

"Not at all over the past couple of days?"

Greenwell raised his dark eyebrows, a sharp contrast to the gray hair.

"No. I keep special orders for him, the best ground beef we produce. Liam loves an Earth-style hamburger. Probably one of the few *Bellagos*-born who even know what that is. Andy hasn't been in for days. Missing too, is he?"

Sue stared up at the ceiling, then down at the soothing blue carpet. She wished she *could* call in a separate Security unit on this and get back to her own domain. She wasn't cut out for this kind of face-to-face work, for deciding in the moment what to tell and what to keep to herself.

In the first decade of this mission, neither she nor anyone else had had any need for more security than what the tracking systems and vids provided.

"Like you said, Mr. Greenwell, no one can actually disappear from the ship. We just need to locate them. You seem to have thought a lot about this. If they never got here when people expected them to, where do you think they might have gotten…dislocated? Any ideas?"

He shook his head slowly, never looking away from Sue's eyes.

"My only idea would be to check the vids. Systems and Security knows where every one of us is at all hours, in case we need help of some kind. That's what all those recordings are *supposed* to be for, right?"

Sue took a deep breath, wishing again for a full sleep cycle. She wasn't yet sure if Mr. Greenwell would prefer to be on her side or not. Either way, he was too quick for her to deal with in her stim-weary state.

Might as well try to sway the balance to her side.

"That is indeed what the recordings are for, Mr. Greenwell. As I'm sure you already suspect, the systems problems are keeping us from accessing those for the moment. May I ask what your background is? What did you do back on Earth?"

He smiled with half his face, as if the other half was unable—or unwilling—to shed the stony expression.

"Have I been a tank wrangler all my life, you mean? No. My family was in that line of work, some of the first to pioneer tank-grown protein back in the old days. I went into the military instead, then law enforcement."

"Systems and Security didn't try to recruit you?"

Dan Greenwell finally smiled all the way. Sue was surprised at how the hard planes and angles of his face were transformed into warm and welcoming by a simple movement of his facial muscles.

"They did. Earth HQ still sends a new and improved offer every few months. They can't quite seem to understand that I did my time and was ready to move on to something else. *Somewhere* else. If I'd wanted to stay in my old line of work, I would have stayed on Old Earth."

Sue laughed at that, doing her best to keep it quiet so Liam wouldn't hear. Greenwell had just about repeated her reasons for joining this mission. She suspected he was another like her, unattached and past the time for adding to the ship's population, and certain to die before they ever reached their destination.

And as unable to resist the adventure as she was.

"I can't argue," she said. "You sound a lot like me. I won't try to recruit you, but I may want to ask you more questions at some point. I spend too much time cooped up in my command pod to know what's going on in people's lives. With your background and training, I'd bet *you* know more than you let on."

Dan tilted his head forward in an oddly old-fashioned half bow, half acknowledgement.

"I admit I pay attention to folks. One of those lifelong habits that was impossible to leave behind. I'll help if I can. Ask anytime. But you know better than I do that nothing's likely to get sorted out until you can get a good look at those recordings."

This time he did hold out his hand, and Sue was surprised at how warm and pleasant it was to touch another person. Especially when Dan Greenwell held on a bit longer than strictly necessary.

She *did* spend too much time isolated in that command pod.

"I'll take you up on that offer, then," Sue said. "We could have some kind of serious issue with the ship itself, doors getting jammed or something like that, but Maintenance isn't reporting anything. I'll admit to you for your ears only that I noticed a sensor anomaly over at the frozen treats pod just now. It could be that simple."

"But the people are actually missing," Dan said. "Like Liam's father. So either we have crewmembers getting trapped by the ship…"

"Or they're getting trapped by other crewmembers. Have you heard any chatter along those lines? Someone upset enough to consider something like this? Someone you felt like you should be paying closer attention to?"

Dan rubbed his chin, watching Liam and Evans.

"For your ears only, right?" He waited for Sue to nod. "We're not the only ones to notice problems with ship systems. That's unsettling the crew more than I'd like. Unsettled people behave in predictable and unpredictable ways. None of them good."

"Understood," Sue said. "Anything before the systems trouble? I don't have suspects before you ask, but I need to know what we may be dealing with."

"I do hear rumblings here and there, but nothing more serious than what young people generally get up to. I'm sure you know the kind. Barely grown up enough to know they're not kids anymore, not quite grown up enough to have any sense."

"I know the type. I distantly remember *being* the type."

"Yeah, me too," Dan said with another of those brilliant smiles. "Dealt with them a lot over the years. No one onboard got my attention enough to report to the good people over at Systems and Security."

"Fair enough," she said. "If memory serves, it's a lot more talk than action. We're planning to reboot and try to bring the recordings up as soon as we can. I'll be in touch."

He flashed that smile again. "Good."

Sue did her best to ignore Evans and his raised eyebrows and grin as they left.

Chapter 6

NONE of the yellow Invalid systems had flashed back over to orange by the time Sue got back to her chilly, cramped command pod. Tima reassured her that no new orange lights had popped up, either.

But Tima's fidgety stance and restless eyes gave the bad news away before she'd finished talking.

Three more crew members had shown up missing. And Invalid.

Eight thousand seven hundred forty-nine, when there should be eight thousand seven hundred fifty-four.

As soon as Tima left, Sue slapped the command override for silence and no interruptions into effect again, relieved a thousand times over that she'd sent Evans off-duty to take Liam home to his own pod for the night-cycle.

A boy that age didn't need to stay alone, or hear the words she muttered as she read the crewmember notes.

Nothing in common in the two men and one woman who had now vanished into thin, cleaned, and re-circulated air. Only that they'd all disappeared during the last twelve hours. And the Invalid status flashing next to their names, along with the others.

Sue leaned forward, letting her command chair carry her the rest of the way. A quick comm to each reporting family member verified what she'd suspected but refused to assume.

All three had been on their way to the protein pod. The meat kind.

She let out one last string of obscenities for the moment. Sure, she'd meant to get back in touch with Dan Greenwell. She'd even been looking forward to it. But not today, barely an hour after she'd met him.

And not with news like this.

News that had her suspecting she needed to *question* him rather than ask him questions.

A scroll and a few taps, and his handsome face filled her view screen. He even smiled.

"Chief Warrell. Glad to see you again, but I'm afraid it can't be good news so quickly."

"No, Mr. Greenwell, it's not. We've had three more reports come in. All missing. All headed your way. I need to ask if any of them actually made it there."

He listened intently as she gave names and descriptions, his brown eyes narrowed in concentration. He leaned to the side for a second, accessing his own systems.

"I don't recall any of them being here over the last few days, and they're not showing up in our records, either."

Sue rubbed her face. "Okay. I'm going to check from here, but do you have any thoughts on what they could have in common? From those stubborn habits of yours? There are five of them now."

"Nothing jumps to mind, no. I'll run their records to make sure."

Sue nodded, thinking of a thousand questions she could ask someone with a career in law enforcement. She was an outstanding troubleshooter, and she knew every single system on this ship inside and out. Hell, she'd installed more than a few of them.

But she had no training and hardly any experience in investigating people.

The mission planners had optimistically assumed demand for such investigations would be low to none with so much surveillance on board.

Surveillance that was still locked out.

"Great," she said. "Thank you. Let me know if you find anything, or think of anything. I'll do the same."

Dan smiled again, and despite her anxiety, Sue smiled back. He only said one word.

"Good."

Sue scrubbed her fingers through her hair, recognizing the start of one of the other annoying side-effects from prolonged use of stims. Her scalp itched horribly, and she knew her back, palms, and toes would be next.

Still, the combination of a walk in the programmed sunlight and a good dose of ice cream had cleared her thinking enough to do something besides fight alert status lights.

She checked the time of her last transmission to Earth HQ. Still half the day cycle before she could expect a reply, and that was assuming they'd replied right away rather than meeting and discussing and wasting time debating every possible action and outcome. Sue had been part of all that and more with this mission's planning and startup, to the point that she'd been tempted to deliberately break the communications systems after launch.

But until now, the Earth HQ updates had made her job and her life easier, every single time. Those programmers—safely on the birthplace of humanity rather than out here expanding its boundaries—had time to analyze and improve the software more than she ever would.

With five crewmembers missing but presumably still alive, she was willing to give HQ that time to respond. Unless the situation here out on the boundary worsened.

She pulled up all five of the missing crew members on her main screen, including Liam McHugh's father.

Not a thing in common, just as she suspected. McHugh in Systems and Security, the others in Physical Maintenance, Medical, Entertainment, and Horticultural. Each a vital department and job in their own way, especially for thousands of humans spending entire lifetimes inside a massive spaceship. All of them from different sections of the living pods.

No reason Sue could see that each of them would turn up missing. No reason *any* of them would.

That sensor in the frozen treats pod was damn strange, too. She couldn't quite put it out of her mind.

Liam's face flashed into her mind, and not the worried or sad version. This one was more like a typical little boy, with a broad smile and sparkling eyes.

He'd been walking with Evans in front of her, crossing the rounded intersections from one pod branch to another. Liam had said something low, clearly meant for Evans and not her.

Something about…a shortcut.

Sue pulled up a map of *Bellagos*, then zoomed in and tapped the home location for each missing person. No pattern there, only scattered random dots. She zoomed out, located the supply pods, and highlighted the protein pods.

Her mind traced the routes like a decision tree in a systems schematic.

Finally, something she could at least investigate.

Chapter 7

BELLAGOS HAD BEEN BUILT in orbit around Earth, with massive sections assembled and hauled into place over several years. Some sections like spokes in a wheel, some long tubes. Others bulky square or rounded shapes that joined the rest together.

Environmental and health engineers had designed corridors that were broad and inviting to connect the main sections of the ship. Like the ones Sue had walked through with Liam and Evans today, they held simulated sunlight and sometimes even birdsongs or breezes.

They were also designed to help crewmembers get a big part of their exercise needs by walking or running from the living pods to work, play, or gather supplies.

Sue kept to the designated corridors like most other crewmembers. Not because of some long-buried desire to follow the rules.

Sue only followed the rules that suited her or the ones that made things easier.

Keeping to the corridors was definitely the latter.

To her, the idea of wandering around in the old junctions—used for construction and maintenance but otherwise empty—held no appeal whatsoever. They were utilitarian to the point of being unpleasant. Bare steel surfaces, lighting either dim or glaring. Not well-ventilated or overly clean, full of the odd creaks and groans of *Bellagos* talking to herself.

Sue hated to admit it, but those echoing, dim spaces went beyond lonely and deserted. They were downright creepy.

But on the tracking displays, she'd noticed several crewmembers passing through those old passageways. Including one that led from several of the living pod wings to the supply wings, cutting off the longer and far more pleasant main corridor.

Was that what happened here?

Had the corrupted systems update turned the shortcuts into the trap Sue had always worried they could be?

She saw Liam and Evans in her mind again, looking back over their shoulders at her and grinning.

Sue sat up, her heart pounding faster than even her overabundance of stims could account for, moving faster than the chair could compensate for. She scrolled through the comm and keyed her emergency code.

"Damnit Evans, report. Report!"

After a couple of minutes of what would be a piercing alarm in a small living pod, Sue ended the comm.

She couldn't remember ever shying away from a report or a survey or facing an angry superior in her entire career. Her whole life, really. She hadn't thought it was in her DNA to put off an unpleasant thing she'd have to face later on.

But Sue's hand shook when she reached toward the ship status console.

Personnel tracking. Crew count.

The already missing had the count down to eight thousand seven hundred forty-nine.

And the current count had it down to eight thousand seven hundred forty-seven.

Sue knew what she would see, but she had to confirm it for herself.

Both Liam and Evans with Invalid yellow flashing under their names.

She jumped so hard the seat jerked and tried to compensate

when an emergency status comm rang through. Sue hit accept without caring who it was for a change.

"Chief Warrell, Dan Greenwell here." His face, back to its usual stony visage, fell into a frown when he saw her. "What's happened? You're paler than you were before."

"We're up to…up to seven missing now, Mr. Greenwell." Sue took a deep breath. "Why don't you tell me why you used emergency status before I say any more? And how the hell you have an emergency status code to begin with."

Dan's face relaxed into a tiny smile with one raised eyebrow.

"Earth HQ pushed it on me, to be honest. Someone there couldn't tolerate such a distinguished and decorated veteran or some such nonsense not having some kind of special privileges. Never used it before. I'd never planned to, either, had to look the code up just now."

"Because…"

"Because the two crewmembers who are supposed to be on shift now haven't reported in. I know, I know, a couple of kids barely an hour late isn't cause to be interrupting you with everything else going on. But you did say to let you know if my stubborn instincts kicked in. They just did."

Sue opened her mouth to ask for names and where the two lived, but a change on the ship status console caught her eye.

"Would those two missing kids happen to be Charlie Haslett and Debora Hahn?"

Dan's face switched to a full-on scowl. Sue knew anyone who'd run across that look in his former military or law enforcement lives would have had good reason to be scared half to death.

"Care to tell me exactly how you knew that? They both live alone, no one to report them missing but me."

"They just switched to Invalid status on my end. Listen, can you meet me now? I need to check something out, and I could use your instincts on this one if you're willing."

"You bet. Just tell me where and when. This horseshit has gone on long enough."

Sue told him the intersection she'd pinpointed earlier, the one between the living pods and his protein supply pod. She wasn't sure whether she liked his decidedly Old Earth swearing or the fierce light in his brown eyes more.

"Got it. Need me to bring anything else?" he said.

"I'm calling in someone from Maintenance and someone from the Security side to meet us. Bring your old habits and we should be just fine."

Sue made one more call before she headed out, and just as she'd hoped, Tima Chou was outside the door before Sue opened it. A crowd of people passed back and forth behind her, strolling and chatting.

A crowd that was only going to get bigger as the evening cycle wore on, and possibly make the number of missing and Invalid bigger, too.

"Chief! There aren't more missing?"

"There are, Tima. I'm heading out to meet Maintenance to see if we can get ahead of this before it gets worse." Sue checked the time on her comm. "We're down to within an hour of the window for hearing back from Earth HQ, assuming they're not hashing this out in an endless bullshit meeting. You prepared for that?"

Tima's restless motion vanished, and she stood at rigid attention.

"You bet I am, Chief. What are your orders?"

"Watch ship status for more..."

Sue stared, eyes unfocused, over-stimmed mind jittering and yelling at her to not walk away. Not yet!

Not until she made the rest of *Bellagos* as safe as she possibly could without the risky reboot.

Tima jumped out of the way as Sue ducked back into her command pod.

She keyed in the emergency ship-wide address code she'd never expected to use.

Anyone who wasn't sound asleep would see the words on all comms and screens, hear her voice on all ship audio systems. Even the ones sleeping would get the recorded alert as soon as they woke.

"This is Systems and Security Chief Warrell. Effective immediately, all crewmember access to unauthorized passageways on *Bellagos* is forbidden until further notice. I say again, all access to unauthorized passageways on *Bellagos* is forbidden. Any attempt to enter these passageways without my direct permission will be punished with confinement to quarters and restriction to basic food rations."

She followed that up by restricting access to all Maintenance areas onboard, again to levels she'd never expected to use. Now only the two Maintenance crewmembers she was meeting were cleared for access. No one else—working in Maintenance and normally cleared—would be able to go in or out without pinging Sue's own wrist comm.

She stepped back out into the corridor, unruly belly knotting as her own voice echoed all around her.

The busy crowd stopped, staring at their wrist comms and each other.

Tima stared wide-eyed at Sue, but she only said one word.

"Understood."

Sue nodded once.

"Honestly, that should do it. Still, watch for crew members to flip to Invalid. I hope not, but humans have been known to do crazier things. Now, if I give the word, are you willing to shut down all systems and reboot? No matter what my status shows, or what you hear from Earth HQ?"

Tima stared up at Sue with unblinking brown eyes. Sue would have sworn the girl—correction, young woman—vibrated with energy and indecision.

Tima was more of a rule-follower than Sue had ever been.

Despite Sue's best efforts to train that out of her.

"Yes, Chief. You're highest on any chain of command out here. Give the word, and it's done."

"Good. If that crew number count changes or you hear from Earth HQ, I want to hear it from you before anyone else. Otherwise, I trust your judgment to act as needed. You should too. Okay. Here's what I'm going to try."

Chapter 8

Sue worked her way through the streams of nervous and chattering walkers, continuing her best efforts not to meet anyone's eyes. Her habit of overwork and basically avoiding people on the few hours she had off was paying off beautifully, with no one recognizing her.

If one person managed to remember her face from some long-ago command list, she knew everyone would swarm her with questions she was in no position to answer. Especially with no sleep and the stim-itch flaring up like mad. It was everything she could do to stop herself from digging at her palms or stopping to scratch her back against the corridor wall.

A faster walk than she thought possible had her leaving the spotless white corridor with light changing to the warm, reddish glow of evening behind. The floor was bare, bone-jarring steel instead of springy carpeting. Rather than curving and welcoming, the walls of this junction met at hard right angles, and the white was more utilitarian, almost grubby.

Sue doubted any of the Health and Morale engineers had given a thought to this space.

Mainly because none of the crew were supposed to *be* here besides Maintenance. And then only if they had to be. People standing beside a rectangular doorway set so flat into the wall that it nearly disappeared let her know she was in the right place.

Jacinda Kim was familiar from Sue's own team. Older and more experienced than Tima, but she stood just as rigidly at attention. Sue hated to admit it, but she was relieved to see Jacinda looked as rumpled and tired as she herself felt, with brown circles under her eyes and curly brown hair flattened on one side.

The Maintenance tech, Martinez according to his uniform, waited beside Jacinda. Like her, his wide, black belt had several storage compartments and pouches, and he carried a metallic fabric bag slung over his shoulder. His gleaming bald head didn't reveal whether he'd recently tried to catch a nap, but his expression was attentive. His green eyes secure and confident.

Exactly what Sue needed.

She turned at the echo of boots on the metal floor and was relived to see Dan Greenwell. He'd shed the white service uniform and wore casual pants and shirt in a muted green that suited him better than she wanted to admit.

"Okay, we're all in place," Sue said into her comm. "Any changes?"

"Two more missing, ma'am," Tima's amplified voice replied. "Nowhere near you, though."

"*Damn* it. Understood. Note their records for my follow-up and stand by."

Sue turned to Martinez. "We need to get into the Maintenance area here. I know people use it as a shortcut, and you know crewmembers are going missing. We need to see if those two things are related."

Martinez scowled for a second, rubbing his smooth head.

"I know I don't have clearance to ask this, Chief Warrell. Like you know you don't have clearance to ask me to let all of you into the Maintenance passages without an emergency, especially after you yourself just locked them down. Does this have to do with the systems trouble since the last Earth HQ update?"

Sue met Dan's smiling eyes for a second before she turned to Martinez.

"One thing I've learned over the last few hours is how much everyone outside of Systems and Security knows about operations I thought were secure. At least when they go wrong. Yes, Martinez. This is related to the bad update, and the reason for the lock-down. I'm trying to keep it from getting worse. Right now you and Jacinda are cleared to access Maintenance areas, but no one else."

Martinez stared into her eyes for several seconds, then shrugged and smiled.

"Good enough for me, as long as you don't put me on those nasty basic food rations."

He waved his wrist-comm across the center of the door, counted to three, then pushed it open.

The air in the little-used passage they stood in wasn't kept as fresh and invigorating as in the main corridors, but Sue and everyone else flinched away from a stale mechanical odor that rushed out of the passage, like overused synthetic lubricants and warm plastics.

"Sorry for the stink," Martinez said. "Normally circulation is better than this, even in maintenance passages."

"Your systems have been Invalid for twenty-eight hours," Sue said, amazed at how the accurate number popped so effortlessly into her mind. "It's happening all over the ship."

Sue started forward, then felt a hand on her shoulder. Jacinda Kim's cheeks were flushed, but she held her head high.

"I'm sorry, Chief. You have good reason to suspect a problem here, and I trust good reason to declare these passageways off-limits. That's why you called me. I'm going in first."

Sue stepped back, waving her arm toward the door.

"You and Martinez be my guests to work that out between you." A tingle in the back of Sue's overworked and under-rested brain made her hold up one hand. "Only far enough for us to close the door, then hold there."

Martinez laughed under his breath, but he smiled at Jacinda.

"The shortcut toward the supply pods is to the right. Watch your heads. Lighting should activate with motion, but that's been iffy over the past couple of day cycles."

Jacinda pushed her curls behind her ears and pulled a finger-sized trouble light off her belt. She held her breath, hesitating for only a second before she stepped into the darker passage.

Martinez followed.

Sue spoke into her comm. "We're going in, Tima. Let me know if anything changes on our status."

Sue glanced at Dan. "You willing to go last? See if those old law enforcement skills keep us out of a breakdown or ambush or whatever else we're walking into?"

Dan tilted his head and waved his arm toward the door, much like Sue had done for Jacinda.

"I'll do my best."

Chapter 9

The overhead lights in the passage were barely flickering by the time Sue stepped inside. She hadn't been in the Maintenance areas for years, and she still didn't like them. A narrow and angular hallway stretched on to the left, right, and straight ahead, with walls, floor, and ceiling a dark, non-reflective gray.

When the lights finally managed to stay on at full, harsh brightness, the surfaces seemed to absorb the light so they could hold onto their shadows.

The surface absorbed sound, too, leaving Sue feeling like her ears were stuffed full of cotton. Normal shifting and shuffling noises of four humans crowded together barely registered.

Her flattened sense of hearing only brought the stim-induced ringing in her ears back into her awareness in full unpleasant force.

Martinez sighed and rolled his eyes, tension draining from his body. His scalp reflected more than the walls did.

"I was afraid we were going to make the whole walk in the dark."

Jacinda kept her light in her hand as she stared down the right-side passage, clearly not surprised by the darkness just ahead.

"Listen, Martinez," Sue said. "How are people getting in here? The ones not in Maintenance. Or Security. The way I have access set right now, even how it's normally set, Mr. Greenwell's comm won't let him in, correct?"

Martinez crossed his arms and leaned against the wall.

"That all depends, Chief. From what I hear, crewmembers trade favors to get their comms hacked if they don't know how to do it themselves. That or they follow someone. Or sometimes they just push on every maintenance door until they catch one that's not locked properly."

Sue shook her head, unable to stop a grunt of surprise.

"And how often is this happening? Doors unlocked, or comms hacked?"

Martinez grinned. From the looks of him, he wasn't directly involved in any of the illicit activity. But he wasn't concerned and wasn't afraid to say so.

He shrugged. "We do our best to keep the doors secured. Where we are right now is an access passage. A little dull, not all that dangerous. The deeper you get into the ship—away from the living areas—the more people can get hurt or break things. I honestly don't know much about the comms since I've never hacked one. People taking shortcuts is annoying, but it's never been a real problem before."

Sue peered down the dim central passage in front of them, spotting doorways on both sides before it got too dark to see. The stink of the ship's guts was stronger there, too.

"That sound about right to you?" she said to Dan right beside her. "If there are no problems that you've heard about, leave it alone?"

"Martinez here just described every military base I've ever seen. Every college campus, too, and a hell of a lot of municipal buildings back on Earth. People are going to see how much they can get away with no matter what you do to stop it. I always figured it was better to let the small things go as long as it never escalated."

"Yeah, it all worked fine until the latest great Earth HQ update," Sue said. "Close and secure that door, would you, Martinez?" She waited until he had, then raised her wrist comm. "Still seeing us, Tima?"

The silence stretched on, long enough for Sue to count to twenty.

"I was afraid of that. Okay, Martinez, see if you can get back out."

Martinez blinked, then stepped back over to the door. When his wrist comm didn't work, he moved to the side and held his hand flat against a recessed panel Sue hadn't noticed. He shook his head, but he was reaching for the metallic bag over his shoulder.

"No good, not responding to me at all. I've got the tools to get any door on *Bellagos* open, but anyone outside of Maintenance would have a hell of a time of it."

He pulled out a silvery tool that seemed to have three tiny flattened heads protruding a few centimeters out of a rounded body. He fitted the tool into slots Sue couldn't make out even while she was watching him. One on each side of the door, one top, one bottom, with a muted grinding noise and flashing movement from the ends each time.

The door gave a low thump and slid open.

"Good work," Sue said. "Let's all go back out and see if we still exist."

As soon as she stepped clear of the door, Sue's comm let out the jarring screech of an emergency alert, and Jacinda's did the same. Sue's heart pounded even though she was sure she knew what she was about to hear.

"Tima? What's happening?"

"There you are! You all dropped off, just like you thought."

"But we're back on the status screen now?"

Dan frowned at Sue when several seconds passed before Tima's reply.

"I'm sorry, Chief, but no. All four of you are still showing as Invalid."

"That's why your comm didn't work," Dan said to Martinez. "In theory, I'd guess all access should switch off if something like that happened. Crew members switching to Invalid."

Sue nodded. She rubbed her temples, trying to catch the thoughts her weary mind must have missed earlier. Way back when something as simple as the sensors on her ice cream cup not working seemed like a huge clue, and her biggest concern was dealing with the stim-itch that now crawled across her scalp again.

"I'll have to reset us all if a full system reboot doesn't do it," she said. "But that doesn't explain what's been happening here. Liam McHugh's father has been missing for hours. Now Liam and Evans are, too. None of them instantly tripped into Invalid status. It took time."

"Maybe the changes you made to shipwide access accelerated whatever is happening," Jacinda said.

Sue nodded. "That may be, makes sense. Tima, we're heading back into the shortcut. I need you to verify the last several missing crewmembers. After Evans. I did the first few, but then we all assumed that status was the truth."

"You already said that, Chief," Tima said, "before you headed out. Verified one as missing, another as safe and sound, but in Invalid status. Working on the others. Still no word from Earth HQ. Let me know when…whatever you know."

Sue looked at Dan Greenwell. If she didn't already know, she would have guessed he had some kind of investigative background by the gleam in his eyes, the flush in his cheeks. He might have been perfectly happy over the last several years working with his protein vats.

But that wasn't what he was *made* for.

"Those old instincts back in gear, Mr. Greenwell?" she said. "Still willing to go with us?"

"Try and stop me. You solved a big part of it, Chief. But something besides faulty sensors is going on here."

Chapter 10

Sᴜᴇ, Dan, and Martinez followed Jacinda back into the Maintenance passage. Jacinda had run her fingers through her hair enough that it wasn't the least bit flat, on the one side or anywhere else. When the door refused to respond to his comm, Martinez used the same whirling gadget to close the door behind them.

They headed deeper into the ship.

Sue remembered from the map that they were cutting off two of the long main corridors, turning an hour's steady walk into about fifteen minutes. But by the time Jacinda gave up on waiting for the motion sensor lights to kick on and charged ahead with her trouble light, Sue was sure they'd been walking for hours.

The wall to the right remained the same unbroken, dull gray, while passage after passage jutted off to the left. Several sloped sharply up or down, and Sue suspected ladders waited just out of sight. Designers of the mechanical areas of *Bellagos* hadn't worried about keeping a level, human-friendly plane like they had for living areas. Certainly not when so much of it was built in orbit with no worries about gravity, artificial or otherwise.

The stink rose and fell as they walked, but never quite disappeared. The lack of sound, from footsteps or breathing or much of anything else, set Sue's nerves on edge. It was everything she could do not to scratch at her scalp and the palms of her hands.

Finally Jacinda stopped, turning around with her light held toward the floor. The overhead lights weren't even flickering, but Sue could see a door behind Jacinda. Their access passage had come to an end.

Martinez stepped forward, waving his wrist comm and touching the recessed panel, then working on the top of the door as he had before.

Nothing happened. He examined the silvery heads, then tried one of the sides. He leaned closer with his own trouble light.

He shook his head and scowled. "This isn't right. Even if my comm is bad, every door on this ship is designed to work with this tool. It's hard to tell without magnification, but I think the access points have been jammed."

"Part of the system update?" Sue said.

"I don't think so." Martinez was rubbing his head again. "The port isn't even engaging. The other door worked fine until the ship thought we disappeared, then I got it open anyway. This one is physically jammed."

Dan turned in a slow circle. "So we, and probably the others, were meant to get in but not get out."

Jacinda joined Dan, shining her light all around them. Nothing but the dark passage they'd come through, the jammed door, and a passage heading off to the left.

"I didn't see the map, Chief," Jacinda said. "And honestly, this isn't one of the passages I normally use. Will anyone hear us if we shout or beat on this door? Out in the main corridor, I mean?"

"I doubt it. This comes out in another one of those side corridors. And if this end has been jammed for a few days, I'd bet people have stopped trying it as a shortcut."

"Someone in *here* might hear us, though," Dan said. "If we're loud enough over this sound damping. Someone we're not ready to meet just yet."

Martinez stowed the door tool back in his pouch and stood with his hands on his hips.

"I can head down any of these other passages and find a way around. Or I can get bigger tools and get us out of here by force. But I have no idea what I'll run into or if I'll make it back out."

"Forget it," Dan said. "We're not splitting up. Either we got funneled down here on purpose and they're hesitating for some reason, or they're busy and not paying attention. We know for certain that at least one person has disappeared from here."

"Probably three," Sue said. "I'm sure this is the shortcut Liam wanted to show Evans."

"Well then," Jacinda said, her voice tight, "we should head back to the door we know is working. Bring a bigger crew back, more Security and more Maintenance. Figure out what the hell is going on."

Dan started to speak, but Sue touched his arm.

"I think we're out of time for that."

Chapter 11

In the horrible silence, a soft shuffling sound grew steadily louder.

Sue didn't protest when Dan joined her and Jacinda shoulder to shoulder across the narrow passage in front of the jammed door. None of them could tell where the noise came from, but with exactly none of them armed, that didn't seem to matter much.

Jacinda jerking her light around and Martinez darting his between their heads only added to the disorientation.

"Whoever it is can only be another crewmember," Dan said in a low voice. "There are no energy weapons or even projectile weapons onboard. Not unless someone built them."

"We have no need for such crude devices," a soft voice said from somewhere to their right. "One easily jammed door and human nature are doing everything we need and more, aren't they?"

Jacinda and a beat later Martinez swung their trouble lights down the passage. Two men and two women waited, one of the women out in front. All of them wore leisure clothing like Dan, soft gray with no rank or name visible. No weapons of any kind visible, either.

Sue didn't recognize them, but she heard and felt Dan let out a breath beside her.

"Mayam," he said. "What's going on here?"

"Where's the boy?" Sue said, stepping forward. "My crew?"

Now that they were only a couple of meters away, Sue could see they were younger than she'd thought. The woman, Mayam, didn't look like she'd reached her second decade. She was tall but not filled out yet, wavy black hair chopped in bunches around her narrow face. Still very much an angular and gawky kid to Sue's eyes.

"*Your* crew, Chief?" Mayam said, shaking her head. "That may be true of the ones who volunteered for this mission. Maybe the ones born here. But not all of us."

Dan raised his hands. "Listen to me. This isn't going to accomplish whatever you want. Especially not holding people against their will."

"What's my other option, then?" Mayam waved an empty hand at Sue. "Petition the warden here for early release? Jump off at the next stop?"

"How will capturing and holding people change any of that?" Sue said. "They can't turn *Bellagos* around any more than I can. Why are you doing this?

Mayam stepped forward until stood almost nose to nose with Sue. At Jacinda's defensive movement to her side, Sue held up her hand.

"This is at least doing *something*!" Mayam shouted, fists clenched in front of her stomach. "Making a decision, having a bloody choice. For the first time in our lives we're not... inert!"

Dan moved toward Sue and a little bit in front of her. Rather than someone trying to downplay her own authority, he was clearly putting on his old role in law enforcement.

And acting on whatever his relationship to this Mayam really was.

"I know you were young when you were brought on board," he said. "Many of you were, long before you could have made such a choice for yourselves. We can't fix it, no. But we can't do anything to help if you keep taking the choices of others away."

"Is the boy safe?" Sue said. "Liam? He was born here, and he loves it here. This is his only home."

Mayam scowled and waved her arm. "Do you think I'm trying to set up some kind of hostage trading program? Keep rounding them up until there aren't enough people left to keep this floating prison ship working?"

"Did you sabotage our systems?" Sue said. "Disable the tracking units in this passageway? I don't remember your name from the list of missing."

Mayam tried to hide it, but a flash of pride lit her eyes. She stepped back and crossed her arms.

"Earth HQ isn't quite as all-powerful as we've been led to believe. That bit wasn't even hard to do. If you check your *infallible* snooping systems, you'll see me and everyone with me still where we're supposed to be. Vital signs, movements, everything. Just like normal."

Sue clenched her fists, surprised at how badly she wanted to use them.

"You're disrupting the lives of everyone on board to do what? Prove a point? What's your next target, Mayam? Life support? I asked you if you sabotaged our systems. I suggest you give me an answer."

"We don't have a death wish," Mayam said. "I'm not stupid enough to take out life support. This wasn't some random impulse action."

Sue crossed her arms, doing her best to put on Dan's confidence in a situation that terrified her to her bones. With someone who didn't know the ship's systems well enough to safely modify the systems updates, it might as well have been an impulse action

Even Sue herself didn't know the software well enough to make those kinds of changes.

"You haven't seen the screens I do in the command center," Sue said. "You have no idea what you've changed, what effects every single change has. Humanity has never built anything as complex as *Bellagos* and ships like her. The changes cascade. The changes are *still* cascading, and even I don't know what's going to fail next."

Mayam scowled, but her defiant stance softened.

"All I did was spike the update. Left instructions for how the changes would be carried out that overwrote the ones from Earth HQ. I modified our sensors and the sweep field in these passages. Nothing more than that. Getting your attention was the point. It worked."

Sue steeled herself for the lie, needing to know what kind of systems and coding knowledge she was up against.

"Then what was the point of rigging the sensors ship-wide to trigger alarms for no reason? When Evans and I took Liam out to calm him down, Liam who is *still* a frightened little boy who needs his father, we couldn't help but notice the trouble they're having in the frozen food pod. Every single bowl sets off the alarm, even when you're nowhere near their boundary."

"I never touched those systems!" Mayam finally took a step back. "The only thing that changed is in here, in the maintenance passages."

Dan followed the step backward with a near-charge forward of his own. His voice was colder than the depths of the frozen food pod, and all the more dangerous for it.

"Chief Warrell has asked you repeatedly about the health and whereabouts of several of her crew members. Liam McHugh, his father, and Senior Tech Evans, to be specific. If you have any expectations of continuing this mission outside of a prison pod, which I will *happily* create just for you, answer her. Now."

"I'm already in prison," Mayam said, her whole body seeming to deflate. "We all are. Some of us just can't manage to pretend it's anything else. Liam and his father are fine. So is everyone else. They're in a storage pod not far from here. Did you really believe I would hurt them, Uncle Dan? Hurt a little boy?"

"You did hurt Liam," Dan said in a softer voice. "You took his father away. The boy had no idea where, or why. How many other people have you hurt and upset, Mayam? What did you think you could possibly gain with all this?"

Mayam stared into Dan's eyes, leaving Sue free to watch the three who were with her. The woman and two men were still and silent, either looking at Mayam or at the gray floor. They might have been willing to follow her, to respond to her actions or whatever she accomplished. But without her, they should be easy to calm down.

And easy to control. Direct where Sue wanted them to go.

"We don't have any prison pods onboard," Sue said, looking at the other three. "But we have plans to convert pods if the need ever arises. I don't want to do that, not now, not ever if I can help it. We need every crewmember to help make this mission a success."

She shifted her gaze to Mayam. "What you're doing is causing the kind of disruption we most need to avoid. More and more people are getting upset, and not just the families of people you abducted. I'm sure you have no idea what's happening since you're been hidden away out here. We *are* losing vital systems. Not just sensors, either. Food production is faltering. People know there's trouble. We're one of the first few colonization ships to ever leave Earth, but we know what happens in big communities or sailing ships. When people lose confidence, everything starts to break down."

Dan picked up on her lead exactly like Sue hoped.

"You know that's what I spent decades dealing with back on Earth," he said. "I watched systems break down, in uglier ways than you can imagine. Ways I don't ever want you or anyone else on board to experience. If we end up with riots on a contained ship because of this kind of disruption, exactly how do you think Chief Warrell should handle that?"

Chapter 12

Mayam stood with her arms crossed staring up at Dan, leaving Sue wondering if she'd mimicked the gesture in her uncle when she was growing up. The three behind Mayam shifted their feet and glanced nervously at each other.

Martinez spoke up from beside Sue.

"We don't have the capacity or crew to handle anything like this in Maintenance, much less riots or a bunch of people locked up. Just me being offline right now is going to play hell with our schedules. Especially in the emergency situation you created. You get too many of us trapped back here or trying to deal with the trouble the corrupted update has caused, and life support systems won't have to fail."

He paused, looking at Mayam and the other three for a few seconds. "If this keeps up, *Bellagos* will take herself apart all around us. But at least your *inconvenience* would be at an end, right?"

Slowly enough that it would have been easy to miss if Sue hadn't been watching for it, the three behind Mayam moved back a step. They moved closer together, too, almost shoulder to shoulder, leaving Mayam standing alone.

"I'm not stupid," Mayam said so quietly that Sue had to strain to hear her. "I'm not a kid, either. I don't want everyone to die." She shook her head. "I don't want *any*one to die. I just don't want this. I never did. No one should have been hauled out here against their will."

Dan nodded, and the warmth and sympathy in his face stirred up a pleasant heat in Sue's middle, even while her eyes prickled with tears.

"You were brought against your will, you're right. That wasn't fair." He looked at all of the group behind Mayam. "It wasn't fair to any of you. I can't change it, but I can say I'm sorry. I truly am. I can't speak for all of your families, but I know my brother was thrilled to be able to give you this chance to help build a new human homeworld. That was your mother's dream, too."

Mayam turned her head to the side, but not before Sue saw her blinking back tears.

"I know. I remember her talking about it before she died. Barely, but I remember. This all might have been different if she were here. Or I might hate it even more with both of them telling me how wonderful it is. How damn *lucky* I am to be here."

Jacinda spoke then, surprising Sue until she realized Mayam was only a couple of years younger.

"Having them both here might have helped a little. Both my mothers are, and my bio-dad. They drove me crazy the whole time I lived with them, though, carrying on about The Great Dream and Carrying Humanity to the Stars and all the other capitalized slogans they came up with."

Mayam looked Jacinda up and down, her eyes narrowed.

"You believe in all that stuff?" she said. "All the hype and propaganda?"

Jacinda shrugged, holding up one hand.

"Not exactly the way my moms put it, no. I'm pretty sure the galaxy would have been just fine without a bunch of humans cluttering up the place like we did on Earth. Probably better off. I didn't much like feeling like I had no choice in being here myself. But I'd rather see it work than see it all fall apart around us."

"I was angry when I asked you before," Sue said, "so let me try again. What would make this better? We all know what we *can't* do to change things. What are your ideas for what we *can* do?"

Mayam turned her head, then her whole body to face the three behind her. A few steps behind her now, and all of them staring at their feet. The other young woman finally raised her head.

Sue saw her give a sad half-smile, then shake her head. Leaving Mayam on her own, exactly as Sue expected.

A soft sigh from Dan let her know he'd expected the same.

Mayam turned slowly, blinking back tears again and rolling her eyes at the same time.

"Okay, now that I know where we all stand," she said. "We want…*I* want to have a say in what happens here. What I'm supposed to do. What's supposed to happen for the rest of this journey I won't live to see the end of."

"You have as much right to choose what you do as the rest of us," Dan said, not quite back to his military voice, but edging toward it.

Mayam shook her head, hands on her slender hips again.

"No, Uncle Dan, we don't. We all got the same training from the second we stepped on board. Or the second we were carried on board, too many of us. We serve the same apprenticeships, get sorted into the career paths *you* or Earth HQ say will suit us best. I'm supposed to get funneled into Security like a good little drone. Preparing us to live useful lives to best serve the mission. Not one thought given to what would serve ourselves or make us happy."

"That's what we're all doing," Dan said, holding up both hands. "But maybe things can change. You're right. Odds are high you won't live to see the end of this mission, but some of you might. I know I won't. So what you want and how you want to run things matters."

"The rules we have aren't inflexible," Sue said. The three behind Mayam shifted, paying attention now. "Earth HQ only gave us guidelines. No one knew for sure how any of this would go, and they can't exactly punish us. I'll admit I wondered if that's what they were doing with that damn botched systems update. Trying to shake us up so we'll keep paying attention to them instead of depending more and more on ourselves."

"I know what all this trouble has really caused," Jacinda said. "Everyone on the Security side does. People on board got a reminder that we're all in trapped together in a huge metal ship in the dead of space. Even if they'd made their peace with our situation, worked out how to live with it, you pushed it into their faces. If you wanted everyone to be more aware of that, you succeeded."

Jacinda and Mayam locked gazes, and Sue had no doubt the two of them understood each other in a way neither she or Dan ever would.

After all, she and Dan and others of their generation had not only chosen to come on this mission, they'd fought for the chance.

Mayam blew air out through her lips.

"That wasn't quite what we were trying to do, but maybe it's a good thing. I never forget that for a second. I wanted to start with letting us choose what we want to study once we get past the basics. What we want to learn how to do. Maybe learn as many different duties as we can. I know we must have all the functions on *Bellagos* filled, and we'll have to deal with that. But maybe if we branch out and learn more, we could rotate through."

Dan smiled at Sue, surprising her yet again when he winked.

"I'm on my third career, hoping to have more ahead. And, I've been resisting Earth HQ's idea of how I could best support the mission since before I came onboard. I'm not the one in charge, but I can't think of any reason to argue. What do you think, Chief?"

"I'm not in charge either," Sue said. "Humans couldn't possibly go out into space without recreating committees and other such nonsense, no matter what they call it. I suspect it would do crewmembers a hell of a lot of good to know more about how *Bellagos* operates. How fragile she is, and how strong. What you ask makes sense to me."

Sue stepped forward and held out her hand to Mayam.

"I'll bring it up, I promise. As soon as everyone is back with their families. And, if you agree to come to the command pod so you can see how many systems you actually disrupted whether you meant to or not."

Before Mayam could respond, a low thud rumbled through the floor, and all the harsh overhead lights in the passages they could see switched on at full strength. Screeching alarms from all seven comms had everyone scrambling to silence them.

"…please, Chief. Report and confirm status."

Sue raised her comm, unable to hold back a wide grin. For the first time in her life, she welcomed the stim-itch flaring up over her whole body with the jolt of adrenaline.

"Here and fine, Tima. Get word back from Earth HQ? A new update?"

"Glad to hear your voice, ma'am. We got word from HQ, but no new update. After I verified the missing or Invalid crewmembers, I dug into the systems interface and located code that didn't fit protocol. Earth HQ said to act on our own best information while they analyze the problem. So I removed that code and rolled back to the last clean version. When you give the word, HQ will resend the update, hardened against that code. Crew numbers are back to full, all on the tracking board."

"I think you and Mayam here will have a lot to talk about," Sue said, laughing. "You both seem to know the software better than I do. Maybe it's past time I stopped being so hands-off with the software that keeps this place running myself. Well done not *quite* obeying orders, Tima. I knew I could train that rule-following out of you. You ready to stay on shift for a few more hours?"

Sue could just about see her second, mouth opening and closing, cheeks red, blinking. Trying to decide whether she'd done good or bad.

Tima's calm, confident voice shifted the balance toward good.

"Thank you, ma'am. Ready and glad to stand for a full shift."

"I'll bring everyone out and check in," Sue said. "Then I'm off for at least a full sleep cycle. Three if I can manage it. Call in someone else when you need a break, hold steady on the old systems software. The rest will be there when we're all ready to face it."

Chapter 13

THE CLASSROOM POD had been designed for older students—well into their second decade and even beginning their third—but Sue was surprised to feel a bit cramped.

The space was the full dimensions of a standard living pod without any walls or divisions, so that didn't quite make sense. Four rows of long white tables left plenty of room for everyone, even with a larger crowd than anyone expected for the last day of their first software coding workshop.

Every attendee had an arm's length on both sides. The white chairs weren't nearly as comfortable as Sue's in her command pod, but they were workable. The lighting was set to full Earth daylight and reflected nicely off the bright yellow walls. Even the full-wall instructional monitor up front showed an open vista of a calm Earth ocean around the unused edges, adding to the expansive feeling.

A fresh ocean breeze completed the scene and somehow enhanced concentration rather than distracting it.

Sue finally decided the confines around her physical body weren't causing her discomfort. She simply wasn't used to being in a room full of thirty people. They ranged from members of her own Systems and Security Team to Martinez from Maintenance to at least one from every occupation onboard *Bellagos*.

The ages ranged as well, and Sue and Dan were far from the only gray heads in attendance.

Up front, Dan's niece Mayam and Sue's second-in-command Tima continued to do a fine job of explaining the basics of the code language that made everything surrounding them function. Mayam in particular had high color and obvious enthusiasm that warmed Sue's heart.

Whether Mayam decided to stay in teaching or working in code or transitioned into her original path of Security, she'd be a natural at the job.

Sue felt a bit less happy about Tima taking so well to teaching, but couldn't deny she was good at it.

Dan's chair did sit quite a bit closer than was required, and Sue was happier about that by the day. Since she and everyone else in Systems and Security had gone back to regular leisure days, more than a few of hers had coordinated with Dan's.

It seemed wanting the company of another human outside of work hours wasn't quite as far behind Sue as she'd thought.

Not when it was the right human.

He caught her glancing his way and winked with the half-smile that spoke volumes. Sue knew her cheeks and throat were flushed from memory and promise, but she didn't care. She focused on the front of the classroom just as Mayam switched the display to full ocean.

"Everyone has done a fantastic job this week," she said, beaming at Tima, then at Sue. "We appreciate the opportunity more than we can say, and we hope you all enjoyed it as much as we did."

Both of them basked in well-deserved, hearty applause. Sue felt like her brain was straining at the edges, and she'd taken more notes than when she was a student herself decades ago.

And she was thrilled to admit that understanding how the software was constructed was already helping her manage onboard systems.

The replacement update from Earth HQ had installed flawlessly, and Sue expected the same from future versions. No one would be touching live software anytime soon, or making changes to existing systems.

But she had no doubt teaching the next generation of programmers would be vital to their mission's independence, and their eventual success.

The changes they were making in this room—and in similar classrooms all over *Bellagos*—would cascade and grow and branch off into the future in unpredictable ways.

Exactly as Mayam's changes to ship systems had not so long ago.

But Sue was certain the simple fact of crewmembers working together now, with full understanding and growing respect for the vital role they all filled, would help make these new changes positive ones.

And leave everyone onboard *Bellagos* and future generations stretching all the way forward to their eventual settlement on Junos 7 better equipped to handle whatever came their way.

Dan stood and walked to the front of the room and Sue joined him, her cheeks flaming again when he reached for her hand. She held tight and spoke over the general commotion of people getting ready to leave.

"We want to thank both Mayam and Tima for doing such a great job teaching," she said. "As well as congratulate ourselves and everyone else on a job well done keeping up with them."

"Everyone in this room has earned a treat," Dan said.

At a tap on Sue's comm, the doors to the side opened. Liam McHugh pushed a hover-cart full of double-sided frozen treat bowls, head high and bursting with pride. Liam's father followed close behind with Senior Tech Evans, both pushing silver hover-carts Sue knew were full of almost every flavor people could put into those bowls.

Cassie from the frozen treat pod came last. Her smile was a thousand light years from the fake customer service version Sue had seen when none of them had any idea what they were facing.

More importantly, Sue knew the hover-cart Cassie pushed was full of chocolate, cherry, and her own favorite mix of the two.

As everyone else gathered around the celebratory treats, Sue leaned up and whispered in Dan's ear, breathing in the warm scent of his skin.

"We still on for a private celebration later, Mr. Greenwell?"

This time she got his full smile, and went a bit weak in the knees.

"You bet we are, Chief. *Bellagos* will just have to manage without us for a couple of leisure days."

Sue surprised herself by kissing Dan full on the mouth, right there in view of the whole group.

"Good."

KARI KILGORE

RESTRICTED SPECIES

To my Dad, Jim Steffey

*For his incredible ability to grow anything,
his love of helping people,
and his endless curiosity.*

Chapter 1

Jim Turhan couldn't quite remember why he'd started his nighttime habit of strolling around his cadet training lab on Mossera 4. He rarely saw another living creature, human or otherwise. No one wandering through empty xeno-botany classrooms or huddled in front of a holo-comm, homesick and lonely. Even when he looped outside into the crop supply planet's dim twilight, Jim was alone.

Jim had no doubt the rotating groups of ConSpace recruits got homesick all the time. Most were so young, humans still in their teens, aliens in the same awkward, confusing life stage. None of them were from the neighborhood or within a month's travel. Even with great clusters of stars close enough to leach darkness from the night sky, the Mossera System was as far from habitable worlds as you could get without a few years of hyper-sleep.

The structure and schedule for first year cadets at the Mosslea Academy focused on one thing. Keep them just overwhelmed and exhausted enough that they won't have time or energy to get into trouble. Sure, they'd retain a good bit of what they learned in their weary brain cells, and they'd make lifelong friends along the way. Those were side benefits.

Keeping them out of mischief until they grew some common

sense was the only way to end up with graduates rather than washouts. Or worse.

Passing the outermost rows of octo-triticale, Jim brushed his hand across the waist high plants, faintly brown and green in the twilight. Wispy tassels and spiky rows of seeds tickled his palm and wrist. The nutrient-packed wheat seemed to thrive no matter where humanity scattered their seeds, even on a planet with no native pollinators or any other kind of insect.

Jim was mostly glad they only had the pollinator drones he specialized in, ranging from barely visible midge-bots to metallic hummingbirds. He'd read about the biting, stinging kind that died out on Earth before he was born.

Mossera 4 had no life forms that weren't firmly rooted in the ground. And everything turning this formerly wet but lifeless hunk of rock into a lush farmworld came from somewhere else.

He followed the faintly glowing plas-rock path that crunched under his feet, back toward the academy's domes powered down to essential lighting and systems. Jim could easily make out the rounded roofs of greenhouses and square classrooms. A breeze funneled between buildings carried the scent of rosemary bushes after the day's rainstorm. He hardly ever worked in the herb sector, but Jim never grew tired of those surprise bursts of aroma.

Mosslea wasn't a lively entertainment region, not like Mosserrania, the leisure continent around the warm equatorial zone of Mossera 4. ConSpace usually did their best to pair up supply and leisure when they sent miners into less than hospitable conditions.

Mossera 5, the ore- and energy-rich planet every operation on 4 supported, fit that definition better than most. Well below freezing, almost non-existent atmosphere, no water to speak of.

Jim had never set foot on the arid, treacherous orange and black surface, much less beneath in the kilometers of mines. He had no desire to change that. All he needed to know about 5 was ConSpace needed those resources enough to dedicate an entire planet to supporting those miners.

A faint, bluish light inside the pollinator drone lab pulled Jim out of his visions of the hellish landscape barely two hundred million kilometers away. Every light system in the lab complex powered down automatically for evening, powering up only if someone triggered it.

Only one other resident would possibly be wandering around so late into sleep hours. And working, at that.

Sure enough, a head full of spiky blond hair was visible in the drone assembly and maintenance section. Rob Martinez leaned over one of the oval tables adjusted as high as it would go, elbows sunk into the pale blue moss surface just like when he was a raw cadet more than ten years ago. He'd finally grown into his lanky arms and legs, and into his quick and sometimes troublesome mind, turning into the natural xeno-farmer Jim suspected he'd be.

Not that it wasn't a near thing for a while there. Rob's struggle to believe in himself had been long and painful to watch.

"You authorized to be in here alone, kid?" Jim said, smiling when Rob's head popped up.

"Someone's gotta keep the place organized. The old man in charge keeps wandering off in the middle of the night."

Jim snorted as he joined Rob at the table. Seemed silly to call a man in his early thirties a kid. Looking back from pushing eighty himself made just about everyone seem like a kid. Lifespans and medical advances, not to mention living several decades on such a pure, clean planet meant he likely had a good forty years ahead of him.

The kilometers added up though, especially from when he was younger than Rob.

War years always seemed to add double.

"Night's the only time I can get some peace and quiet around this place." Jim glanced at the drifts and piles of disassembled drones covering the flat blue surface. Moth, fly, maybe a honeybee or two. "Did the cadets break more than their usual quota today?"

"No more than usual, no. I doubt any of them could come close to my personal record." Rob ran his hands through already messy hair, a habit from his challenging cadet years. "Wish it was something that easy to deal with."

Jim brushed the surface of the moss, smoothing some of the

divots his former troublesome student still made. The moss not only helped keep the air clean and smelling more like a hardwood forest after the rain instead of nervous sweat. All the pollination drones, from nearly invisible midges up to dive bomb hummingbirds, were programed to land there in case they got away.

They always got away from new cadets. Every single time.

"What's going on?"

Rob picked up an empty pollen sack from one of the mechanical honeybees. The rice grain-sized pouches were soft transparent poly-plas. Or at least they should have been transparent. Some careless cadet, combined with careless supervision, had left these dusted with yellowish powder.

"These were last used a few days ago." Rob held the sack up toward the overhead grow-lights. The rubbery black wrist-mag he wore created the static field he needed for a good grip. "Put away a mess, as you can see."

"I know you're not out here late at night cleaning up after a bunch of sloppy cadets."

"Nope. I checked out the summer squash vines this afternoon. The ones we got a few years ago from old Earth stock? The plants look great, growing like wildfire. And not one blossom is setting fruit."

Jim scowled. "That can't be right. We ran those drones…well, a few days ago, just like you said. I watched your sloppy cadets load up the pollen myself."

"Same way you watched me load it up way back when, I know. I took the cadets out that day to see the drones in action since the squash blossoms are so big. Everything seemed normal. No heavy wind, no rain until yesterday."

"From the looks of these pollen sacks," Jim said, "they used up most of it out there. Even if they didn't bother to clean up." He picked up several of the sacks and shook them in his palm. The rattling motion rewarded him with a fine coating of yellow dust. "Anything strange about this batch?"

Rob straightened to his full height, several hands taller than Jim, stretching his arms above his head.

"Not that I can see. We collected it last season from the male blossoms. Standard procedure with a new strain."

Jim shivered, remembering his grandparents' tales of failed crops back on Earth. How they thought it was isolated at first, but the problem continued and spread. How waves of shortages and starvation led to conflicts that lasted long enough to catch Jim up in their final gasps of violence. Rapid colonization, and ConSpace developing the drones scattered in front of him, turned humanity's descent into triumph.

"We need to check the other crops," Jim said, dropping the cleaner pollen sacks and rubbing his palms on the table moss. "Have we sent any of this pollen out to other xeno-farms?"

"Not yet. We hadn't established our own supplies enough. This strain has grown true on at least a hundred other planets and moons. Think it could be a local problem? Soil or water, maybe?"

"That or some kind of problem we haven't seen before. Much as we screen out cadets from disease-prone planets and sterilize everything, we know something could get through. Got enough to keep the kids busy tomorrow?"

Rob grinned. "Already got it planned. Every single drone gets broken down and cleaned. Perfect opportunity to explain how problems spread without letting anyone know what's going on. And to watch the cadets who left this mess do it the right way."

"They won't soon forget you looming over their shoulders. Glad to help if you need it. It's been a while since I got to intimidate a bunch of lazy kids." Jim helped Rob sort the drones back into their proper bins. "Good call on keeping this quiet, too. If this is a simple fix, we don't want ConSpace breathing down our necks or causing a panic for no good reason."

"If it's not, we'll have done everything we can on this end." Rob clapped Jim on the shoulder. "Let's get them started cleaning first thing, then we'll check the rest of the new crops. Get some sleep, old man. Long day ahead."

Chapter 2

THE NOSTALGIC GLOW of instilling a bit of healthy respect into new cadets, along with a vital refresher about drone maintenance, faded before Rob and Jim finished inspecting the first five crops. Only Earth species failing would have been bad enough. But they found evidence of the same lack of fruit in the violet protein-rich cassamond fruit from Sitendra 8, pumpkin-sized blue citrus from Piddo 2, and rich, starchy gipla trees.

All perfectly healthy and normal plants, in fields kilometers away from each other. All loaded with multicolored blossoms that fell with very little fruit behind.

Jim tried to push the chill now deep in his gut aside as he landed the hoverpod. The sprawling apple orchard could have been on Earth itself judging by historical photos and primitive videos. Sturdy, compact trunks spaced evenly across the low covergrass landscape, each grafted with different species of planetary heritage apples. The blue tint of Mossera's sun threw everything off, but most of the trees displayed the unmistakable red and yellow of ripening fruit.

Those were all pollinated months before, though. Mossera 4's long, slow orbital tilt - much more gradual than Earth's - combined with a closer orbit to make repeated crops possible. Most of the trees also had several branches with nothing but leaves. Only a few new apples dotted the dusky green with tiny pink or green fruitlets smaller than Jim's fingernail.

"When were these pollinated?" Jim said. He noted everything on his wrist-comm, but that was only out of habit. He never forgot anything that scared him this badly.

"These are the oldest so far. Three weeks from the drone pass." Rob shook the branch closest to him, sending pink and white petals to the already covered ground. Jim counted less than ten infant apples where dozens should have been thriving. "What the hell is going on here?"

They'd walked the rows of every other crop, collecting samples of the flowers and making sure they had a clear picture of the damage. This time, Jim was relieved Rob didn't seem to have the heart for it either.

"I haven't seen or heard of anything like this, not even when Earth failed. That was gradual, such a slow decline that people didn't pay attention until it was too late."

"No disease I've read about hits several unrelated crops at once like this, either." Rob leaned against the curved glass bubble of the hoverpod. "The drones should be able to pollinate these apples without our help, really. The orchard is decades old. We just load the pollen to get a better yield these days."

"That's what we're seeing, Rob. We probably would have had better results if we'd sent out empty drones. We're going to have to check the pollen stores. Maerlis Quan has a group of students studying diseases, doesn't she?"

The younger man's cheeks flushed pink, and he studied his fingernails intently. Jim tried to hide his smile. He hadn't caught the signs before, but now that he thought about it…

"She does, yeah. I think she might be willing to help."

"I'll leave you to discuss it with her, maybe over lunch," Jim said. Rob's face turned nearly as dark as the reddest apple in the orchard, but to his credit, he looked Jim in the eye. "I'll gather pollen from every crop we inspected and meet you in her xeno-lab."

Chapter 3

Jim wished the trouble with the crops were as easy to diagnose as Rob and Maerlis. The xeno-biologist was as friendly and outgoing as Rob, but the two of them acted positively standoffish once Jim arrived. They were a perfectly matched set as far as he could tell.

Both strong and healthy, around the same age. Maerlis was as small and compact as Rob was tall and lanky, with waves of gleaming black hair falling loose past her shoulders. Both loved the odd combination of planetary isolation and intense socialization of repeated swarms of new cadets and departing graduates.

And each almost embarrassingly smitten with the other.

Rob's gaze followed Maerlis as she gathered equipment and supplies from around her compact lab, all gleaming plas-steel and flawlessly clean glass. The orderly straight lines of cabinets, storage and freezer units, and counters made the curvy, organic chaos of the drone section seem like a slow moving disaster.

If they couldn't isolate whatever was causing so many crops to fail, that might turn out to be true.

"Rob tells me you have samples of affected pollen and the sterile flowers?" Maerlis said, stopping in front of Jim. She glanced at Rob for an instant, but she hid her blush better than he did. "We'll see if it could be the pollen and not something else."

Jim handed palm-sized black sample pods directly to her rather than risking touching the spotless surfaces. Each carried a digital code identifying the source and age of the pollen or flowers inside. She dropped them one by one into a slot Jim hadn't noticed on what he thought was a shiny black cabinet along one wall. Maerlis must have noticed his raised eyebrows.

"This tests the chemical composition of each sample. It reads the code on the way down. If we have a mismatch, we'll know in a few seconds."

"Does it check DNA?" Jim said, stepping over for a closer look at the silent machine. "In case there's some kind of hybridization going on?"

"You'd think she'd have that equipment here, wouldn't you?" Rob's face was flaming red again, and he looked like he wanted to inhale the words back out of the air.

Jim had the clear impression the kid had just spilled the nerdiest pillow talk of all time.

"That *is* something I've discussed with ConSpace," Maerlis said. She smiled openly at Rob, apparently deciding to drop what little façade they had left. "The technology is cheap and fast these days, but it's not considered any kind of mission priority. This scanner will catch anything we should be worried about, they say."

"And ConSpace considers hybridization a good thing if it happens," Rob said. "If it helps crop adaptation to the planet, so much the better. If not, we go back to our pure pollen stores and that takes care of it."

"Exactly." Maerlis touched a flat yellow button in the middle of the scanner, and a huge screen filled with blue letters. The data took up the whole wall, as long and tall as Jim's arm. "We check nutritional content, potential toxins, digestibility. No need to waste our time worrying about genetics. ConSpace has that handled, right? At least officially."

Jim stepped closer to the screen on one side, Rob on the other. Jim was no chemist or biologist, but he could read the species names and varieties with no trouble. Maerlis confirmed his impression before he could speak.

"Nothing unexpected here, Jim. According to this, every single grain and petal come from the species you coded onto the sample. We've got some other kind of problem."

Maerlis leaned against the table behind her, giving Jim and Rob the cue to do the same.

"I don't understand this then," Rob said, shaking his head. "Any chance of an airborne fungus or even an insect?"

Maerlis shrugged. "Not a trace of pathogen from what you gave me. I can't imagine insect life spontaneously evolving since we arrived here."

"And we sterilize anything before it comes to the surface," Jim said. "Cadets, visitors, miners, or anything they receive."

"What's next, Maerlis?" Rob said. "Send these off-planet for testing?"

She sighed and pushed herself away from the table. Jim and Rob followed her into a tiny office off the lab. Jim was amused to see her desk and the table behind it were as disorderly as the lab had been neat.

"Have a seat and I'll check the freighter schedule." Maerlis sat behind the drifts of equipment, sheets of slippery plas-paper, and several honest-to-goodness printed and bound books. She retrieved a flat touchscreen comm from the mess. "I'm pretty sure it won't be what you want to hear."

After a moment of touches and swipes, the xeno-biologist looked up with a half-smile.

"I'm afraid I was right. No ore pickups or supply deliveries for about five months. And all those ships are already inbound."

"So they won't have emergency supplies or testing equipment," Jim said. The chill had settled into his bones. "And we can't send anything out for what, at least a month or two after that?"

"At the soonest." Maerlis leaned forward, holding the comm in her lap. "I know we're a fresh food outpost, so I hate to ask. What happens to our supplies in that time?"

"Considering that the freighters won't bring a damn thing with them?" Jim said. "Besides what little we can't grow here. Even if we warn them, they won't likely be able to detour to another supply planet."

"There aren't any other ones close by." Rob's face was as pale as it had been flushed.

"Not that they could re-route to." Jim scrubbed his face. His brain didn't want to see the answer, much less say it out loud. "We won't actually starve to death. At least I don't think so. You'll know the nutritional deficiencies we'll run into better than I do, Maerlis, with a year or more before we get a good harvest. But we'll have a planet full of miserable cadets and furious miners on our hands."

Jim kept his true worries, and his memories, to himself. He'd seen people as rough and hardened as the miners on a desolate planet. At the end of the last wars on Earth.

He knew how more shortages and hardships they weren't prepared for could turn a difficult situation into a nasty one. Rob seemed to read his thoughts.

"Any chance ConSpace Security out here could help us? With emergency supplies? I hate to say this, but having them more visible down here might help if things get really bad."

"They depend on us for supplies too," Jim said. "That's why the system is set up the way it is. We have backup supplies, untouched seed and pollen, multiple sources and formulas for keeping the soil healthy. We can design and build new pollinator drones if we have to."

"But when our whole purpose here is to provide food," Maerlis said, "no one plans for a link in that chain to break."

Jim's mind reeled, thoughts, images, feelings best left in the past storming through like a thousand drones released at once. The only idea he could grasp was a question.

"Maerlis, I don't want to offend you. But what you said, about ConSpace handling genetics. Officially."

"I'm right with you, Jim. This is more than unofficial, you know. It's completely unauthorized."

Rob drummed his fingers on his leg.

"You told me that thing is older than we are, Maer."

"I sure did." She slapped her hands against her own thighs, then grabbed the comm and got to her feet. "More like fifty Earth years, to tell the truth. But if it solves our problem, it's worth the risk."

She paused to eject the sample pods from the scanner and drop them into Jim's bag. The two men followed her out into the echoing corridor, empty with all the available cadets pulled into drone sanitizing duty. Jim held his questions and tried to still his panic-tinged thoughts as they turned toward the residential pods.

They didn't follow any sort of gender or species divisions, but general planet seniority arrangements had grown up over time. Jim lived in the oldest section, adjacent to the working facilities. Maerlis and Rob were further out, almost in the cadet wings.

Maerlis led them into a cozy pod neither as neat as the lab nor as messy as her office. Jim would call it comfortable and lived in, and Rob obviously would, too. He headed toward a small door to the left of the living area before he realized what he was doing. This time he added pulling his hand back from the doorknob to his flushed face.

"I doubt we fooled Jim for a second," Maerlis said, laughing. "Go ahead."

"We don't have nearly enough families on this planet," Jim said. "Assuming we make it through the next year, I'm delighted for both of you."

Rob had the grace to simply open the door and stand aside for Maerlis and Jim to enter.

The room beyond wasn't much more than a closet. A few shelves were jammed with more of the ancient bound books and clothing for the various climates on Mossera 4. A small, scarred wooden table along one wall held a black box, nearly a meter on each side. Jim could tell it was electronic from dormant lights and touchscreens all over it. He didn't doubt the bulky thing was nearly his own age.

"My great-grandmother gave it to me." Maerlis sat on a wooden chair that looked nearly as old. "She was a geneticist. Worked for ConSpace, like most of the rest of us. When her orbital lab upgraded gene sequencers, they let her take this hulk with her."

She touched a button flush on the top, and the machine started up. Jim hadn't heard anything whir like that for decades.

"How do you keep it running?" he said.

"She taught me how. She gathered up all the spare parts she could find, then asked around for what everyone else had. I've been repairing it since I was about twelve. I couldn't leave it behind when I came out here. Not much use on a planet with no native species, but I figured I might not be here forever. She gave me all these musty old genetics books, too."

She winked up at Rob, then pulled out the first sample pod.

"This won't be nearly as fast as the scanner in my lab." She picked up a thin, flat tool that Jim recognized from drone maintenance. The pick opened the pod as easily as it did one of the big drone casings. She handed the comm to Rob.

"I transferred all our results to this," she said. "I'll give you the code, you note it."

She turned to look at Jim, mouth drawn to one side.

"This is going to take days if I work randomly, and we probably need to move faster than that. Any ideas where I should start?"

"Find the code for the squash," he said. "The first ones we caught. That's all fresh seed and pollen from old Earth stock. We need to start there."

Chapter 4

Several hours later, well into Jim's usual nighttime strolling hour, they had results from three species of pollen and flowers. And not the normal results from the modern scanner.

Maerlis pushed the chair back and rubbed her eyes.

"Same thing as before. The flower is a perfect match. The pollen has several sequences altered. Every one related to reproduction."

"But no trace of a ConSpace marker, right?" Rob rubbed her shoulders, finally getting over his shyness around Jim. "How is that possible?"

All three of them stumbled back into the kitchen to pick at their half-eaten meals. Jim knew he wasn't the only one wondering how long fresh food would hold out.

"It shouldn't *be* possible," Maerlis said. "There are a few of these ancient sequencers around, sure. But the means to manipulate the DNA itself, to make specific changes like this, was taken out of private hands after the final bio-attacks on Fassey decades ago."

Jim remembered that war, the only one he knew of that was more destructive than the last conflicts on Earth. Centuries-old fears and paranoia about genetically engineered weapons had surpassed imagination during those long years in the Fassey system. Turned out one species could indeed create a weapon that would completely annihilate another if they were willing.

The Drephana had been willing.

Maerlis stared out at the twilit fields. "There's no evidence of tampering at all. Yet the changes are almost identical. This has to have been done on purpose."

"But who?" Rob said. He'd taken up Jim's walking habit, but confined to the tiny living pod he was going in circles. His questions were too. "And why?"

"We're never going to get there without how," Jim said.

He sat forward, squeezing his temples with the heels of his hands. Something, fluttering around from his own schoolboy days. Whispering through too many years of memories.

"A restricted species," he said. Not as quietly as he thought.

"A restricted what?" Rob stood beside Jim, held tilted to the side. "Restricted how?"

"I can't remember," Jim said. "I'd bet your great-grandmother could have, Maerlis."

The xeno-biologist jumped up fast enough to spill her water.

"She would have, yes." She dashed back into the sequencer closet and came back out with the comm. "We have the next best thing here!"

Jim met Rob's gaze, but the younger man shook his head. Maerlis tapped on the screen a few times, waited, then tapped again. She looked up, her eyes fierce and bright. Jim knew in that second exactly how Rob felt when he fell in love with her.

"She's awake, come on. I would have woken her up anyway, but this is easier. Crithiens are beasts when they've been asleep."

"Crithiens?" Rob stood frozen, staring at the floor. "You mean Kayren?"

Maerlis was already standing by the open door.

"Of course, Kayren. No one in the Mossera System knows more about history than she does. No one in *any* system, short of an artificial, knows more than a Crithien."

Jim took a step toward the door, trying to force his anxious and weary mind to keep up.

"They have…"

"Multiple brains and eidetic memory, yes." Maerlis waved toward the corridor. "They make connections faster than any human can. Move if you're coming with me!"

The tone of her voice cut straight through to Jim's spinal nerves, and Rob's as well from the look of it. Both men got out the door as fast as they could.

Chapter 5

Kayren lived closer to Jim's section, as befitted the colony's history professor and historian. She'd settled with the first wave, as Crithiens often did. Their deep, broad memories had led them to careers as explorers, investigators, and on permanent system juries as well. Computers were wonderful devices, as far as they went. Organic brains, especially Crithien brains, were still by far the best in the galaxy at making connections.

Kayren was still young by her species standards at just over two hundred Earth years. She only had five segments, each holding one of her brain structures. Jim wasn't nearly as disturbed as the new cadets often were when meeting what looked like a gigantic soft-shelled insect for the first time. But he braced himself when Maerlis knocked on the door.

The historian's leathery abdomen was a glowing magenta, a sure sign that she was about to molt again. She still had recognizable facial features, though, her compound eyes not quite as indistinct as they would soon be.

Seven limbs, thin and sharp like an old Earth shellfish, moved her three meter long bulk easily. Her mouth parts, shaped eerily like a triangular beak, managed to imitate human speech quite clearly. The purring buzz was downright pleasant once you got used to it.

"You have a mystery for me, Maerlis? Greetings, Jim, Rob. Please come inside."

Kayren's lounge was long and low, curved to suit her body, but she had human chairs and a couch as well. She wouldn't leave her quarters again until she finished the messy process of shedding her too-small shell.

"Thank you for inviting us, Kayren," Maerlis said, sitting closest to the Crithien. "We need to ask you about a restricted species."

"What is the nature of the restriction?"

Everyone looked at Jim, including a dozen glittering compound eyes.

"I, uh, I think it had to do with genetic manipulation. I can't remember, maybe a travel restriction?"

Kayren closed all of her eyes, and Jim noticed Rob letting out a breath the same way he did. The respite only lasted a couple of seconds.

"You speak of the Dalsoria. They are restricted from travel, ever since the ban on genetic engineering in the private sector. There have been reports of smuggled groups, however. Dalsoria are simple creatures, not well-suited to deal with questions of morality."

"They've been found recently?" Rob said. He sounded fascinated despite his unease. "In inhabited systems?"

"They have," Kayren said. "ConSpace and other authorities keep such matters secret so as not to inspire more questionable behavior. But Dalsoria have been found as recently as nine Earth years ago."

"What are they used for?" Jim said.

"Often blackmail, often against the larger corporate systems. Forcing others to bend to the criminal will. Or for espionage among governments."

"How would we..." Maerlis shook her head. "How are they found, Kayren? Are there signs?"

"Their own genetics are mutable, changeable. Your grandmother likely would have studied them before the restriction. The Dalsor homeworld has high levels of radiation from an unstable atmosphere. It's a large moon orbiting a gas giant, rather like the moons of Jupiter in the old Earth system. They never developed a stable genome as a result, as defense against the constant damage. This leaves their bodies changeable as well."

"Changeable how?" Rob said. He was pale, but his drawn brow showed how closely he was listening.

"They can adapt to almost any environment once they touch a creature native to that world. They slowly change shape, but never an exact match. Close enough in less advanced populations, but deeply disturbing in more advanced ones. The ability they had to develop to survive on such a dangerous and unstable homeworld gives them nearly unlimited flexibility wherever they are taken."

"How could they possibly alter DNA without technology?" Maerlis said. She chewed her bottom lip and stared off into space. "Without hundreds or thousands of generations for breeding, that's not possible."

"Not for humans, no," Kayren said. "Nor for any other known species. The Dalsoria always retain a porous section somewhere on their bodies. If the target species is small enough, they absorb them and make the adjustments. If the target is large, they can absorb only part. Something as small as a human hand or foot would be enough. The crucial addition is a sort of virus that spreads the modification throughout the entire body, and then the entire population."

Jim shivered, his earlier chill taking over *his* body, along with his heart and mind. If this spread on its own, they might never be able to recover without starting over.

With supplies they couldn't get until it was too late.

"Will you share what you're searching for with me, my friend?" Kayren said, extending a limb toward Maerlis. Jim couldn't stop himself from staring at the soft human hand in the grip of five pincers. "For my history?"

"Of course I will, Kayren. We may end up sharing this with the entire galaxy."

"You will need to search for genetic modifications," Kayren said, "but not complicated ones. The pattern, once successfully altered, rarely deviates with the Dalsoria. They are not good at covering their tracks."

"Where would we look for them?" Rob said. "The Dalsoria. If one were in Mosslea or somewhere else on the planet?"

Kayren slowly knotted all of her limbs together across her torso.

"They would be found in groups, at least three or four. They are warm water creatures from a volatile homeworld, unable to stand the coolness of most of Mossera 4. Dalsoria would only be found around the equatorial zone."

"Mosserrania." Jim shook his head, horrified and amazed at the simplicity of the thing. "Where aliens and humans aren't paying attention to anything related to science or survival."

Kayren tilted her upper segment forward in a clear imitation of a human nod.

"Indeed. A place designed for relaxation and pleasure, but with vast unspoiled natural waterways would be ideal."

Maerlis stood, followed by Jim and Rob. Jim wasn't sure if his lightheadedness was because of the late hour or all the puzzle pieces swirling into place in his brain.

"Thank you, Kayren," Maerlis said, gripping the Crithien's limb again. "I apologize for leaving so quickly. I promise to share everything we learn with you."

"I trust that you will, Maerlis. One more thing you must know. When searching for the shelter of Dalsoria who want to remain hidden, the acidic balance of the water is key. They excrete base rather than acid. The water nearby will be soft and sweet."

Chapter 6

Jim kept the quick pace with Maerlis and Rob, but his thinking was considerably slower. It was one thing to walk around late at night, letting his mind wander and his body relax. Trying to force his brain into mystery solving mode without at least a few hours of rest wasn't going to end well.

Thankfully Rob spoke up before Jim figured out how to, and before they got all the way back to the newer quarters.

"Listen Maer. I want to figure this out and I know Jim does too. But we've all got to get some rest."

She kept charging ahead with the same determined stride until Rob touched her arm. Jim saw her shoulders rise and fall in a slow breath before she turned.

"I don't think I *can* sleep. Not with starvation hanging over our heads. And all these kids…"

"If you don't mind a little detour," Jim said, "I believe I can help with that. Remember the fulmenberry fruit, Rob? You had that a time or two, back when you were a scared, green cadet."

Rob shook his head and laughed under his breath.

"Every night for a couple of months." He put his arm around Maerlis. "I wouldn't have made it through my first cycle without Jim here. You never saw a more pathetic, homesick cadet in your life."

"I doubt that," she said, smiling at up Rob. "I've known a few sad cases."

"Well, don't send them all my way at once." Jim turned toward his quarters, willing to bet the lovebirds would follow him. "I can only grow so many fulmenbushes in a season."

One corridor over and three doors down brought them to Jim's home for most of his adult life. As often happened when he had company younger than himself, he was shy about opening the door. Not because of clutter, but because of lack of it.

Everyone old enough to remember the last Earth Wars tended to fall into one of two patterns. They either hoarded everything, surrounding themselves with more supplies and belongings than anyone could possibly need. Or they lived with the bare minimum for human survival.

Jim fell squarely into the latter group. He'd never wanted much besides the standard issue equipment, either as a soldier or as a teacher. Blank tan walls, a brown sofa and two matching chairs. Bare floors made of nearly indestructible strips of bamblewood. Even his kitchen and wardrobe were spare and easy to maintain. A couple of plates, bowls, and utensils. Several of exactly the same pants and shirts.

Neither Jim nor anyone else who remembered those difficult times found his empty quarters depressing or sad, any more than they found the cramped quarters dirty or undisciplined. Jim thought of each response as a way of making sure you always had enough.

You either got attached or detached.

"Same old Jim," Rob said, softening his words with a smile. "Can't lose what you never had in the first place."

"You got it. Come on through to the greenhouse. I have a fresh batch drying out there now."

The one well-supplied, even crowded, area of Jim's quarters was the huge greenhouse space. He'd picked this apartment not for the windows looking out over the fields, but for the chance to have his own miniature test lab. Four rows across and several of his strides long, the plas-glass enclosed room was still fragrant and warm even so late into the night cycle.

Jim did test new drone designs out here, and he sometimes tested new crop strains. But he loved this room for the same reason he'd wanted this assignment when the war was over.

The peace and calm of growing things

An unknown threat to that calm all over the planet terrified him to his bones.

"Did they model the big grow houses on this one?" Maerlis said. She stopped and peered at every new group of plants in the waist-high row.

"More the other way around. They had the big ones started before I got here. I just wanted somewhere to putter."

The fulmenbushes grew along the back row, perpendicular to the rest. They were nearly a meter high, covered with deep orange leaves nearly as big as Jim's hand all season long. The berries, huge and bright green and shiny, sprouted all along the trunk and branches.

"I'll spoil a bit of Jim's fun," Rob said, taking Maerlis's hand. "Don't let him convince you to try one of the fresh ones. They're bitter enough to make your throat hurt, right before your whole mouth goes numb for a couple of hours."

"You never tried anything without knowing exactly what it was after that, did you?" Jim pulled a heavy metal tray from the row under the bushes. The lights down there left the tray warm, but not too hot to handle. "They dry up sweet, and the concentrated fruit works a lot better."

The shriveled berries were much smaller, about the size of old Earth blueberries. He dropped one into each outstretched hand.

"Only one," Rob said, nodding to himself. "More than that, and you'll wake up with a hell of a headache. Not to mention your guts get plugged up tight for a couple of days."

Rob's face flashed red when he met Maerlis's eyes, and she burst into laughter.

"I'll keep that in mind. Thanks, Jim. Late breakfast at my place?"

"I could use that extra hour or two of sleep," Jim said. "We just have to figure out an excuse to run off for a vacation."

Chapter 7

Just as Jim had expected, Rob was already with Maerlis when she opened her door the next morning. And Rob hadn't yet changed out of his brown robe, made extra long to suit his height. Maerlis at least was fully dressed and ready for the day, and handed Jim a cup of coffee before he could say a word.

"I tested a few samples from the pollen stores," she said, walking back to her small kitchen table. "While Rob was still snoozing. The sealed ones are fine, no mutations. Whatever happened was outside those secured units."

"Thank goodness for that," Jim said. He drained half his coffee in one steaming hot gulp. "At least we know where the problem is *not*. Kayren said whatever the Dalsoria touch spreads like a virus, though. If it is them, we'll have a challenge getting everything cleaned up again."

"We have to work out a good way to get to Mosserrania first," Rob said. He had a nearly empty cup of coffee in front of him, and an empty plate and bowl. "Shuttles leave every couple of hours even this time of year. We just need a reason we can admit to."

"Got that covered." Jim helped himself to a bowlful of hot porridge, with orange and red fruit from last harvest. He hoped it wasn't the last for a while. "I woke up thinking about how we're always wanting to establish a larger food growing area around the equatorial zone. Things we can't grow in Mosslea outside of the greenhouses."

"Sure," Maerlis said. "We could all use more fresh fruit. But they're not going to give up enough of the leisure zone for something as unexciting as food."

"Probably not," Jim said. "But that doesn't stop us from going down to consult. They actually do want us to manufacture drones for them, to pollinate their flowers and enough fruit for the resorts to use."

Rob snorted. "Yeah, the decorative drones I keep hearing about. Jewel tones to match each resort's colors. They even want each set to buzz in a different key so they can tell them apart. Last time I checked, how well the drones work matters a lot more than how pretty they are."

"Silly as it sounds," Jim said, "this all works to our advantage. No one knows more about drone design than we do. And Maerlis here would be the best choice for making sure all these new exotic fruits don't cause contamination with our existing crops."

"You think ConSpace will go along with this?" Maerlis had cleared her own place except for what looked like a very cold cup of coffee.

"They already have," Jim said, grinning. "Our shuttle leaves in three hours. That enough time for you two to get packed and ready?"

Chapter 8

THE CONSPACE EMPLOYEE shuttle was hardly luxurious, certainly not compared to what occasional tourists or the wealthier long-term miners were treated to. Jim, Maerlis, and Rob sat on uncomfortable, barely padded seats rather than recliners with cushions that felt like a massage. They were free to bring their own drinks or snacks for the two-hour trip, but they wouldn't have attendants and menus to choose from. Of course a cost of free made minimal accommodations a lot easier to accept.

Best of all, the odd travel day and travel season meant they had the small, boxy aircraft to themselves. Not even a human pilot to worry about hearing them.

Jim already expected Maerlis to be the best prepared of all of them, and she didn't let him down. Her palm-sized touchscreen was loaded with everything she could find about Dalsoria, their abilities, and their restrictions. He suspected Kayren and her advanced security clearance had helped.

Even the most hidden data wouldn't say how they were possibly going to locate a banned species on a vast, unfamiliar continent.

"This is tragic, really," Maerlis said. "Dalsoria never have understood the trouble they've caused, or the trouble they're in. Genetic modifications are as natural as breathing to them. Their biggest flaw is they trust strangers far too easily."

"I'd never even heard of them," Rob said.

Jim shrugged. "You wouldn't have. They were restricted long before you were born. I had no idea they'd cropped up so recently. You can imagine how often that would happen if they were better known."

"But why?" Maerlis said. She put the screen on the table between them. "Why target us like this? An agricultural post is about as far from warlike as it gets."

"Sure, down here," Jim said. "But remember what we support. ConSpace isn't the only player when it comes to resource extraction or transport. Kayren didn't mention corporations, but she mentioned espionage and governments. ConSpace is bigger than any planetary government, and wealthier than most systems."

"They have to have made enemies along the way," Rob said. "Just going by their public history, much less what never gets passed along to us farmers. Are you sure this is something we can handle? Shouldn't we bring in ConSpace for something this dangerous?"

"I thought a lot about that this morning," Jim said. "Even started to do just that. Have you ever had to call them in, Maerlis? To solve a problem before you understood what was going on yourself?"

She swore under her breath, turning toward the window.

"A teacher of mine did, once. An unknown disease on a new colony. They charged in and took over everything. By the time they were finished, the native populations were nearly wiped out. Most of the early colonists were, too, mainly from panic."

Jim frowned and nodded at the same time.

"That's what I've found, too. Once I know what's going on and what I need, ConSpace is the most powerful ally in any system. Before that, they're the most destructive force. I'm afraid we'd have a panic down here and up on Mossera 5."

The three of them fell silent, watching a vast desert wasteland underneath their shuttle. Jim knew ConSpace had hopes of bringing this arid continent into food and resource production to support the miners someday. Assuming the colony lasted that long

"I hate to sound like a warning loop," he said, "but we're getting ahead of ourselves. Knowing *why* won't help us. Not yet. If Kayren is right, we have to find these creatures first."

"Have you ever known a Crithien to be wrong?" Maerlis said, smiling. "I haven't spent much time on Mosserrania. Either of you know how we might find them?"

Rob shrugged, shaking his head.

"I haven't been there much," Jim said. "Not for a long time. An old buddy dragged me down there, a couple of months after I got here and before he shipped back out. He was a lot more into the entertainment side of things than I was by then. I spent most of my time…"

Both Rob and Maerlis responded to Jim's slow smile.

"Spill it, old man," Rob said.

Maerlis picked up her tablet, ready to search.

"I spent most of my time getting to know everyone who was already here. Everything, too. There's a delightful species we need to seek out. Greponians might be just who we're looking for."

"They…they're like giant old Earth sea otters," Maerlis said, grinning like a little girl. Rob's expression matched as soon as she held up the tablet.

"Violet sea otters?" he said.

"That's the ones," Jim said. "They work as entertainers, and they're whip smart. Funny, too. I bet they'll jump at the chance to do something different."

"Kind of like we did," Maerlis said.

Chapter 9

Mosserrania was as carefully designed and engineered as anything else ConSpace invested in. Visitors could always find what they sought, but they were never confronted with anything else. A family with small children wouldn't accidentally wander into a gambling palace, or a resort devoted to adult entertainment. And no adults would be forced to wander through pastel fairy tale landscapes when they sought only more mature activities.

There was no need for such surprises, not with a string of vast islands circling the planet, each dedicated to a specific sort of recreation.

What Jim and his friends sought waited in the middle of one of the larger family complexes, only a short air-bus ride from the main arrival terminal. The flat, sandy expanse had been converted into a water park. Bright, open buildings surrounded warm lagoons and bays, all sculpted and maintained to child-friendly perfection.

The natural greenish sand remained around the outskirts, with pastel beach houses lining the shore. Inland, the sand changed to sky blue, lavender, pink, every cheerful shade with buildings and walk-ways to match. The heady floral scents from flowers in every possible shape and size were overwhelming compared to the more mundane vegetal smells Jim was used to.

Jim understood Rob's annoyance at something mistaking their vital drones as coordinating toys, but he thought jewel-colored versions would be lovely flying through the wild varieties of plants and flowers. Not to mention a great way to educate miners and tourists alike on the critical work of the farming zone and Mosslea Academy.

Work that was well on the way to disaster if they couldn't figure out why crops were failing.

The busier season on Mosserrania matched the cycles of the mining planet they supported, like all of Mossera 4. Gigantic ConSpace freighters had departed a few weeks earlier, loaded with several months' worth of precious ores and metals. Now with the new extraction cycle underway, only a few off-system tourists wandered in a vacation daze.

Jim, Maerlis, and Rob ignored the temptation of warm water and nearly deserted beaches, heading instead for the performance areas in the middle of the island. A deep, vast pool lined in warm gold tones, surrounded by rows of tiered seating, served as the professional home for many of the water performers.

"This place is beautiful and all," Maerlis said, staring at the rows of palm trees behind the seating area. Their broad leaves and trunks ranged from palest pink and blue to deep burgundy and indigo. "But no one's here. Are any Greponians around?"

"They take their vacations when the miners get back to work," Jim said. "But they usually have a show once a week or so for the off-worlders. I put in a call before we left to see if one of them could speak to us."

A ripple broke the surface of the perfectly clear water, and a violet streak crossed from the opposite side of the pool. Jim's eyes couldn't track the speed, but he knew what was coming. Rob and Maerlis gasped when a fuzzy head bigger than a human's splashed up by their feet.

The Greponian was the largest and oldest Jim had ever seen, easily twice his own size. The fur around its mouth, eyes, and most of its face had faded to black, covering up the distinctive coppery markings that made it easy to tell individuals apart.

Her mouth, he amended, when he caught sight of her elongated deep blue fangs. He didn't know the specialized teeth could extend so far, nearly past the creature's rounded chin.

A clear reminder that while the giant violet otters seemed friendly and joyful during performances, and they usually were with tourists, they were also fierce hunters and fighters.

Jim slipped a tiny translation bud into his ear, noticing the Greponian already wore a water-proof version in her flat, oval ear opening. Rob and Maerlis did the same.

"Greetings to you, ma'am," he said. "Thank you for taking the time to speak with us."

She regarded the three of them with deep green eyes, then shook herself. She took care not to spray water onto the humans, unlike during a performance. Her voice sounded like a range of low-pitched growls and barks to his open ear.

"No one calls me ma'am but the wretched pups I try to train some sense into. Junima will do."

Jim knelt on the warm, rough concrete, waiting while Maerlis and Rob joined him. Junima's rich aroma of fish and seaweed rose all around them.

"I'm Jim, this is Maerlis and Rob. We do our best to train cadets on Mosslea. You have my sympathy."

"Sympathy or not, you're keeping me from my work. What do you want from me, Jim?"

Her tone, even through the translator, reminded Jim of his commanders during the Earth Wars. Might as well get to the point, and hope she had more sympathy than they ever had.

"We won't keep you, Junima. You may know we've been working to expand food production into warmer climates. Hoping to grow more varieties of fruit and such."

Junima snorted water from around her dark purple nose.

"Enough of my pups already waste time working in the seafood facilities. No other species working for ConSpace is forced to take shifts growing their own food. We cater to the miners enough as it is."

Jim decided not to mention how many farmers labored to do exactly that.

"Nothing like that, no. We just need to scout for a specific location, one we think the Greponians can help us find."

"This whole blasted planet has been mapped," Junima said. "Every inch of the land and sea. You want to go exploring, find another world."

"No ma'am," Maerlis said. "Junima, I mean. It's not something we can see on a map. We seek a certain type of water environment."

Junima heaved half of her torso out of the water, this time not bothering to be careful of the splash. Her four back legs, webbed into great flippers, stayed under. Her front feet, with six fingers ending in curved black claws, flexed on the concrete.

Rob and Maerlis stood and took a step back, but Jim stayed put. Junima's eyes, and fangs, were inches from his face now.

"Seems you don't train your pups all that well, Jim. They don't even know not to speak out of turn."

"Maerlis and Rob are leaders themselves, no longer cadets." Jim put a hand on Rob's knee, trying to keep him from coming forward. "All we ask is to work with some of your most mature pups for a couple of days. I know they'll be more than well-trained enough to help us."

"They're not trained to do any such thing. They don't have to be. Unlike humans, Greponians have more than enough senses and instincts for such simple tasks."

"So you'll help us," Maerlis said. Jim was proud of how her voice didn't even tremble.

Junima glared at her, then back at Jim.

"If ConSpace is actually supporting this nonsense, I don't have much choice. Just show me your authorization, and I'll decide how to proceed."

"Our travel auth is right here," Rob said, reaching into his pocket.

"I don't need to see a damn travel auth." Junima flipped her broad tail, sending ripples through the pool. "You couldn't even get down here without that. Show me the ConSpace authorization for my pups to search for your special water. Or, tell me what you're actually after."

Jim didn't need the translator to know this wasn't going to work. Junima had the trick of narrowing her eyes perfected as well as any human commander. They were going to have to find another way.

"Unless I miss my guess, ma'am," he said, "you have enough military or government experience to know we can't share the details of every mission. ConSpace approved our travel. They did not approve my sharing the details of what we're here to do."

"Right. Likely because they don't know. You've wasted enough of my time, and you won't be wasting any of my pups' time. If you bother any of us with this nonsense again, I'll report all of you. Then we'll see who knows what."

Jim stood and pulled the others back just as Junima submerged, sending a wave rushing over the edge of the pool.

"Great," Rob said, stomping water off his boots. "Nice manners on that one. Glad she wasn't my teacher when I was a pup."

"We can't risk telling her what's really going on," Jim said. "She'd go right to ConSpace Security."

Maerlis stepped to the edge of the pool and leaned forward, looking into the still agitated water.

"Any other ideas how we can find the Dalsoria? From what Kayren said, they're going to be pretty well hidden."

"Not yet," Jim said. He thought he heard soft ripples in one of the smaller pools behind them, but he didn't see anything moving. "Not without causing exactly the panic we need to avoid. The only thing worse than food shortages would be telling anyone we have a restricted species loose on the planet."

Chapter 10

A MEAL rich with the seafood Junima's pups helped maintain and a long conversation afterward left them no closer to a solution. The hotel's elaborate fairy tale decorations, sparkling light fixtures, and overly attentive service felt decadent after years spent in Mosslea's utilitarian spaces.

Jim enjoyed watching the young couple marvel at everything, but it made him uncomfortable. Especially with trouble he couldn't figure out how to solve hanging over his head, sinking into his tense shoulders.

Mossera's bluish sun set hours earlier than Jim was used to so close to the equator, but he knew he'd never be able to get to sleep so early. Not with his nighttime prowling habits on top of his worry.

He set out wandering the lush tropical landscape shortly after Maerlis and Rob retired for the night, wishing he'd brought a supply of dried fulmenberries with him. Lighted paths through the flowers and along the beach gave him more than enough to explore on an island that could easily accommodate a few thousand people. He hoped the mindless walking would let his mind relax and come up with something. Anything.

The warm sand felt good under Jim's bare feet and between his toes, almost as good as the soothing rhythm of waves sounded to his ears. Aching calves sent him back to the paths before long. He passed through a fruit picking area designed for children, gathering handfuls of everything he recognized. His favorite was tiny yellow starecks that started off tart enough to make his jaws ache, then turned sweet when he crunched them between his teeth.

He was sure someone in Mosserrania would have equipment that could test the water. There were too many aquaculture habitats set up and maintained for diving and other recreational uses, along with the underwater food production zones. But Jim knew anyone he talked to about using that equipment would be even more suspicious than Junima, and with good reason.

He headed toward the lagoons and pools, deserted and silent. He hadn't seen or heard from Junima after her abrupt departure. The possibility of a year without a good harvest wouldn't impact Greponians or any other species that depended on seafood nearly as much as it would everyone else.

At least not until ConSpace claimed everything they could to support the essential mining operations, leaving the rest to fend for themselves.

He stopped at the edge of the big performing pool, wondering if the soft light around the edges was organic or electric. The Greponians he'd spent time with years ago hadn't been nearly so grouchy or worried about rules and regulations. They'd been a lot more like his rowdy older cadets, willing and eager to get into trouble any chance they got.

Of course the ones he'd known had been around that same age, not crusty old veterans like Junima. Or like he was now.

Jim spun around at the same ripple and soft splash he'd heard earlier. The small pool wasn't nearly as well-lit as the big one, but he could just make out a dark shape moving toward him. He fumbled in his pocket for his translator bud, pulling out the hotel-issue flashlight at the same time.

The Greponian floating at the edge didn't have a trace of black fur in the violet. The metallic coppery markings were clear and distinct, swirling around her eyes and cheeks like the ripples spreading away from her body. Her fangs only showed a few millimeters past her mouth, and she wasn't much bigger than Maerlis. Still, she stared up at Jim, bold and not bothering to hide.

"I'm sorry," he said, finally slipping the translator into place. "You startled me. I'm Jim."

"I did not mean to startle you, Jim." Her grunts and growls were higher and softer than Junima's. "I am Belles."

"Were you here earlier? When we were speaking to Junima?"

"I was. All these pools are connected by tunnels. I was finished with my practice drills and helping the younger pups. And I was bored. So I followed her."

Jim sat on the soft grass that surrounded the pool, grunting at how sore his hips and back were. He'd walked a lot more than he usually did tonight.

"I'm guessing you overheard what we were talking about."

"Of course I did. We long ago learned it's in our best interest to hear whatever Junima says. At least we can try to be prepared. Sounds to me like you're worried about something you didn't want to tell her."

Jim recognized the curiosity and defiance from his earlier encounters with these delightful creatures in her voice and the way her whiskers twitched forward.

"And if I am?"

"Some of us aren't determined to follow *all* the rules," Belles said. "We might be able to help you."

"Not afraid of getting in trouble if she finds out what you're up to?"

Jim recognized the rising and falling hiss, a Greponian's version of laughter. Hope sparked and glowed in his belly for the first time since Rob showed him the messy drones.

"We're old enough to have vacation time, no matter what Junima thinks. We've earned it. I'm not about to tell her where we're going or why. Are you, Jim?"

Jim laughed himself then. No matter the decade or the species, cadets never truly changed. And this situation certainly warranted breaking a few rules.

"Not a word from me. Got a suggestion of where we could meet and talk a little more? See if this is something you really want to get mixed up in?"

"Unlike Junima, many of us enjoy our time in the aquaculture areas and the diving zones. I worked in a particularly lovely one last season. Humans seem to enjoy visiting as well. If you're comfortable with diving, I could meet you there."

Jim got to his feet a little more slowly than usual, but the weight in his heart had lightened considerably. At least they had a chance now. At least they could try *something*.

"We'll manage, I'm sure. Got a couple of friends as brave as you?"

Belles ducked her face under the water for a second. When she came back up, Jim was sure he saw her smiling.

"A few. As Junima says, we have instincts for such work already. We would be neglecting our training if we didn't exercise those as well as our performance muscles."

Chapter 11

BELLES WIPED out any lingering doubts Jim had about her willing participation before he woke up the next morning. Along with a message confirming a diving outing for himself, Rob, and Maerlis, they found all the equipment they'd need waiting in the hotel lobby.

The snorkels and goggles were decidedly old-fashioned, as were the long flippers. Even if they were in bright shades of green and yellow. The modern tech upgrade of ear and mouthpieces for communication and translation were welcome additions.

"We're not going to get Belles into trouble?" Maerlis said. They were all out front, dressed for the water, waiting for their Greponian escort and co-conspirator to arrive. "Sounds to me like she's just a kid. Junima doesn't seem like a good one to cross."

"She's young, sure," Jim said. He hoped his farmer legs weren't too painfully white in swim shorts. "But she's already working with younger pups of her own. And she came to me."

"She went through all the official channels to set this dive up," Rob said. "I doubt this is her first go round with bucking authority. She's better than I was at such things."

Maerlis rolled her eyes and took Rob's hand. Unlike the two men, she looked stunning in her bright red swimsuit, with muscles and curves in all the right places. Between that and her sharp intelligence and curiosity, Jim wondered if the younger man would be concentrating on anything besides her all day long.

"You're still not good at such things, Rob," she said. "I guess we're about to find out about the rest."

A low hum from the left warned them right before their diving tug came into view. Only a few paces across in either direction, the flat craft had rows of seating along all four sides. The space in the middle was open to the water.

Two sleek violet shapes bounded and splashed along just in front of the boat, with three more alongside. They all seemed around the same size as Belles, and Jim spotted three with visible female fangs. The humans walked along a short, vibrant pink dock to meet the pups.

"Good morning, Jim," Belles called. "My friends hope you don't mind if they accompany you on your dive. This is Suma, Alor, Nesil, and Tafen."

Each of the pups ducked their heads in turn. Jim grinned, noticing his friends doing the same.

"Not at all. Happy to meet all of you. This is Maerlis and Rob."

"We're ready to get underway, then." Belles swam in a quick circle around the boat, coming back up beside the dock. "This craft is already set to take us to my favorite diving area, only a few minutes away. You may sit or float in the tank, to get used to the water."

Maerlis immediately slipped into the water. Rob hesitated and moved slowly, but once he stood on the bottom of the tank, he seemed to relax. Belles and the one she'd called Nesil joined them, while Jim got comfortable on one of the benches.

"Is such a close location the best choice for today?" Maerlis said. "With what we have planned?"

"It's perfectly fine," Belles said. "The rumor is Junima resents ocean duty because she's grown to hate the open water. I think she's been in the pools too long, myself."

The boat moved out, slow enough that Jim could have swam alongside and kept up. He noticed several small speakers just under the bench seats, probably for larger groups, and louder ones. The craft itself was nearly silent.

"How much do your friends know, Belles?" he said.

"As much as I do. I have to point out that that's not much of anything."

"No one knows besides the three of us," Rob said. "We could be in for some serious trouble over the next several months."

"Whatever you say is safe with us, Rob," the male called Nesil said. His copper markings streaked like lightning away from his nose and eyes. "We've kept plenty of secrets for a long, long time."

Jim shared what he knew, pausing to let Rob and Maerlis add as much as they could. By the time they arrived at the dive site, a wide, perfect circle of multicolored sand with trees and bushes to match, all the Greponians had fallen silent. Instead of splashing and jumping, they swam quietly.

"I'm sorry to give you so much bad news." Jim stepped off the boat onto the hot lime green sand. "But we've got to find these Dalsoria as soon as we can, assuming that's what's happening."

"You have to be careful if you do find them," Maerlis said. "Don't touch them, no matter what else happens. Don't let them touch you. They don't mean to, but they can make you sick and spread it to every Greponian on Mossera 4."

"I only hope we can manage," Belles said, "in time to stop a disaster. When can we start?"

Rob blinked, then smiled at Jim. "We're ready right now. We just don't have any idea *where* to start."

"Do you know any of the coves and bays Kayren was talking about?" Maerlis said. "Quiet, isolated. Maybe with caves, and she said the water nearby would be soft and sweet."

The five otter-like creatures ducked under the water, heads close together. Jim couldn't hear a thing, but he was certain they were speaking too fast for human ears or electronic translators to keep up. After a couple of minutes, all five popped up at once.

"We can think of fifteen such areas," Belles said. "We'll probably find more when we can look at a map."

"Fifteen?" Jim rubbed at the back of his neck, trying not to get upset. Time was already desperately short. "How long will it take to search that many?"

"That depends on how much diving you plan to do on your vacation," Nesil said. "A few weeks, maybe five with what we have here. If you're enthusiastic enough to charter one of the big, fast hoverboats, though, the kind with warm water tanks built in, we could get that down to a few days."

Maerlis whistled. "You mean the kind a huge group usually rents. I'd love to dive off one of those things, someday when Rob finally lets me teach him how. But I can't afford one room, much less the whole thing."

"That's way above my pay grade," Rob said, shaking his head. "Even if I could swim."

"Don't know what I need a big retirement fund for anyway," Jim said. "It's not like I ever plan to quit. Starving to death isn't exactly the way I'd want to go out in any case. Make the arrangements, Belles."

Jim tried his best not to focus on the cost, or the weeks of vacation he could have bought instead. All the leisure time on Mosserrania or anywhere else wouldn't matter if the whole system collapsed, or if some kind of sinister outside group was responsible for the genetic modifications. Bad as the trouble already was, he was certain whoever this was wouldn't stop at interfering with their food supply.

All he could do was help map out the list of bays Belles and her friends gave them, and hope that list wouldn't get too much longer by the time they headed out in the morning.

No one back at the hotel had ever heard of fulmenberries. They were too rare for even a fully stocked leisure continent. But the human concierge gave all of them drinks to help them sleep without asking any questions.

Jim tried to remind himself to ask Belles if she'd had anything to do with that as he drifted off.

He fell sound asleep without his nighttime walk for the first time in decades.

Chapter 12

By the end of the second day of searching, the excitement and adventure had worn off for everyone. Even the young Greponians. Each cove was lush with human-seeded plants and grasses that didn't require specialized pollination. Each was pristine and beautiful, with no visible trace of habitation or even recent visits. Each remained empty, all the way to the back of every possible cave and habitat.

A few sites held faint remains of water that was sweeter than normal, lingering in the furthest reaches of the caves. Belles and Nesil felt sure that meant the Dalsoria must have been there. Neither they nor any of the other searchers had ever sensed water like that anywhere else on Mossera 4.

Those maddening clues didn't bring them any closer to locating the restricted species, or to understanding why they'd been altering the pollen stores.

Even the strange sense of exhilaration from being the only occupants on a glamorous vessel meant to host dozens of celebrating humans and performing Greponians wore thin. The boat was an engineering marvel, capable of sailing, cruising at typical air speeds over the water, and even closing up tight enough to fly faster than anything but ConSpace Security aircraft.

As sleek and modern as the family-style resort had been colorful and charming, their new home gave Jim, Maerlis, and Rob enough distractions to stay calm at first. The floors, walls, and ceilings were gleaming silver and black, accented with bright, angular artwork that changed throughout the day. Sails that glittered and changed color with every burst of wind towered overhead when they were moving slow. Maerlis in particular was fascinated with watching the moving parts as the ship shifted and transformed between different configurations.

The contract Jim signed stated in no uncertain terms that the three human crew members would be polite, respectful, and above all, discrete. The three women had given a tour of the ship, explained how the human diving equipment, small boats, and a miniature submarine functioned, and disappeared. Jim had to agree the crew were discrete, since he'd only caught sight of them when the ship dropped anchor or departed for a new location.

The full-body dive suits were far more advanced than the snorkel gear from a few days ago, and more than a little intimidating. Only Maerlis was enthusiastic about the equipment, trying all of it before the first day of searching was over.

Every failed search sent Jim further into worry about how much he was spending. Nearly a month's salary for every day that passed. And no matter how delicious the food was that they all enjoyed from the ship's stores, Rob spoke for everyone when he said every bite made him a little more fearful of the shortages to come.

As Mossera 4's blue-tinted sun headed toward the horizon on the second day, the ship waited still and quiet rather than shifting to its airborne configuration. Belles and Nesil had organized their targets so they could sail or cruise at high speeds between locations during the day, then the crew would set the autonav overnight to their next destination. All five of the violet Greponians were still out searching.

Jim found Rob walking along the still-open deck, the first time he'd seen Rob without Maerlis since they'd left Mosslea. The set of the younger man's shoulders, the way he rubbed his thumbs back and forth over his fingertips as he walked, reminded Jim of the more difficult times of Rob's long ago cadet days.

"You authorized to be up here alone?"

Instead of turning, Rob only stopped walking. He gripped the transparent rail and stared out toward the open ocean. Whenever they were ready for flight, a similarly clear shield would drop for protection without blocking the view. But for now, the fresh salty breeze dried the sweat on Jim's face and neck.

"What are we doing out here, Jim? Every day we keep at it is another step toward some kind of food riots. Or these things we're looking for turning us all into some kind of mutants."

Jim stood beside him, watching the sunlight blazing on distant waves.

"What do you think we should be doing instead?"

"I think we should call this whole thing off and bring ConSpace Security in to handle it. Now, before the whole damn planet falls apart!" Rob took a deep breath, held it for a second, then turned to face Jim. "I'm sorry. I shouldn't have snapped like that."

"Don't you dare apologize. Not for speaking your mind when you need to. You may be right. It seemed like a good idea to try to figure this out ourselves when we started. I've been here way too long to deny that ConSpace functions a lot better when we bring them a solution ready to go. If a bunch of corporate types jump in and try to solve the problem before they understand it, a lot gets broken along the way."

"You sound just like Maerlis," Rob said. He smiled, but his features all turned down at once when he closed his eyes.

"Is she wanting to call them in, too?"

"Not even a little bit. She deals with them a lot more than I do, even more than you do. You heard what she said about trying to convince them to let her have simple gene sequencing equipment. She's wanting to get in the water and search herself."

He sighed, blowing air out through his lips. "She's none too happy with me right now, either."

Jim resisted a strong urge to put his arm around Rob's shoulders. What helped a scared teenager would probably upset or embarrass a grown man.

"First fight?" Jim said.

"No, we've had… Well, yeah. First real fight. First one that feels this bad."

"I won't pretend to give you relationship advice, since I don't have much to give. I do think you two are going to be just fine. I'm not going to ignore how you feel about this whole mess, either. Listen, we've got this thing hired for another two days. If we still come up empty, we'll all sit down and talk about what to do next. Okay?"

Rob focused on his hands for a couple of seconds, then he looked back up at Jim and nodded. Before either man could say more, a flurry of splashes and high-pitched squealing rounded the front of the ship.

Five violet streaks headed straight for the underwater portal and disappeared. By the time Rob and Jim raced down two flights of stairs to the tank level, Maerlis was already sitting cross-legged on the wet floor in front of the wall full of diving equipment.

"Slow down, the translator can't keep up," she said, holding both hands toward Belles. The other Greponians darted around behind the lead female, chattering and grunting to themselves. At least they'd stopped the ear-splitting squeals.

Belles looked up at Jim and Rob. Without turning, she raised her tail and hit the water with a huge, booming splash. The other four immediately stopped where they were and floated without a sound.

"No wonder she clashes with Junima," Rob said under his breath.

He stood beside Maerlis, rubbing his thumbs and fingertips again. When she held up her hand, he took it and sank to the floor beside her.

All five Greponians stared at Jim until he managed to sit on Maerlis's other side.

"Did you find it?" Rob said.

"Not the sweet water, no," Belles said. "We met a group of Greponians working on a bed of grasses, a green one we don't have on Grepon."

"Seaweed, maybe laver or nori," Jim said. "An old Earth delicacy."

"Yes, seaweed. I've worked in those beds many times. They're having a problem with their crop, too."

"It's not growing?" Maerlis said. "Even when they seed them?"

"Not like that," Belles said. "They have the same fertility rate as before. The problem starts when the grasses grow and mature. They don't grow the soft leaves. They remain tough and spiny."

"The parts we eat," Jim said. His head spun, catching his stomach up in the whirling feeling of motion. "The parts any of us eat."

"Any sign of disease?" Maerlis said. "Maybe problems with the water?"

Nesil moved beside Belles.

"None," he said. "They've been trying to figure this out for several days now."

"And they're hearing of similar problems from other groups," Belles said. "All in this region for now."

"But probably not for long." Rob moved closer to Maerlis and put his arm around her waist. "They've been here, the Dalsoria. How fast does the seaweed get to this stage?"

"This species grows very quickly," Belles said. "They're seeing trouble in plants only a few days old."

"They're *still* here," Jim said. "Still active. Our pollen was altered long before this. The only way I can think to survive a long crop failure in the farm zone is to turn to the oceans."

"Now that's going, too." Maerlis pounded her fist on her knee. "What the hell for? If they're making some kind of demands or threats, they're being awfully damn quiet about it!"

Jim leaned forward, trailing his fingertips in the warm water. He remembered the danger and suffering of war far too clearly, even from so long ago. He'd rather jump into the tank and let Belles hold him under than see a peaceful world go through that again.

"They're not finished," he said. "Whoever's behind this. They want to make it clear how much power they hold before we ever find out what they want. If we can't figure this out and stop it, I'd bet they'll hit every food source we have. Probably fresh water, too."

"Should we…" Rob glanced behind Maerlis and met Jim's gaze. "Do we need to call in help?"

"We have to be close," she said, shaking her head. "If this is starting in the oceans, the Dalsoria must be nearby."

"Where's the next search, Belles?" Jim said. "How far away?"

"The next target on our map is several islands away from here," she said. "Another overnight flight. But we don't want to go that direction. We need to go back to an area we missed."

"What have you found?" Rob grinned like his young cadet self. No matter what else was going on, that smile warmed Jim's heart.

"The seeds for the sea grass, seaweed, all come from a central storage facility. The group here has heard of problems starting in several growing areas, in different seaweed crops. It would be much easier to work from there to infect many places at once."

"Are there caves close by?" Jim said. "I don't remember any from the map."

"A couple of pups from this group tend to explore where they're not supposed to," Nesil said. The other Greponians hissed laughter. "Not exactly unusual for us. They found a cave system with an entrance underwater. Human mappers probably missed it."

"Whoever we're up against didn't," Maerlis said. "The Dalsoria aren't exactly master strategists, not going by what Kayren told us. Whoever's directing them would have a hard time moving them without getting caught."

"Better to put them in the middle of everything," Rob said. "No tourist is going to bother with an underwater cave in the middle of nowhere with hundreds of more interesting diving spots by the resorts. How far away is this seed storage?"

"Three hours fast over the water," Nesil said. "Less than an hour if we fly."

Chapter 13

Jim had never had a clear understanding of how much the equatorial zone had developed around Mossera 4 in the decades he'd lived there. When he'd first arrived and taken his brief tour of Mosserrania, he'd seen mostly resorts and rec complexes on the existing islands ringing the middle of the planet. There were a few half-constructed diving habitats and rumors of more on the way, but not much else.

The vast expanse dedicated to relaxation had seemed like an unimaginable paradise to him so soon after a time of horrible war.

During the brief flight just ahead of the sunset with Rob and Maerlis at his side, the ship passed over dozens of diving or recreation islands, too round and perfect to be natural. They also passed over more aquaculture zones than he could keep count of. Most would be invisible from the water, or to a tourist or miner who didn't know what they were seeing.

Mossera's clear water revealed rows cultivated under the surface that weren't all that different from where he and Rob worked much further north. Some round, some in a standard rectangular grid. The plants flashed from browns to reds, purples to barely visible greens against the sandy seabed.

Knowing the Dalsoria were somewhere nearby, and that whoever controlled them was already active in this rich ocean farmland, only increased his anxiety about stopping the attack before it got worse.

"That's got to be the storage facility." Maerlis pointed dead ahead, drawing Jim's focus from a perfectly square mat of luminescence off to the left. "Those must be constructed pools."

Sharp bright squares and circles stood out against the darkening waters, each nearly as large as the growing fields they'd just passed over. Jim gave up when his count passed thirty, all on one side of a rocky island. He couldn't see how many were hidden by the mountains.

"Isn't this a secured facility?" he said. "They're not just going to let a pleasure craft land close by."

"You'd be right." Rob tapped his breast pocket. "If it weren't for the useful travel auth you secured for us, old man. Scouting for farming expansion, remember?"

"I have a meeting scheduled with the supervisor tomorrow afternoon," Maerlis said. "Have to make sure the species they're growing are compatible with ours."

"Except they don't know what species they're growing," Jim said. "Not any more."

The boat circled past the growing pools and their high concrete edges, settling on the right side of the island. Jim spotted a few more pools in the distance, but not as many on the other side.

"How could Dalsoria be this close to a ConSpace growing facility?" Maerlis said as they headed downstairs to the tanks. "Wouldn't they notice the change in the water?"

"This might be the perfect place," Rob said. "I'm sure those big concrete pools out there go all the way to the bottom, to keep each species isolated. Just like we do in the greenhouses. Then they transfer the crops out to the open ocean. They'd probably be a lot more worried about the water quality inside the pools than out."

"That's what we thought we were doing," Jim said. "The attack made it to our pollen stores already, at least some of them. I hope we're in time to save these crops."

All five Greponians were circling in the tank, growling and barking. They'd always searched during daylight so far, but they were clearly eager to get started.

"If they attack the moving seafood," Maerlis said, gripping Rob's hand, "mollusks and fish, we might not ever be able to stop it. Not if they spawn in the ocean."

Belles and her mighty tail splash pulled Jim's attention away from the nightmare scenario he'd been worried about for days now.

"Nesil and I scouted as soon as we landed. We smell traces of the sweet water we've been seeking."

Nesil bobbed his head, his coppery lightning streaks glinting.

"The plume extends in several directions with the currents, but we think it's coming from the island. Exactly where the cave is supposed to be."

"Do you need to wait until morning?" Jim said, glancing at the portals behind them. They were underwater, but he could see only a trace of sunlight filtering through.

"This search is by smell," Belles said. "And by taste. The question is whether humans can search by night."

"Humans?" Jim said before he could stop himself.

Of course they'd have to be involved in this part. He could ask the Greponians to locate the cave they needed, and maybe identify the Dalsoria. But he couldn't, and would not, allow them to confront whoever was behind these attacks.

"Yes, humans!" Maerlis had already pulled diving equipment down for herself, a gleaming black suit and transparent goggles. "We've let you do all the work long enough."

"We can't..." Rob said, swallowing hard. "I wasn't joking about not being able to swim, Maer."

"Just use one of these," she said. She dropped a larger version of the diving suit at his feet. "You can breathe with the mask, and one of us will tow you. Or you can use the submarine, but that might not make it into the cave."

Rob shook his head, but Jim jumped in before he could speak.

"I'm not the best swimmer myself. We'll all go out in the boat, get as close to the cave as we can. Then we'll know exactly where the cave is instead of having to wander around."

"Yes, this makes sense to us," Belles said. "Waiting for humans to swim would be too slow. We will find the cave, then direct you to it."

Maerlis shook her head, clearly ready to argue. When she caught sight of Rob's pale face and wide-eyed expression, she relented.

"I'll get the boat ready. You two try out the suits, make sure they fit and you know how to use the breather." She tapped her bare foot for a few seconds, then looked at Jim. "Think it may be time to let someone know where we are? What's going on?"

Jim picked up the slick rubbery suit, holding it up against his body. It looked a few sizes too small, but he knew they stretched quite a bit.

"I'll ask the crew to send a message to the leader of the growing facility here. And I'll send a message to one of my buddies in ConSpace Security. Nothing detailed, not yet. But I'll let her know to keep an ear to the ground for us. Or to the water."

Maerlis nodded once, then headed toward the boat docks up front.

"Ready for this?" Jim said. He held the larger suit out toward Rob.

"No. Not even a little. I thought I might get to paddle around before I jumped right into an underwater cave." He gripped one arm of the suit, stretching it between his hands. "I'm not letting her go out there without me, though. You either."

Chapter 14

Before Jim or Rob quite managed to get comfortable in the suits but after he'd sent his messages, the Greponians returned in a burst of more ear-piercing squealing. The thickening streams of sweet water led to a cave entrance a few meters below the surface. No signs of guards or defenses, but they hadn't gone all the way inside.

Jim had the clear impression they didn't like it, especially Belles and Nesil, but they'd listened to the humans begging them not to face whatever was in the cave. Their impatience while waiting for the boat to reach the jagged face of the cliff showed even more clearly.

Thanks to the huge pleasure craft's supply of night diving equipment, Jim could watch the Greponians circling the small boat. The close-fitting goggles he, Rob, and Maerlis wore let them see a few meters under the water as well as the rock wall ahead of them. Red-shifted dive lights would help illuminate the cave once they headed inside.

Rob gripped the edge of the small bamblewood boat, staring at his flippered feet more than the open water around them. Jim wished the younger man had admitted he wasn't just unable to swim. Rob was obviously frightened of being in such a small, fast-moving boat, dreading whatever lay ahead.

Jim tried to stop himself from running his fingertips over the emergency beacon the leader of their pleasure craft crew had pressed into his palm, refusing to let him leave without it. The round thumb key wasn't going to fall out of the rubbery inside of the suit's hip pocket, no matter how much he worried about it. One sharp press with his thumb, and they'd have whatever backup the crew could provide.

He kept his own emergency beacon, a souvenir of gratitude for his military service, to himself. Jim had never had to use the slim medallion implanted into an indigo bracelet. He hadn't worn it for longer than he could remember back on Mosslea, but it never left his pocket. He hoped he wouldn't need the direct link to ConSpace Security now or any time in the future.

That hadn't stopped him from fitting the bracelet just under the sleeve of the dive suit before they set out.

Maerlis stood up in front of the boat, where she'd been crouching to talk to Belles. Rob managed to hold out a hand to her when she reached the two men instead of asking her to be careful. Again.

"There's a rock just to the right of the cave where we can anchor, about a meter down. Still no signs of guards or any kind of barrier. We don't know what's inside there, though."

"Think it's big enough for us to fit through?" Rob was finally staring at the rock wall rising above them rather than at his own feet.

"If the Dalsoria are there, someone has to be visiting them," Jim said. "Or something. Otherwise they couldn't get anything in or out for them to modify."

Rob nodded slowly, still gripping the sides of the boat. Maerlis sat beside him, gently turning his face toward hers.

"We'll have five natural swimmers with us, sweetheart. Jim and I will be fine. Would you please stay with the boat in case we need help?"

He let go long enough to brush his fingertips through the water, keeping a tight grip on the other side as he leaned. Jim pretended not to notice Rob's shaking hand.

"I'll go behind you two, okay? You showed me how to use the

mask, so I know I can breathe. Just make sure someone knows to pull me back out if I get into trouble."

Maerlis stared into Rob's eyes, then turned to Jim.

"You're a much better swimmer than I am," Jim said. "You stay with Belles, and I'll keep hold of Rob. We'll tell the other Greponians to do the same."

Belles surfaced with two more furry heads close behind her.

"The boat is anchored. None of us can hear anything, but the smell and taste of the water is strong. We're in the right place."

"We're ready." Maerlis turned to Rob again, smiling. "Just remember, breathe normally once you have your mask on. Belles and the others will make sure you're safe."

"We're accustomed to keeping up with humans," Belles said. "Any of us with dive training know you are new to the water."

"Thanks for that." Rob pulled the teardrop-shaped transparent mask up over his nose and mouth. Jim saw his chest rise and fall before he held up both thumbs.

"You're doing great," Maerlis said. She pulled her own mask up, and Jim heard her voice through the speaker built into his diving cap. "We can all speak, and Belles has a transmitter."

She moved to the flattened edge of the boat, grinned at Rob and Jim, then flipped backward into the water. Jim scooted until he was beside the ladder instead, gesturing to Rob to go first.

"I'm right here," he said. "Stay close, and come back out if you need to."

Rob climbed down the ladder and went under the surface. Jim saw two red dive lights flip on. Nothing left to do but jump in himself.

And hope for the best.

Chapter 15

THE CAVE WAS MUCH WIDER than Jim feared, leaving room for him and Maerlis to swim side by side. Belles and Nesil went in front, and the other three followed behind Rob. The red lights showed irregular dark rock all around them. No signs of machinery or anything other than a natural cave.

"Light up ahead," Belles said. "Faint, but clear. Someone's in here."

Maerlis darted ahead. Jim touched her foot before she got too far away.

"You're not going to let me go first, are you? Just promise you'll look, not engage. If anything serious is going on, or if there are guards, we back out of here and call in the professionals."

"I got it, Jim. And no, you're not going first. You're too slow."

She joined the two Greponians in front, and they swam out of sight around a bend in the cave.

Jim touched Rob's shoulder, and they moved forward together.

"Check in, Maer," Rob said, his breathing fast in the speaker. "Let me know what's happening."

"Still moving. Turning my dive light off. Definitely something glowing ahead." Several seconds passed, with only her slow, steady breaths. Her voice dropped to a whisper. "There's the surface. Staying back against the cave wall. Hang on."

Jim pointed up ahead. They'd passed the same curve, and he could see the yellowish glow. He turned off his dive light. Rob looked in a circle around and in front of them before he did the same.

"Someone here," Maerlis whispered, almost too soft to understand. "Some*thing*. Two, no, three of them. A whole shelter in here, supplies and all. May have been here for-"

She gasped, and Jim jerked when she yelled.

"In the water! Belles, it's in-"

She yelled again, too loud for Jim to make out the words. Before he could grab Rob, furry bodies passed over both of them. The Greponians gripped both men with their back feet and surged forward.

"Maerlis!" Rob shouted, flailing his arms, knocking into Jim more than moving himself in the water. "What's happening?"

"-got Nesil! Belles, watch out!"

The cave streaked by, growing brighter until Jim's face burst out of the water. Too much noise and motion made it impossible to understand what he was seeing. Rob's bellowing only made matters worse.

"Where are you! Maerlis!"

A huge hand smacked Jim's mask, driving pain into his nose and making him see spots. He caught Rob's wrist and squeezed hard.

"Stop it, Rob! Let me find her!"

Jim yanked his mask and goggles off, holding tight to Rob. A horrifying, oily thick stench coated his nose and throat. Worse than a spoiling compost pile full of maggots and flies, worse than acres of rotting old Earth battlefields filled with the dead and dying.

A shelf of rock rose up a few meters away. Several lights along the back wall made it hard to distinguish the shapes moving along the edge.

Rob screamed then, trying to jerk his wrist away.

"Something in the water, grabbed at my foot. Maerlis!"

Chapter 16

Splashes exploded in front of Jim and Rob, right in front of the shelf.

Maerlis with her arm wrapped around Nesil, trying to drag him out of the water.

Belles pushing from behind, grunting loud enough to make deep ripples.

Neither Maerlis nor the Greponians saw the things waiting along the cave wall.

"Watch out!" Jim let go of Rob and lunged forward, trying to get to Maerlis. Strong paws gripped his waist, nearly throwing him onto the rock.

Jim raised his arms, hoping he looked more threatening than he felt. Hoping he wouldn't throw up before he could protect anyone. Or himself.

"Stay back! Don't get near her!"

The things could have been human if glimpsed through wavy glass, or maybe through watering eyes.

Heads and limbs slumped like melting wax, sickly green and mottled grey.

What should have been eyes were sunken, bruised looking pits, and irregular gaping holes held space for mouths. He could barely hear the noises coming from the creatures, not with shouting humans and grunting Greponians.

What he heard sounded more like cries from dying artificial babies, a deranged child's toy, than any attempt at communication.

"Maerlis, watch out behind you!" Jim got to his feet, ducking to avoid the low ceiling. "Stay back!"

The things, Dalsoria he guessed, cowered back from his waving arms. But they immediately started moving forward again, oozing and undulating across the cave floor.

"Something got Nesil," Maerlis said, her voice loud but not panicked. "One of them, I think. Rob! Get your head up!"

Jim glanced over his shoulder, long enough to see a violet paw shove his red-faced and choking cadet onto the edge. He also saw Nesil, kicking and struggling with five limbs.

The sixth limb sank into the middle of what had to be another Dalsoria. This one a horrifying version of a Greponian. Seven limbs more like rotting tentacles, purple and blue and black streaks on sticky, matted fur.

Jim grabbed under Rob's shoulders, hauling him up onto the rock.

"Help me, Rob. Get up, but watch your head."

Rob sputtered and coughed, dragging himself up onto his knees. "Maerlis…"

"She's fine, Belles is helping her. I need you, right now!"

The three shapes moved forward again, almost close enough reach the water. Jim lunged at them.

"Get closer and we'll kill that one!"

All three turned their sagging faces toward him, unable to blink but clearly paying attention now. Rob grabbed Jim's hand, pulling until he stood, hands on his knees.

"You understand me," Jim said. The Dalsoria made no reply, but they didn't move, either. He pointed toward Nesil, still twisting and trying to free his limb. "Tell that one to let go. We don't want to hurt any of you."

Three faces flowed around the sides of the heads, pointing more or less toward Maerlis and the Greponians. The crazed, slippery creature holding Nesil's limb lay half in, half out of the water.

"Tell it to let go!" Maerlis yelled. "Now!"

The awful sing-song babble started up again, wavering and slipping from one pitch to another. The one holding Nesil responded, sounding like a Greponian struggling to speak through a throat full of sludge.

"What the hell are they?" Rob said, gasping for breath. "Dalsoria?"

"I think so," Jim said. "That one's letting go of Nesil, so they understand us."

Nesil's paw gradually slipped free, making a horribly loud squelch.

"Are you hurt?" Belles said. She moved to pull Nesil toward her.

"No, Belles!" Maerlis reached between the two. "If he's infected, he may be contagious. Nesil?"

"I don't feel hurt." He cradled his paw with the other three. "My foot feels sick, like it wants to vomit."

"Watch that one," Jim said, pointing at the Dalsoria trying to slip back into the water. "Don't touch its belly."

Belles and the other three grabbed the slimy, diseased-looking version of themselves and threw it up onto the rock.

"How do you talk to them?" Jim said, turning toward the fleshy Dalsoria. "The ones who put you here? How do you know what to do next? We promise not to hurt you if you help us. We may even get you out of here."

After a moment, all three faces slipped and turned toward the wall to Jim's right. The sleek comm boxes weren't any kind he'd seen before, but it was clearly human technology. Advanced models, too, much newer than anything Jim had seen on Mossera 4.

"We need to get Nesil out of here," he said. "Maybe you can help him in your lab, Maerlis." He turned back to the Dalsoria. "Do you have anything here now? Something they told you to modify?"

One of them moved toward the back wall of the cave, slouching like a human with no bones to keep them from collapsing. Jim's stomach protested again, but he bit his tongue to force himself to focus.

He stepped over to a wide tank, easily big enough for him and Rob to fit into. Inside swam dozens of fish, all different species. Another tank close by held shellfish, oysters, and other shelled creatures Jim didn't recognize.

The next phase of the attack.

But they still didn't know who was behind all of this.

"Do you have a way to call them?" he said. "The ones who bring things to you? Just show me, don't call them right now."

Another of the humanoid Dalsoria shifted toward the wall with the comm unit. Jim saw its stomach, or whatever it would be called. This one was where a human's chest would be, soft and caved in. The flesh glistened in the low light.

The Dalsoria tapped three soft appendages just below the comm, making a pattern too fast for Jim to recognize.

"Okay, good." He waved toward the middle of the rock shelf. "Get back together now, where we can see you. What do we do now?"

Maerlis pulled herself up onto the ledge, keep clear of the watery Dalsoria crawling toward the other three.

"We have to get Nesil out of here. And we have to call for help. What's in the tanks, Jim?"

"Fish, mollusks. Just what we were afraid of happening next."

"Call them now," Rob said. He dropped to his knees beside Maerlis, hands on her shoulders. Jim thought he wanted to hold a lot more of her than that. "Get back to the boat, call them, and get the hell out of here. They have more than enough to find."

"No, not enough." Belles darted back and forth in front of Nesil, more distressed than Jim had ever seen a Greponian. "Catch who did this. Stop them from doing more."

"Get Nesil back to the big boat," Jim said. "Rob, help Maerlis. Once you're on board, let me know. I'll have the Dalsoria call their handlers. Then I'll alert ConSpace Security."

"You can just do that?" Rob said. "Call them up?"

Jim pulled his dive suit sleeve down, revealing the blue bracelet.

"A little reminder of my military service. Yeah, I can just call them up."

"The dive suit systems won't work inside the caves," Belles said. She'd stopped darting around, but she watched Nesil closely. "Not as far away as the ship. Suma, you wait outside. When Nesil is on board, tell us, then head back yourself. Jim will make his calls. I'll get him out of here."

Chapter 17

"Now, Jim," Belles said when they surfaced outside the cave. "We must get Nesil to safety before these attackers show up. They've done more than enough damage."

Jim took a deep breath, letting the fresh, salty air wash the last of the reek of the cave away. He had no way to know how long the Dalsoria handlers would take to arrive, or even what the creatures had said in their message.

None of that mattered, not anymore. They had their proof. They needed help.

His dread of dealing with ConSpace Security didn't matter any more, either.

As soon as his fingertips pressed the medallion, a woman's tinny voice spoke.

"Planetary Security. Name and identity code, please."

Jim rattled off his ancient soldier's credentials without hesitation. He doubted he could have called them to mind before that second.

"James Turhan," the tinny voice said. "Director of Educational Services, Mosslea Academy. Current location, Mosserrania. Secured ConSpace seafood growing facility. Please explain your unauthorized location and your call."

"I…there's been a report of a restricted species. I can confirm the report. Extreme danger to Mossera 4 and all ConSpace operations."

"Please identify the restricted species."

"Dalsoria. Four of them. There's evidence of tampering with our food supplies. Ongoing tampering."

The unit fell silent except for a series of clicks.

A churning hum rose from the opposite side of the island, getting louder and closer.

"Jim," Belles said.

"Please explain your location and how you know of this threat."

"No ma'am. Respectfully, not right now. I'll explain everything to Mossera 4 Command in person, please. I'm requesting an immediate response to the presence of a restricted species."

Belles tugged Jim's arm, dragging him away from the rock. The hum resolved into a powerful motor, and a boat came around the edge of the cliff.

"Jim, we must submerge."

"I hear it. ConSpace Security, situation escalating down here. Immediate physical danger. Please respond to restricted species. Be prepared for armed conflict. We're about to have company."

The motor stopped, and the boat drifted into the same spot where they'd been anchored just a few minutes ago. Belles started pulling Jim backward.

"Breather on," she said, her voice barely carrying over the translator bud. "We must submerge."

Jim shook his head, holding the bracelet closer to his mouth. Hoping the tinny voice wouldn't carry the few meters across the water.

His goggles showed several dark suited figures moving around on the boat.

All of them much bigger than Rob.

All of them armed with some kind of heavy rifle.

"Units dispatched. Can you remain at your location?"

Belles froze, just like everyone on the boat. One of them dropped his rifle and picked up an electric torch. The blinding white beam moved across the water in widening circles.

"No ma'am, too dangerous," Jim whispered. "I'll wear my link for the next few days."

"We will find you. Move to safety immediately."

The light flashed into Jim's eyes. He was too blinded to see anyone pointing rifles his way, but he heard a shouted command.

"Okay, Belles. Get us out of here."

Chapter 18

FIVE WEEKS LATER:

Kayren leaned back in her lounger, folding her seven limbs across her leathery abdomen. The Crithien's color had faded from the brilliant magenta of pre-molting back to her normal sky blue. Her latest messy transformation gave her a sixth segment, smaller than the others but complete with a new brain.

She tilted her head from one side to the other, regarding Jim with dozens of glittering compound eyes. He sat calmly in one of her human-specific chairs, looking back at her. Kayren gazed at Rob and Maerlis in turn, sitting close together on her sofa.

After their adventure with the Dalsoria, all three of them were decidedly calmer in the presence of a massive, super-intelligent insect. At least Kayren's genetics were stable, and theirs were in no danger of being altered no matter how intently she stared at them.

"And the Greponian, Belles," Kayren said, her insectile buzzing clear and easy to understand. "She pulled you to safety, Jim?"

"She did. I just about drowned myself, though. I didn't get my breather on in time, so I had to hold my breath most of the way. Not an easy thing at the speed she swims."

Rob shook his head, smiling at his teacher. "You had us scared, old man. Took a couple of good thumps on the chest to get you to cough up all that seawater."

"Yeah, I appreciate that." Jim rubbed at his chest. "Could have done without the cracked ribs, though."

"The spies, they did not pursue you?"

"They got interrupted by Jim's buddies at ConSpace Security," Maerlis said. "We heard their energy rifles blast a few times, then what sounded like an explosion over our heads. A full troop transport, bearing down with heavy arms and thirty soldiers, against seven guys on a boat. Wish I could have seen their faces."

"We can still see their faces," Rob said. "Thanks to Kayren here."

"It seemed the least I could do," Kayren said. "Your actions saved the Mossera System considerable hardship, if not total collapse. I'm sure ConSpace would allow you to attend their galactic court trial even without my influence."

"I'd rather not go, given the choice." Jim finished his beer, then got up to pour more for himself and Rob. Maerlis was still sipping water. "I've had enough of courts and testifying and questions to last five lifetimes."

"Yes, I've reviewed your testimony, Jim." Kayren nodded when Jim offered her more of her own fermented beverage. After seeing the luminescent orange color, he'd decided not to ask questions. "You handled yourself very well for such a serious situation."

"I managed not to get thrown into prison, is that what you mean?" Jim said, laughing. "Junima would still love to see me locked up for dragging her precious pups along on our crazy expedition."

Rob held up his glass, grinning. "I think the only thing that saved any of us was working ourselves half to death getting this new pollination cycle underway in record time. They can't exactly throw us in prison when we're heroes, can they?"

"Especially not when only a handful of us ever knew the real danger." Maerlis touched her glass to Rob's. "Planetwide panic, averted."

Jim held up his own glass before taking a long drink. They'd finished final inspection earlier that day. Pollen from their secured stores, carried in carefully sterilized drones. Fields washed down with great loads of water carried from the oceans to remove as much of the mutated pollen as they could.

So far new fruit was setting on all but a few of the affected species.

They'd have to be vigilant for years, watching for that Dalsoria virus to return. But at least now they understood what they were looking for. And they had an ally in understanding and fighting the problem if it ever did come back.

"We'll have a couple of lean months," Jim said. "Shortages of a few fruits and vegetables. Easy enough to explain one bad season than survive a bad year. We'll get through."

"How is the wounded one faring?" Kayren said.

"Nesil is doing well," Maerlis said. "I was able to arrest the damage to his DNA before it spread beyond his paw. He did lose it, though."

"He would have lost his life if not for you." Rob reached for her hand. "Him and a bunch of other Greponians, probably."

"We don't know what the manipulations would have been," Maerlis said, swatting his hand away. "The Dalsoria might have been improving him for all you know. Should have let them get hold of you."

Kayren picked up a touch screen designed to respond to Crithien limbs.

"That's how you helped Nesil, Maerlis? By studying the Dalsoria?"

"My new guests were quite happy to help once they understood the problem. And once we learned how to adapt the translators to them."

Jim shuddered, trying to hide his reaction. He understood why the creatures couldn't leave, not with their restricted status and the crimes they'd been involved in. Creating a highly secured and tightly controlled habitat for them, deep under Maerlis's lab, seemed like the most humane solution.

They were, after all, innocent of the crimes, acting on human instruction.

"I still don't like you working with them, Maer," Rob said. He sat forward, rubbing his hands against his knees.

"You think I'd pass up the research opportunity of a lifetime?" she said. "Several lifetimes? Thousands of scientists across the known systems would give anything to study the Dalsoria. And I never get close to them, you know that. Thick plas-glass walls, guards everywhere. Dalsoria are very sweet once you get to know them."

"I look forward to meeting them as well," Kayren said. "Perhaps when the galactic trial has concluded. I do wonder what the sentence will be."

"They tried to destroy everything we've built here," Jim said, more sharply than he intended. "All so PittGalactic could swoop in, buy up the Mossera System, and rescue us all. If there's any justice, they'll get a lifetime of hard labor on Mossera 5."

Jim struggled with himself, as he had countless times since his own trial. His friend in ConSpace Security had admitted, to him and in private, that he'd probably made the right choice in not calling them sooner. Any overreaction and resulting panic would have played right into PittGalactic's hands.

He figured he'd admit that much to Maerlis, and maybe Rob. Someday. When all this fuss and bother finally died down.

As the silence stretched out, Rob started fidgeting, then shifting around the same way Maerlis had. Jim recognized the signs from years of experience.

"All right, kid," he said, glad for an excuse to speak up after his outburst. "What are you wanting to say?"

Rob shook his head, staring into the corner for a few seconds. He didn't manage to hide his broad smile. As Jim knew he would, he started talking.

"We…Maerlis and I want to…" Rob's face flushed as red as when Jim first saw the two of them together. "Go ahead, Maer."

"I'm pregnant," she said, throwing her hands up and smiling. "Got confirmation today. We figure it happened sometime during our grand adventure down on Mosserrania. Just like all the tourists and miners, right?"

Jim jumped up and caught the two of them in a hug. He smiled while Maerlis, and even Rob, hugged Kayren as best they could.

"You are well-matched," the Crithien said. "I look forward to welcoming a new member of your family."

"Congratulations don't even come close," Jim said. "I couldn't be happier for both of you."

"I'm glad you feel that way, Jim." Rob looked into Maerlis's eyes, then settled his hand on her belly. She covered it with hers. "I hope you won't mind company on your twilight walks once I'm carrying a fussy baby around half the night."

"You know," Maerlis said, turning back to Jim. "Since none of our parents are here."

"Makes things a little harder." Rob ducked his head and grinned, sending Jim back to his earliest days trying to keep up with him as an unruly cadet. "We were kinda hoping…"

Maerlis took her turn. "If you wanted to…"

"I'd be the luckiest man in the whole system, being a part of this baby's life. Any way you need me to." Jim paused to wipe a tear before it could get away. "That's what Granddads are for."

Author of Restricted Species and Renovations

KARI KILGORE

THE BECALMED

To my father-in-law Frank Adams

*For his love of science fiction,
his love of helping others,
and his great big dream of flying all over the world
that he made come true.*

Chapter 1

Luis Ahmad had tried every anti-nausea drug in all the galaxy and every home remedy from a hundred AlliedSystems planets. And without fail, as soon as a sub-light transport smaller than a vast ore freighter decelerated for orbit, he was sweaty and shaking, huddled beside the nearest receptacle.

His own specialty of deep psych-hypnosis didn't work any better than transdermal herb infusions from Beta Handsos. He'd even entered orbit submerged in a buoyant vat of Jemushian violet nectar. He had to admit that he smelled wonderful after that, but he still felt awful.

For a man with a body so ill-suited for interstellar travel, Luis often wondered how he'd stumbled into a career demanding just that. He'd never quite given up hope that hibernation technology, and safety regulations, would eventually allow him to wake up on his destination planet rather than hours before braking. A guy had to hope.

One reason he'd taken an assignment so far from Earth, on the edge of the far-flung Abrams System, was passage on the biggest ore freighter in the TransGalactic fleet. His hypersleep recovery cabin onboard the *Bountyfield* resembled nothing more than a dull steel rectangle, with five empty bunks wedged in around the floor-level spot he'd assigned himself. A few grunts and groans when he got up and down were a small price to pay for less gut-twisting motion.

The bass rumble as the ship's braking engines kicked in were the cue to keep himself focused with sensations other than his belly. Stretched out on the rock-hard mattress with his eyes closed, he ran his fingertips across the nubby blanket on his neatly made bed, pointedly ignoring the unfortunate shade of green.

He held his other palm flat on the cold, ridged floor. A mouth full of plain old Earth-style mint candies didn't do much to settle his stomach, but the sharp chill in his throat and nostrils gave him something else to concentrate on.

His position as TransGalactic's head psych-officer, not to mention the absurd amount they were paying him for this assignment, gave Luis the choice of far more luxurious recovery staterooms on board. Even the most rugged freighter carried a few for VIPs, and the *Bountyfield* was hardly rugged.

Commissioned only ten years ago specifically to make runs to the vital Abrams System, the forward section of the kilometers-long freighter could pass for TransGalactic's corporate headquarters. Silks from the moons of Kayren, mood-sensing crystal lighting from Outer Rigia. The finest chefs from around the known civilized systems. All standing ready for hypersleep recovery, on-board meetings, whatever the elite demanded.

And unfortunately for Luis, the staterooms were close to those gourmet kitchens, the better to waft tempting aromas through circulated air. Most humans woke ravenous. Avoiding food, no matter how expertly prepared, until he was planetside worked far better for Luis.

He opened his eyes when the braking engines cut out, leaving only the sound of his own breathing. The worst was over as far as gastric upset, but he was better off staying right where he was. The small crew on a big ship would work like ants racing ahead of a flooding river preparing for space dock. All Luis and any other passengers could do was get in the way.

He sat up carefully in case the grav-dampers still needed to adjust and pulled on a black wool jacket to match his pants. Luis pressed his back against the smooth, steadying wall. No bored long-haul crews had scratched or decorated it yet. One perfect coat of shiny TransGalactic blue would eventually give way to patches and repairs.

An hour until dock. May as well refresh his memory about the case that brought him such a long way. And focus his attention anywhere but on movement he could neither see nor control.

Luis pulled a spherical holo-reader out of his small woven aluminum daypack. He held the reader cupped in his palm, then pressed three fingers into the top to activate the display. He'd resisted the feather-light device at first, preferring the flat touch screen reader he'd grown up with.

The versatility of the display and the simple beauty of the nearly transparent ball won him over in the end. He adjusted the height until what looked like solid paper sat the perfect distance from his eyes before letting the reader float in place.

If Luis had been in one of those posh corporate staterooms several levels above, he would have a sprawling view of Bitanthra by now. More surface water than Earth on a smaller planet resulted in a thick grey and white cloud cover.

Native plants remained primitive and mostly safe, though humans with spring allergies tended to suffer greatly on the surface. A young, blue-tinted star left all that water looking especially brilliant if the observers weren't dealing with watering eyes.

The truth was nothing in particular recommended Bitanthra until TransGalactic got the sparkling deep-green ore scattered all over the rocky surface into their research and development labs. Decades later, Luis and most other sentient creatures understood what Bitan did. Only a handful outside of TransGalactic personnel ever had a chance to actually touch any.

Even the smallest grains were too valuable to remain unused.

Luis shifted his display, changing from text to images almost life-like enough to take the place of touch. An uncut stone turned slowly in mid-air, gleaming pine forest green interrupted by brilliant flashes of purple, red, and orange.

A fine specimen like this, the actual size not much larger than a grown man's thumbnail, was worth more than a thousand homes on Earth.

Two quick metallic raps pulled Luis out of wondering if he'd have a chance to touch a piece of Bitan. He pushed himself to his feet, only grunting a couple of times. He slipped the reader into his day pack and activated the pack's magnetic seal.

Chapter 2

A TransGalactic escort, obviously dispatched from the state-rooms judging by her perfectly pressed midnight blue pantsuit and gleaming gold buttons, waited in the corridor. She looked about thirty, but with people in this line of work spending so much time in hypersleep, Luis never guessed about such things.

He didn't guess about TransGalactic pairing her with him, either. There were no classes or official documents admitting to it, but anyone on long-term hypersleep duty understood the open secret. Luis matched well with men or women with reddish hair, blue or green eyes, and fair skin. Her warm smile made it clear his brown eyes and hair and easily tanned skin fit her preferences as well.

"Dr. Ahmad. I trust your recovery has been smooth."

"Smoother than usual. Please, call me Luis."

"As you wish, Luis. I'm Tegwin Fairbrooke. We're boarding the first shuttle, if you're ready?"

"Lead the way."

The utilitarian steel hallway was decorated only with stripes of paint along the floor. Luis wasn't sure what the black, red, or green paths led to. He'd been told to follow the TransGalactic blue, and Tegwin did the same. Several crew members rushing past them wore sturdy canvas coveralls in colors matching the floor, but he didn't have a chance to see if they followed their proper stripes.

"Your first time on Bitanthra?" Tegwin said.

"It is. I've heard it's lovely."

She shrugged, continuing her quick pace. "Definitely peaceful. I don't mind ten days or so, but I think I'd struggle on a long ore loading stop with nothing else to do."

"Aren't they loading this time? I thought we were here for forty days."

Tegwin stopped in front of a personnel tri-axis motivator. Luis didn't love the unpredictable motion of a tri-ax, but it was unavoidable on a ship this size.

"I'll have plenty to do, Luis. I'm your corporate and planetary liaison. We can always catch a smaller freighter out if you're finished early, but the *Bountyfield* will be here for the duration. Before you ask, I trained in psych before I signed on with TransGalactic. Never had a chance to work much with hypnosis, though."

She waved her wrist in front of a round black sensor beside the tri-ax door. Luis hadn't noticed the thin silver com-bracelet she wore. He wondered how much Bitan it held, and how much a civilian would have to pay for one.

"You'll get plenty of chances to watch deep psych-hypnosis in practice if all goes well," he said.

The lift had the same boxy design as his recovery cabin had, with unpainted steel walls and a textured floor. Tegwin didn't do anything he saw, but the tri-ax moved smoothly to their right, toward the front of the freighter.

Most people swore they couldn't feel the damped motion and were surprised to find out where they ended up. Luis always knew.

"The shuttle will have us on the ground in about twenty minutes. Do you need medication for the drop?"

Luis laughed. "I see my reputation got here first. I'm usually fine as long as I can see and the shuttle isn't bumpy, thank you."

"You'll be able to see. Maybe better than you want to."

The tri-ax door slid to the side, and the reality of a working ore freighter slammed into Luis's senses. Whirring machinery, the stink of hot gears and human bodies working at top speed, a blur of people and material in motion. Tegwin stepped confidently into the controlled chaos, still following the blue stripe on the floor. Luis took a deep, mint-flavored breath, and followed.

When Luis spotted the curved bottom of the shuttle about a hundred meters away, Tegwin's comment made sense. The forward section was transparent, likely a proprietary TransGalactic alloy. The open cargo doors and the back of the shuttle were solid black, as shiny and new as the rest of the *Bountyfield*.

Luis followed Tegwin up a short flight of portable stairs into the crew seating area. White plastic seats with the thinnest of blue cushions were jammed in three to a side, with only a long, narrow window at shoulder height breaking up the matching white walls.

"You're welcome to stay back here if you think the drop will bother you," Tegwin said. "SteelGlas is every bit as strong as the rest of the ship, but some people prefer an enclosed space."

"I'd like to get a look at Bitanthra on the way down. If I have trouble, I promise I'll let you know before it's too late."

A wave of her wrist-comm, and they passed into another world. An absurdly expensive world created by the magic of that green rock. A black-carpeted walkway ran down the middle of the forward lounge, but the rest of the floor, walls, and ceiling were nearly invisible. The empty chairs up here were more like upright cocoons, all facing toward the center aisle.

Thick TransGalactic blue padding adjusted itself to Luis's body when he sat at the front of the shuttle, creating an odd sensation of both security and floating.

"We drop in about a minute." Tegwin settled in beside him. "I can call the attendant if you'd like refreshments or food."

"No, thank you. Are we the only ones going?"

"For now. There's a board meeting on the *Bountyfield*, so the shuttle will be bringing Bitanthrans back up for that. Most of the execs will be outbound on a smaller freighter in a few days, meeting with another colony. If you want to face out for the drop, press the armrest with your right hand. Another press brings you back."

Luis did a quick internal check. Everything felt secure for the moment. He swung himself out into what looked like solid black empty space.

He heard a faint wavering alarm, probably about a thousand times louder in the cargo hold, ending with a solid thud that jarred the shuttle.

"Outer shuttle door," Tegwin said. She'd positioned her chair beside his. "Drop begins now."

A line of light below Luis's feet broke the darkness, letting in a flood of white and blue light. The light grew upward as the inner door rose over the thick clouds of Bitanthra.

The shuttle glided forward, clearing the sides and top. When Luis saw nothing but clear space and choppy clouds with occasional flashes of dark beneath, the shuttle dropped. Not abruptly like most older models, and not too sharply. Luis hardly noticed his stomach's slow roll.

"We're over the sea right now." Tegwin pointed to flashes of dark blue beneath them. "We'll circle the equator then heard north to the eastern mountain ranges. Smoother entry that way."

"That's where the mines are?"

"The big ones, yes. A few are scattered across all the land masses, and we've recently discovered Bitan deposits in the seas. The highest quality ore is still in the highlands."

Luis wished he could pull up the image of flashing green Bitan again, but he'd never been comfortable reading in motion. The reddish sun was hidden behind the mass of the *Bountyfield*, so he could observe the one source of the most important ore in the galaxy without a trace of glare.

A handful of those stones allowed communication across so far unlimited distances, all in real time. Voices and data traveled hundreds or thousands of light years in an instant, while the fastest transport in any fleet would take years or longer to make the same trip. Rapid colonization and the rise of the AlliedSystems would have been impossible without Bitan.

Luis had started out on this journey to save the most vital, and valuable, human colony in the known galaxy three Earth years ago.

To say the collapse of Bitanthra could lead to the collapse of the

AlliedSystems and the TransGalactic empire, if anyone were brave enough to speak those disturbing words out loud, would be no exaggeration.

The problem here wasn't dissatisfaction with the workers, not like cautionary tales of labor struggles of the distant past on Earth or anywhere else. Everyone involved knew mining, processing, and shipping Bitan was never going to be easy. The stones were too fragile and soft for heavy automation or careless handling. Hours were long under and above ground. But TransGalactic took care of their invaluable colony and the people who made it work.

Luis wasn't here for the families of the workers either, at least not the adults. Several generations had been born and raised on the surface, and people rarely wanted to leave.

The colony was under serious and growing threat because of their children.

Chapter 3

For the last thirty Earth years, a handful of the first native Bitan-thrans, the offspring of the original human workers, seemed typical when they were born. They were physically healthy, curious and energetic, and of normal intelligence.

But over the next few years, the children steadily withdrew from their families and the rest of the world. They simply had no interest in the emotional lives of themselves or anyone else.

"You've been briefed on my mission?" Luis said before he realized how it sounded. "I'm sorry. You probably know more than I do. This isn't exactly open information outside of TransGalactic."

"We've worked hard to keep it that way. I always wake early so I can monitor what's happened while we were out. Several groups of women have been taken off-world for their pregnancies and births. No difference. If either parent was born on Bitanthra, the children are far more likely to have the disorder."

"What's the percentage now?"

Tegwin stared down at a break in the clouds, a sparkling glimpse of the star reflecting off the vast sea.

"It's passed fifty percent now."

The twist in Luis's gut had nothing to do with movement. His last briefing, the day before he'd gone into hypersleep, had put the rate at thirty-seven percent.

"It's accelerating so fast. Any progress on diagnosis or treatments?"

"Nothing useful to report. No detected toxin or other signs of disease. No effective treatment." Tegwin sighed long and low. "They're perfectly healthy aside from the complete lack of emotion. They hardly ever dream, either. That was in my last report. The few they have are mild and calm. No nightmares, for kids or adults."

Medical treatments had all failed, as had the same kind of folk remedies Luis constantly tried for his space sickness. Typical psychiatric treatments and drugs had no effect.

No one said the words, at least to him, about deep psych-hypnosis as a last resort in this case. Luis suspected other than moving hundreds of native families permanently off-world and destroying the society they'd built, Bitanthrans and TransGalactic were running out of options.

"How are the groups of affected children holding up?" he said. "Still living in their own communities?"

"They're doing well under the circumstances. The adults all live together, and they raise several of the affected children now too. They can work in sorting or processing, anything that's not dangerous. They seem to lack fear, or maybe the survival instinct to work underground. They've taken to calling themselves The Becalmed."

"Like an old sailing ship when the wind dies." Luis couldn't help respecting the word choice. He understood the separate communities as well. Neither group would be likely to make sense of the other no matter how hard they tried. "Do they know we're coming? What we're going to try?"

"They know about routine medical examinations, and they've all had regular psych evaluations from the time they were born. The current co-leaders have agreed to participate. Everyone knows no one has ever lied under a deep psych field. Honestly, I believe without the capability for fear or suspicion, it never occurs to them to resist."

Luis raised his eyebrows and focused on the much closer planet.

The shuttle was aiming for a larger break in the clouds, and he could see dark yellow sand with spots of flashing metal down there. The equatorial resort zone was all most visitors to Bitanthra ever saw. Mining zones were too important and valuable.

Too many leaders in too many parts of the galaxy had tried to create a docile and compliant force of workers. Even if their methods hadn't been so horrific, the thoughts of people willing to destroy themselves because they couldn't resist was.

"I hate to bring this up before we even land," he said. "But has TransG considered this may not work? Do they have a plan for what to do then?"

Tegwin shook her head slowly.

"They've considered it obsessively. Just like with the medical treatments, nothing useful to report. Nothing they've passed along to me, at least. They established a colony here because it *is* so remote. That's gotten better with faster transports and more colonies out here on the edge of nowhere, but it will never be an easy trip. Men and women doing hard work are a hell of a lot happier if they go home at the end of the day instead of once every few years."

"Getting the existing colony disbanded wouldn't be easy, either."

"Not at all. They've been here for several generations now. They're not from Earth or Beta Zhir or any other planet. They're from Bitanthra. There's something about this place, too. I'm sure you've heard how the natives feel about it."

Luis nodded. "I know they don't like to leave."

"No, that's not it." Tegwin frowned. "They *don't* leave. Ever. The women were furious at having to go off-world for their pregnancies and births. Men didn't much like it either. It wasn't the separation, really. They did not want to leave. I think they would have literally fought it if they weren't so afraid of what's happening to their kids."

"I've heard they're a fierce bunch."

"That's a mild way to put it. I have an odd theory I've never mentioned to anyone else." She glanced over her shoulder. A dozen or so fabulous chairs still sat empty. "I've wondered if people who are from here, the ones who aren't affected, are even more emotional than usual. Maybe not taking on what The Becalmed never had, but adjusted upward somehow."

Tegwin turned to face Luis, cheeks red and eyes defiant.

"I don't see why not," he said. "Is that any more strange than over fifty percent of their children being born without emotion at all?"

She stared at him for several seconds, then her face relaxed into her warm smile.

"It's not, is it? Listen, we're about to pass through the lower atmosphere. The pilot aimed forth the clearest area she could, but it could get a little bumpy."

Luis unwrapped a green and white striped mint candy for himself, then offered one to Tegwin.

"I haven't seen one of these since my grandfather kept a bowl full." She smiled when she popped it into her mouth, but her eyes were sad. "That was what, sixty, seventy years ago? So hard to keep track with all this hypersleep."

"Impossible."

"About as likely as keeping track of a relationship or anything like a family. Outside of these assignments, I mean."

That was another benefit of the open secret of mission pairings. Not only did everyone know. Most appreciated the opportunity in the middle of an incredibly disjointed life.

Chapter 4

THE TRANSGALACTIC PILOT was as good as her word, bringing the shuttle down with barely a shudder. Luis wished the clouds were a little lighter so he could see the mountains rising up all around them. Short, narrow valleys cut through soaring peaks covered in a dense canopy of trees in every shade of green he could imagine. Broad rivers wound through the larger valleys, many carrying wide barges he guessed were full of ore.

Their landing port sat in a wider valley, but the surrounding town couldn't have held more than ten thousand people. Stone and wooden buildings dominated, with none terribly large or tall. Electric personal transports were plentiful, but more people walked than drove.

Luis had visited many small, slow-paced settlements like this on leisure-heavy planets, or in remote areas of more industrial zones. Their brief flyover of Bitanthra with this being by far the largest settlement made it clear how sparse the population really was.

He turned to Tegwin, supervising the offloading of their luggage. A miniature mountain of his black bags and her TransGalactic blue ones sat neatly arranged in the open door of a transport that could have seated ten people. He didn't see any other passengers waiting.

"How many people live here now, Tegwin?"

"About four hundred thousand residents, mostly human. The tourist zone can accommodate around a hundred thousand more, but I doubt they've ever been full. That's just a side industry, mainly set up for the miners and their families. Bitan provides all they need."

"Looks like it."

Unlike other remote resource extraction colonies Luis had visited, everyone he saw on the perfectly maintained concrete sidewalks wore clean clothes in like-new condition. Simple work clothes to be sure, with old-fashioned Earth blue cotton jeans and cotton shirts and jackets in primary colors. But nothing seemed tattered or stained.

People were pale but healthy looking, sturdy and strong. The air itself was a thousand times cleaner than any other extraction colony as well. Instead of acrid dust or choking smoke, Luis smelled faint wood smoke, trees a bit spicier than Earth pines, and rich cooking smells from close by.

Now that he was on solid ground, his stomach reminded Luis that he hadn't eaten solid food for more than three years. Loudly.

"We're meeting the Bitanthran leadership in a couple of minutes." Tegwin said, her eyes merry. "They'll feed you until you beg for mercy. The Becalmed leaders will be there as well."

"Since they know you…"

"I know the older couple, yes. They've been briefed on the basics, but we'll explain deep psych in as much depth as they want. Or you will, anyway. That technology has advanced too much since I had my basic psych training for me to explain it. You're on your own with the food, though."

"I'll take that challenge."

Chapter 5

LUIS LOST THAT CHALLENGE, giving up after his third plateful of food remarkably like that of old Earth. Like Tegwin, he remembered grandparents a hundred years older than his chronological years, along with their holiday customs and traditions.

Eager young Bitanthrans bustled Luis and Tegwin to a long wooden table covered with a heavy white tablecloth, then stuffed them full of potatoes, carrots, onions, and a lean meat they swore descended from Earth deer. A tall glass of milk from actual cows, not widely available anywhere besides Earth, nearly brought Luis to nostalgic tears.

The official delegation joining them for the meal was just as simple and reassuring. Two from each group, typical and Becalmed. Luis participated in the casual chat about weather, Bitan mining conditions, and polite questions about life off of Bitanthra.

He mostly watched the Becalmed man and woman watching the rest of them.

They looked no different from their counterparts at first glance. Same pale skin, sturdy build, and well-made work clothes. The Becalmed woman's black hair was as close cropped as the man's blond, whereas the typical woman wore hers long and pulled back from her face in glossy chestnut waves.

The most striking difference was Luis had no idea how old the Becalmed pair were. This wasn't the oddly fluid idea of age that years spent in hypersleep produced for himself and Tegwin. The Becalmed were clearly adult in face and body, lines of jaw and brow no longer soft with youth.

But those faces were smooth as a young teenager's, without a trace of lines around their eyes or mouths. The effect, along with the obvious understanding of every word even when they didn't speak, was eerie.

When everyone, meaning Luis, finally finished eating, Tegwin turned toward him.

"I know you understand the general idea of what Luis is here to do. He's the head psych-officer for TransGalactic, so he trains others on how to work with deep psych-hypnosis. He can explain a bit more and answer questions if you'd like."

Myrtle, the typical Bitanthran woman, nodded. Luis guessed she was in her fifties. While she did have lines on her face, she clearly smiled more than she frowned.

"We heard a lot about it over the last few months," she said. "While you two were inbound. I'd like to hear how you'd explain it, Luis."

"Tegwin's right, I've been on a few training assignments lately," Luis said. "So please stop me if I get too long-winded. You probably know hypnosis has been around for hundreds of years in one form or another. The difference with what deep psych can do is we map the brain first, so we get an idea of how your individual brain works."

"So you'll be able to tell why ours are Becalmed," Helen said. Her voice wasn't quite as flat and lifeless as an artificial life form, though it was lacking natural inflection. "Why our emotions are broken."

"I don't think brains are broken." Luis picked up his fork. "Not like a shovel or a fork can be. Each human brain, and mind, is unique. We store things in our own way, and the brain has amazing abilities to recover from traumatic injury. We don't know what's different about your brains yet. I hope we can figure that out."

"So you can fix us?" That was Drew, the Becalmed man. "Make us like everyone else."

Luis didn't miss the way Helen shook her head at Drew's words.

"I'm not going to force you to change anything you don't want to. We just want to figure it out. Get an idea why it's happening."

"If it happens to too many of the children," Myrtle said, her voice soft, "we won't have anyone left to mine Bitan. We may have to leave here."

Helen and Drew both nodded, but they showed no signs of being upset.

"That's the concern, yes," Luis said. "The main mission is to figure all of this out. Until then, I won't know if it's something that can be treated or changed. What deep psych allows me to do is pinpoint where an injury or disease lies in the brain, or where a traumatic memory is stored. Then we know where to target with our work instead of guessing."

"We don't believe there is any evidence of trauma." Tegwin touched Myrtle's shoulder. "Medical scans show no signs of disease, either. We're not sure what's going on yet."

Myrtle's partner Willis nodded. His hair was as dark as Luis's, but his beard was a deep red.

"So after you map the brain, you can do more with the hypnosis. Asking us questions and such. And we can't lie, right? Even if we wanted to."

"That's right. Especially with some traumatic memories, your mind tries to protect you and itself. Or the memory may be hard to access. The deep psych field allows us to get past those blocks and find out what's really going on. We're often able to free the blockage and relieve the trauma. Or in an injury or disease, help the brain find new pathways."

"Have you done that?" Drew said. "Has someone else hypnotized you, Luis?"

Everyone in the room, including Tegwin, turned toward Luis. He was used to students looking at him, but not all staring at once like that. He fought a giggle response involving baby birds out of his mind.

"Sure, several times during my own training. We were pioneering the technique, really, figuring out how to best use it to help people. All of us went under routinely. In groups many times, working together. I expect the next question is what is it like, and I'm sorry I can't answer. Not clearly. Most people don't remember much about their time under the deep psych field. All I remember is feeling relaxed after, like I'd had a good nap."

"How do we know what we told you?" Myrtle said, one eyebrow raised. "If we can't remember any of it?"

"We record the sessions," Luis said, with the same reassuring smile he always wore when answering that question. "The words as well as the data. Nothing is sent outside the room without your permission, not unless there *is* a crime. That's not what we're doing here. Once everything is finished, again with your permission, we delete all the words before I leave."

The four Bitanthrans looked each over for several seconds. Luis knew without asking Tegwin that he was under evaluation and the best thing he could do was stay quiet.

After a signal he didn't catch, Myrtle spoke. Her newly formal words and manner carried the weight of ritual even in such humble surroundings.

"I am Myrtle, and this is Willis." She nodded to the red-bearded man beside her. "We are co-leaders of our people. We understand why you're here, Luis and Tegwin. We have great need of your help. With the consent of our Becalmed leaders, and if you are ready, we clear the way for you to begin your work."

"I am Helen, and this is Drew," the Becalmed woman said. "You have our consent to begin your work."

Luis froze, certain he was going to say something absurd and spoil his time here before it really got started. Tegwin saved him.

"I am Tegwin, and this is Luis. We appreciate your welcome, and your trust. We are ready to begin our work."

Luis managed to get to his feet an instant after everyone else did. He wasn't sure whether to be annoyed at himself for not asking about the protocol, or at Tegwin for not warning him. He hadn't expected to jump right in so soon after landing. But after years of sleep and with a comfortably stuffed belly, he couldn't think of a good reason to decline.

Not that any of the women in charge had asked him for one.

Tegwin followed the Becalmed pair out of the room, so Luis followed all three.

"We will go to the medical center," Helen said. "What will you do to get us ready for psych-hypnosis?"

Luis realized everyone was waiting for him to speak.

"It's painless, sometimes with a mild sedative. I believe the head-gear should be waiting for us."

"It is," Tegwin said. "We have five private suites reserved. I thought we'd start with Helen and Drew. Myrtle and Willis have volunteered to act as a control group for typical Bitanthrans. They'll be here in a couple of hours. If we need other subjects, we'll go from there."

Drew held open a glass door set into a painted wooden building with Medical Center stenciled in white on the glass. Luis was pleasantly surprised to see what looked like a modern medical facility behind such a rustic façade.

A bright waiting room tiled in TransGalactic blue with gold accents, with nurses behind a sealed glass window. Even an airlock door in case of quarantine. Only a handful of chrome and plastic chairs scattered around the compact space, leaving Luis to guess Bitanthrans didn't get sick very often.

A man dressed in a bright blue medical uniform glanced at them from behind the window, then moved to the side. A second later, he opened the airlock door, a huge grin on his dark brown face.

"Good to see you again, Tegwin!" He caught her up in a quick hug. "And you must be Dr. Ahmad. I'm Ben Essena, the head nurse." His broad hand swallowed Luis's, but Ben's grip was easy. "We have everything ready if you are. Need something to drink, anything to eat?"

Luis laughed before he could stop himself. He remembered that from his grandparents as well. The immediate effort to feed anyone who came with their reach.

"Good to meet you, Ben. Call me Luis, please. Nothing to eat, thank you. Myrtle and Willis stuffed us silly. Maybe water for everyone?"

"I'll send some right back." Ben waved his wrist, where the same silver comm-bracelet Tegwin wore caught the light, then held the door open. "This way and we'll get you started."

Luis made a mental note to talk to Ben privately as soon as he could. In a small town hospital, the doctors were wonderful to get to know. But making a friend of the nurses would get him everything he *needed* to know.

Ben probably knew more about the people in this town than Myrtle and Willis. And he'd know who Luis should talk to in town and every tiny settlement tucked into the mountains, and make the introductions to boot.

"Glad to have someone using these suites," Ben said as they followed him down a hallway painted and tiled in cool green. Numbered examination rooms broke up the monotony. "They're usually for new mothers."

The nurse's smile disappeared, and he glanced back at the Becalmed pair.

"Please do not worry." Helen's voice was quiet but clear. "We understand the trouble with new babies. We cannot be offended."

"So the birthrate is dropping?" Luis said, determined to keep Ben talking. And to test how detached the Becalmed truly were.

"Has been for years. People say they're afraid."

"If the birthrate falls too far," Tegwin said, "the colony will collapse on its own."

Chapter 6

Luis did keep his thoughts to himself despite Helen's reassurance. If TransGalactic let that happen, bringing in short-term workers they paid enough to tolerate long stretches in isolation, part of their problem might solve itself. Assuming Bitanthrans allowed themselves to die out and be replaced.

Ben stopped beside the first of several dark wooden doors, with letters instead of numbers. A, B, C, and so on continued around the corner.

"I do worry about that to tell you the truth." Another wave of the wrist to open the door. "This is one of the suites, just like the rest. Plenty of food in stock, though anyone in town would be delighted to have an off-world guest and talk your ears off. All your things are here already. Yours too, Helen and Willis."

Luis saw his drift of black bags and cases along a cheerful yellow wall. The living space he could see was as modern as the rest of the facility, with a wall mounted entertainment and comm terminal, a compact automated kitchen pod, and a row of windows overlooking a huge garden area that would have been his grandmother's pride. No wonder Bitanthrans ate so well.

"This will open your suite for now." Ben said. Luis took the bright blue identi-badge the nurse held out, then pinned the tiny square to his jacket. "You'll have to have one of us let you into the building, though. Will Dr. Ahmad get a wrist-comm, Tegwin?"

"We can do that if you like, Luis." She peeked into her own suite across the hall, then closed the door. Helen and Willis seemed to already know where they'd be staying. "It would only take a few hours. Might make things easier with such a long assignment."

Ben backtracked up the hall to a solid metal white door.

"This is the biggest procedure room we have here. Big enough for four beds and all the monitoring equipment you could ever need. Your headgear arrived not long before you did, Dr. Ahmad."

Luis followed the nurse into a room utterly at odds with the slow-paced, rustic town he knew was outside. The walls and ceiling looked like dimpled cream-colored fabric, perfectly designed to dampen any noise. What Ben called beds were as far away from flat, traditional mattresses, or the bunks even on a ship as fine as the *Bountyfield*.

Thick, tan padding lined a reclining surface that offered adjustments for not only the back, but also for all four limbs and the head. He suspected leaning back into that padding would feel like floating on warm air.

Whatever their motivation, TransGalactic spared no expense in looking after the health of people mining and supporting Bitan.

Sleek, oval pods that adjusted to any height stood beside each bed. Luis would need those for monitoring heartbeat and respiration. His primary equipment, four shiny black cases shaped like human skulls, waited on a table in the middle of the room.

Luis pressed his fingertips into the top of one, much like his sphere reader, then lifted the thin lid. The psych-hypnosis nets were as fine and intricate as black lace, with glittering red sensor nodes instead of hand-tied knots. His subjects always said they couldn't feel the nets at all.

Luis turned back to the group, then blinked. Helen and Willis were each stretched out on an exam table, hands folded over their bellies. Both stared up at the ceiling, faces calm and blank.

"I usually explain things a little more, answer questions," he said. "Before we get started."

Helen turned her eyes toward him without moving her head.

"We have no questions, Dr. Ahmad. You can ask us any questions you want to."

"Please, everyone, call me Luis." He shrugged and shook his head. "If everyone else is ready, we can get started with the initial calibration and setup."

As Luis fitted the nets onto Helen and Willis, thankful for their short hair, he wondered if sedation would be necessary at all with the Becalmed.

"Okay, we're ready to begin," he said. "This might be a little boring, but be patient with me, and with the systems. Once we have your brains mapped, we'll…we'll get to more interesting questions."

Luis shook his head, reminding himself he might have to adjust his usual testing speech. He normally joked about not being afraid of a scan finding nothing in the brain at all, getting down to the fun part and rearranging thoughts and memories, silly things to put the subjects at ease.

Helen and Drew probably wouldn't have a problem with what he said. But joking about the problem he was here to diagnose felt more than a little insensitive to him.

"We're ready, Luis," Drew said.

"You won't feel anything, so just relax." Luis tapped the interface on the skull-shaped control units, linking them to the oval bedside pods. "If you would, please count silently starting with one. However fast or slow you want, but for this part, stay with whole numbers. One, two, three. I'm going to activate a white noise field so you can concentrate. We'll switch it up in a little while."

He started the sound generator embedded in the sensor nets. He heard only a faint whisper of static, but anyone wearing the net would hear nothing else in the room.

Luis crossed his arms and waited for data, watching Helen and Drew's mouths move as they counted. Tegwin stood beside him, her head tilted.

"It's mapping the physical brain?"

"That's the first step. It goes from the outside in, mapping deeper and more complex structures as it goes. There's the first set."

The displays showed a faint blue outline of a human brain, wrinkly with two matched halves. Red dots filled in slowly, marking the curves and folds under the surface.

"We'll switch to more complex numbers, counting by twos and threes. Then the alphabet, and words. What I'm worried about is the next phase."

"Emotional mapping," Tegwin said, glancing at Helen and Drew. "That's getting into memories, right?"

"Exactly. They should do fine with earliest memories, when they started school, when they finished school. Then things like waking up this morning, when they met me, when they put the nets on. But will they even understand when I ask about a happiest moment, times when they were afraid or sad?"

"A whole lot of people are interested in the answer to that."

The emotional mapping questions, and the resulting data, were less dramatic and far less informative than Luis expected. Helen and Drew simply looked straight up at the ceiling when he asked, like they did with all the other questions. But neither of them responded to any questions about strong feelings.

"Okay, that's all we need right now," Luis said. He glanced at Tegwin, raising his eyebrows and shaking his head. "You two can take a break, go out and walk around for a bit. I know it's hard to be still for that long. Thank you."

The two of them sat up, waiting for Luis to remove the nets. Both ran their fingers through their short hair, but they didn't laugh or comment on the experience like most subjects did.

"Thank you, Luis. When should we be back here?"

"What is it here, sweeps instead of hours? We've been here two sweeps. Be back in one?"

Both Helen and Drew nodded, then left without another word.

Luis moved his rolling chair beside the table holding the net's sensor units and sat with a gusty sigh.

"Well, that tells us exactly nothing."

"How so?" Tegwin said.

She leaned over his shoulder, watching the units light up with a replay of the tests. The red dots aligned themselves inside the translucent skulls, recreating Helen and Drew's brains. The marks were unnaturally regular and evenly spaced.

"This is the same thing you'd see in a classroom or textbook. Not one for alternate development or various thinking styles, either. This is the standard, off the rack, learning-the-basics human brain pattern. Helen and Drew show no deviation whatsoever."

"You mean nothing abnormal?"

"I mean nothing at all. Not even normal deviations that we all have. Someone could have assembled their brains out of a beginner textbook. Even though they didn't answer the questions, the emotional responses worked within their brains. But those were identical to each other. That's not possible in humans. Not that I've ever seen."

Tegwin sat beside him, rubbing her face.

"So all we've learned is we're not going to find the problem in their brains."

"Right. Though I'd say this kind of utterly standard development is a problem in itself. If I got these results on any other subject, I'd suspect the units were malfunctioning."

"But these are brand new and calibrated." Tegwin pulled out her own spherical display device, glancing at the surface. "Nine sweeps ago. I did it myself."

Luis shrugged. "I'll run diagnostics again, but I promise they'll come up functioning perfectly. I want to test typical subjects to make sure, of course. Something else is going on here."

"I may not have much authority as your planetary liaison," Tegwin said. She stood, leaning back with her hands on her hips. "But I'm going to use it. Take your own advice, Luis. Start the diagnostics, but get out of here for a little while. Walk around and get some fresh air. Think about something else. That's what I'm going to do."

Chapter 7

As soon as Luis stepped out into the corridor, he knew he was going to ignore part of what Tegwin said. He spotted Ben in the nurses' office, chatting with one of the doctors on duty. Luis was willing to bet the healthy population allowed for a few unscheduled breaks for medical personnel.

Ben smiled when he caught sight of Luis.

"Everything going well back there?"

"Good so far, Ben. Just finished up the initial mapping and calibration. Listen, if you have a few minutes, I'd love to speak to you."

"You bet. When we actually do have an emergency around here, it can be a bad one. But most of the time, we're pretty laid back. Walk with me?"

"Show me your town."

A few minutes of walking through the cool, sunny afternoon with Ben's easy narration revived Luis more than he expected. Several general stores. Banking and travel planning. Charming but modern schools for children. Even a small college to start adults on the paths to careers other than mining.

Luis found nothing out of the ordinary among the wooden and stone buildings, the neat and well-maintained businesses and streets.

But the fresh air and conversation stirred up enough questions that he wasn't sure where to start.

When they settled into a loop around a path that circled downtown, lined with flowerbeds and stone gardens, Ben made it a lot easier.

"I imagine you have more serious things to ask me about than the town gossip," he said with a smile. "Go right ahead. That's what I'm here for."

"TransGalactic warned you about me?"

"I wouldn't say warned. They mentioned that you'd want someone to talk to. Someone who knows more about the people who live here than they do themselves."

"That I want. Promise you'll tell me if I'm asking things you'd rather not answer?"

Ben brushed his fingertips through a chest-high bush covered with tiny burgundy flowers. The stirred up aroma smelled like fresh apples to Luis.

"I've been watching this place try to die out for years now. No matter what any of us do, the trouble is only getting worse. As far as I'm concerned, nothing is off limits."

Luis tried to organize his thoughts for several steps before he gave up.

"I've had the briefings, read the reports. I'll test Myrtle and Willis when we get back, but I don't think I'll find anything out of the ordinary with them, either. What do you think I need to know, Ben?"

"Find anything with Helen and Drew? Anything unusual?"

Luis shook his head. "Probably not the way you mean. The only thing their brains are missing is any kind of deviation. They test out like someone picked up standard human brains off a shelf and installed them. Even the emotional centers are normal. And identical to each other."

"Wish I could say I was surprised. We haven't been able to do anything like your psych-hypnosis or that kind of deep brain scan. But the Becalmed always act like every other kid when they're born.

By the time they start school, though, around five years old, they change."

"No trauma, no difference in their nutrition or experiences?"

"Not a thing. The hardest part has been watching siblings grow up and grow apart. We had several sets of twins over the years, one typical, one Becalmed. The last three sets of twins born are both Becalmed."

Luis watched a group of kids running around outside the primary school. His heart sank at his quick count. About half were laughing and squealing, playing like any kids he'd ever seen.

The other half walked around the edges of the playground, nearly in lockstep. Eerily silent. Their faces weren't sad or angry. They were simply as calm and blank as Helen and Drew.

"How about the rest of the population?" Luis said.

"You mean mentally, emotionally? They're fairly average humans, I'd say. I was off-world for a few years doing my medical training, but I've lived here the rest of my life. The only thing I noticed is how much everyone who's born here loves Bitanthra."

"You too?"

"Absolutely. I hated being away from here, every second of it. Now, I know everyone gets homesick. This is different from what I can tell. Being away, even on the orbital med base to help out with childbirth, feels like a part of me is missing. And that missing part hurts, like a broken bone or something. We have to take shifts up there because none of us can stand it for long."

A warm, tingly space in Luis's chest woke up. That tingle was usually his first hint of how he would find a solution, or at least part of it. He knew better than to worry about that just yet. His idea seed needed time and space to grow.

"How are people reacting? Besides the Becalmed?"

This time Ben took several steps before answering. Luis concentrated on their footsteps crunching through black gravel, not wanting to interrupt or rush.

"I generally see folks once a year for a physical, and that's it. We can schedule those like clockwork, hardly any deviation at all, except for accidents at the mines or somewhere else. Lately, though, people have been coming in at odd times. Mostly women, but a few men."

He walked quietly again, leaving Luis hoping he didn't know the reason for the strange visits. His chest told him he did.

"They're coming in for birth control," Ben said. "Even the ones who don't have any kids. We don't have any problem with that here, not at all. But the whole planet has a problem when more than half the adult population doesn't want children. Not because of some personal reason or to concentrate on their work, or because they have enough. We always had that. People are coming in now because they're too afraid to try."

"How do they feel about the Becalmed, Ben? How do you feel?"

"You met Helen and Drew. They're sweet as they can be, never would hurt anything or anyone. Most people seem to know this isn't contagious, or at least we don't think it is. But it's not just the Becalmed who are happier about their separate community."

Luis tried to find something to say, some way to reassure Ben. But the truth was he had nothing but more questions, and more worries than he had when they'd started walking.

"I'll do everything I can to figure this out, Ben. I give you my word."

Chapter 8

By the time Luis and Ben got back to the medical facility, everybody was waiting for them in the lobby. Luis noticed how Helen and Drew sat quietly off to the side, while Tegwin chatted with Myrtle and Willis.

Humans always sorted themselves into groups, just like almost any living thing. That in itself wasn't a problem. But the lack of basic understanding between these two groups was starting to frighten him after only a few hours.

The separation continued as he got Myrtle and Willis set up for their own calibration and testing. Helen and Drew volunteered to go wait in their rooms instead of observing, and no one besides Luis seemed disturbed by that. The only thing he could think of was to agree and move on.

A couple of sweeps later, with the leaders of the typical Bitanthrans departed for the evening and Helen and Drew still in their rooms, Luis and Tegwin watched the calibration results pop up in the second set of skulls.

"See the difference?" Luis said. He'd left Helen and Drew's sensors active on the other side of the table for comparison.

"They're all over the place." Tegwin walked around the table, leaning down to peer through the two sets of results. "I don't think one point matches between Myrtle and Willis."

"Nope, and they wouldn't between me and you. They're hitting in the typical regions of the brain, sure, but not nearly so regular."

She crossed her arms, looking at Luis.

"They acted different during the testing, too. They weren't just following instructions, were they? They were living those memories. I saw it on their faces, in their bodies. The monitors picked it up in their vital signs, too."

"Especially the bad ones." Luis waited for the soft chime of a completed brain map before pulling one of the oval display pods over to the table. "That's exactly what I think Helen and Drew were doing. Following what I said with no emotional responses, at least not that they were aware of. Their brains reacted accordingly."

He tapped the display to zoom in on the right side of Myrtle's brain, toward the front. The red dots increased in both size and frequency.

"Remember your theory about the typical Bitanthran being a bit more emotional than usual? That's what we see in Myrtle, in response to the bad and good memories." He pulled up Willis's brain. The dots were in different places, but also large and close together. "Same with Willis. This doesn't look like any kind of disorder, but it is on the high end of normal."

Tegwin leaned down again, examining the right sides of each of the translucent skulls.

"But in Helen and Drew, everything is tiny, spaced out. Almost like a grid."

"Right," Luis said. "Regular enough to read as unnatural."

Tegwin walked around the exam room, seeming to peer at every display and piece of equipment. Luis would have bet his credit bonus for this mission she wasn't seeing a single bit of it.

He wished he had one of the sensory nets set on her right now. He'd watched the human mind make connections and leaps countless times in demonstrations and tests, but he never tired of seeing that magic.

"This isn't making sense, Luis." Tegwin still had her back turned, still walking. "Helen and Drew's results may be too normal, but they *are* happening."

"Right."

"And you just said Helen and Drew could be having emotional responses that they're not aware of."

"I did. I'd love to have a sensor net on them when they're asleep. See if they're dreaming and not remembering it, too. Have you seen reports of the scans they can do here or on the orbital med base?"

She turned to face him, one eyebrow raised.

"They show as normal. Nowhere as accurate as what you just did, not as detailed. But still, normal. You think they've got some kind of block."

"With what we've seen so far," he said, "nothing else makes sense. I can't imagine people here are hiding any kind of trauma, and I'm seeing no signs of disease. I can't explain it yet, but yeah. I think there's a block."

"You've dealt with blocks in deep psych-hypnosis before, right?"

Now Luis stood, walking back to the exam beds. He touched the head rest on one, tapping his fingers on the soft surface.

"Many times. But they were usually the result of an injury or emotional trauma. Sometimes a disease or disorder. I'm afraid we'll rule all of that out with our first session tomorrow. Helen and Drew appear to be perfectly healthy. If anything, their brains are *too* healthy. I have no idea what we're dealing with here, Tegwin."

He was surprised to see her smile.

"And I was worried about this being just another boring assign-ment in the middle of nowhere."

Chapter 9

A RESTLESS NIGHT, unlike Luis usually had first night planetside, and a fruitless first morning of psych-hypnosis did nothing to improve his gloomy mood. Just as before, Helen and Drew answered every question, followed every last bit of instruction.

And just as before, even under the deep psych field, they showed no conscious emotional response to any prompt.

The emotional centers of the brain throughout the limbic system continued to react, laying down more perfect and regular dots on their sensor displays. But even with the diagnostic bed's sensory arrays active, Luis detected no physical response. Their placid expressions and voices matched their unchanging heart rate and respiration, body temperature and perspiration.

If he didn't know he was working with flesh and blood humans, Luis would have sworn he was examining the most lifelike simulations ever created.

The only event that broke up the growing frustration, and his hovering sense of hopelessness, was Tegwin returning from her midday break with a fitting bracelet. She slipped what felt like a smooth, silver chain around his left wrist.

"I'm getting my own tiny piece of Bitan?"

"So tiny." The cool metal shifted and formed itself, tickling the hair for a few seconds, before she clicked it open. "You know Earth sand? Or maybe a grain of salt?"

"Hardly worth a fortune, huh?"

"Not exactly. Even the highest level officers of TransGalactic get the same thing. Sadly, since you're technically a contractor on Bitanthra, they'll want this back before you leave."

Luis rolled his eyes and rubbed his wrist. He welcomed Tegwin's touch behind his own, enjoying the warm sensations her fingers stirred up a long way down.

"Think I'll get to touch any Bitan? That I can actually see, I mean?"

Tegwin slipped the silver bracelet into a flat black box.

"We should be able to head up into the mountains at some point. I doubt we can go into the deep mining chambers, but there's always plenty at the surface, where they process the ore."

"That would be something different," Luis said. He activated the second set of sensors, getting ready for the first round of deep psych for Myrtle and Willis. "Unlike what we're getting in here."

"You can't be getting discouraged already. How many days do you usually test each subject before you start working on their problems? Just the one?"

Luis glanced over his shoulder, making sure she was smiling.

"Usually at least a week. Often a lot longer on more complex problems. But I normally see something in the first few tests, you know? Some idea of where to head next."

"You're asking the same questions with Myrtle and Willis?" Tegwin said. She flipped through her notes on her holo-reader.

"That's right, a general hypnosis session. Make sure the psych field is working, gather responses to compare to the Becalmed. Something you think I should be watching for?"

She shook her head, but she was frowning.

"Not really." She jumped at a knock on the exam room door. "That's Myrtle and Willis. I don't know, just remember those high emotional responses. Okay?"

She opened the door before Luis could respond.

"Come on in, he's ready for you."

The contrast from the tranquility of Helen and Drew was obvious from the second Myrtle and Willis walked in. They didn't look angry, exactly, but Luis could see from their hard expressions and stiff gaits that they were nervous. And not happy about feeling that way.

"There's nothing to worry about," he said. "This won't be all that different from the testing and calibration yesterday."

Myrtle pressed her lips together until they were a thin line.

"This is the part where you hypnotize us, right?"

She crossed the room and sat on one of the exam beds, but her entire body remained tense.

"We generate a field from the brain map we made yesterday." Luis touched the skull unit with Myrtle's data, and it glowed with dots, lines, and folds. "This won't make you act strangely or let me control your mind. We'll just be able to ask questions you may not usually be able to answer."

Willis sat on his own bed, looking nearly as anxious as Myrtle.

"They explained all of this to us," he said. "The people from TransG. Before we said we would help, and we still want to help. It's just different walking in here knowing you're going to poke around in our brains."

"You use this for criminals?" Myrtle said. "To make them confess?"

"We can't do that, no." Luis kept the dubious origins of the technology to himself, just like most people in his line of work did. Along with the differing laws for wartime or galactic-level crimes. "Forced confession is illegal. People who work with criminals use deep psych when the accused ask for it. To verify the things they're saying, since no one can lie under the field. We don't force them to do anything. The only similarity here is we record your words along with your data, but like we discussed before, that doesn't leave this room without your permission."

"Do you do that sometimes, though?" Willis said. "With criminals?"

"No, not even during my training. I've always worked with people who have some kind of problem with their brains. Injuries, certain diseases. Sometimes an emotional trauma they need help with."

Myrtle and Willis locked gazes. Luis knew he'd led them right to the questions they really wanted to ask. Myrtle looked into his eyes.

"You think that's what happens to them? Some kind of trauma? Or a disease?"

Luis sat on the rolling chair he'd pulled beside the beds while he was working with Helen and Drew.

"We don't know what's going on, but I don't think it's trauma. I see no signs of disease. With the way it only affects some people in a family, I don't believe this is contagious at all. Mind if I ask you a question?"

Both Bitanthrans shook their heads.

"What do you think is going on? What do people who live here, who've been watching this happen for years, think?"

Willis drew in a slow breath, and Luis saw tears standing in his eyes.

"Some of us are afraid it's poison, something to do with Bitan. It seems to be getting worse over time. Like we've been exposed too much, and we're passing it along to our children."

"Well, I can't rule anything out yet since we just got started. But your medical center here has tested for everything we know of, and off-world facilities have too. Nothing seems out of line with your bodies. Nothing seems to accumulate or get depleted over time."

"Except our kids' feelings," Myrtle said. She didn't look sad like Willis. She looked furious. "That's depleting, more and more every year."

"I can only imagine how hard that's been for all of you," Luis said. "I know you're scared and upset. I'm going to do everything I can to help. I promise I won't hurt you along the way. Okay?"

Myrtle stared into his eyes, and Luis knew any planetary system court's specialized deep psych equipment wouldn't see him any more clearly than she did.

"Okay. We'll do whatever we can to help you do that."

She lay back on the bed, letting it adjust her into the best position for testing. Willis nodded once at Luis, then he did the same.

He and Tegwin fitted the sensor nets, then Luis held his hands over the skull units.

"Starting the field in three…two…one."

He touched the plastic temples with his fingertip and thumb, then tapped the top of the skulls. Myrtle and Willis didn't react, but the maps in front of Luis glowed green. The display of brain waves on the oval viewing pods gradually changed from a chaotic bunch of peaks and valleys to slow rises and falls.

"We're ready to begin," Luis said, sitting down beside the beds again.

He worked through the typical list of baseline questions, letting the field adjust and fine tune itself. Name, occupation, age. Last things they ate or drank, who they talked to on the way to the facility. Myrtle and Willis responded much the same ways Helen and Drew did, as Luis expected.

"Now, Willis, I'm going to ask you a different kind of question. One you answered for me earlier. I'm not trying to trick you. This just lets us get an idea if the field is adjusted to your brains. What do you think is causing the trouble with the Becalmed?"

Willis answered the same way he had before, almost word for word. His emotional responses jumped up, too, all over the right side of his brain. Fear and sadness ticked outside of normal, not quite into disordered levels. Tears escaped his closed eyes, running down his cheeks.

"Thank you, Willis. Myrtle, I didn't ask you this before, but I want to know what you think is going on with the Becalmed."

"Poison, like Willis says." Myrtle's readings lit up bright around the amygdala. Fear, again, and especially high levels of anger. "Not from here, though. Not from the Bitan we bring up out of the ground. Somewhere else. Far away from here."

Luis looked at Tegwin, eyebrows raised. She shrugged and shook her head.

"Can you tell me more about that, Myrtle? Why you'd say that?"

"You asked me what I thought. I told you. That's all."

Her levels calmed when Luis moved on to emotional mapping,

never getting to the same peak of intensity. Not with questions designed to elicit fear, sadness, even anger.

She and Willis both responded within typical human emotional range, all across the spectrum. Neither reached the high peaks brought on by the question about the Becalmed.

Chapter 10

Tegwin's grin when Luis walked into the exam room the next day was too infectious to resist, even after he'd slept less than the night before.

"You're not under house arrest anymore," she said, holding out a small black bag. "You won't have to track me or Ben down to get in or out of this place, either. Or into another apartment if you're interested."

Inside was a thin silver bracelet, less than half the width of Luis's pinkie finger. It was open, hinged in the middle underneath the blue and gold TransGalactic logo. When Luis closed it around his wrist, it fit perfectly against every contour of his flesh and bone.

"I'm very interested in other apartments," he said, returning her smile. "At least one other one. How do I get it back off?"

"You don't," Tegwin said. "Not until you're ready to leave. I've been wearing mine for almost twenty years now. Well, a lot longer than that if you count my hyper-sleep time, but I try not to. If it needs adjustments, let me know. But it should fit close enough that you won't notice it."

Luis made a fist and flexed his wrist in a circle, watching the wrist-comm flash and shift.

"I already can't really feel it. What all will this do for me?"

"Mainly opening the doors in and out of here. There aren't any other secured facilities to speak of in this part of Bitanthra. If you go down to the resorts, this won't get you in to the vaults in the gaming areas or anything like that. Otherwise, you should be set."

She turned to activate the deep psych equipment, then turned back.

"It's a tracker, too. They all are, not just yours. Some people don't like that, I know, but it's more in case someone has an accident than anything else. Just thought you should know."

"Thanks for the warning," Luis said. "I'm not that exciting to track. I might get out and see the town tonight though, instead of huddling in my rooms."

"You told me you wanted to be alone for a couple of days! I would have invited you…" Tegwin stopped, catching sight of his expression. "Well done, you got me. You're still welcome to join me if you want."

The flirty mood evaporated as Luis glanced over his notes from the past couple of days, along with his notes from a nearly sleepless night. If he kept getting the same results, or lack of results, he was going to have to let his superiors know he was out of ideas.

That was a conversation he hadn't had since his fledgling days, when none of them truly understood how the psych fields worked. Luis and everyone else in the field had to read questions from a list back then. He didn't want to have that conversation now after decades of experience, but he was running out of ideas.

Luis knew something had changed as soon as he activated the deep psych field for Helen.

The red dots in the emotional centers, all around the amygdala, glowed more brightly than before. He was sure they were lighting up in different areas, too. Not just the textbook locations from before.

"How you feeling today, Helen?" he said.

"I am fine," she said. The strained tone in her voice made Tegwin and even Drew look up. "No, that's not the truth. I felt normal until I got here. Until you put the sensor net on my head."

"And now?" Luis stood beside her, checking the placement of the glittering red sensory nodes against her short hair. "What's different?"

She shook her head, but not hard enough to dislodge the black netting.

"My shoulders hurt. My jaws." She opened and closed her fists, then rubbed her palms against her thighs. People usually didn't move once they were under the field. "Everything feels too tight."

"Your voice sounds too tight," Drew said. His expression remained calm, but he watched Helen closely. "Are you ill?"

"That's not your business!"

As soon as she said it, Helen's eyes opened wide. She covered her mouth with one hand.

"Luis," Tegwin said. "The readings."

Luis turned the oval readout toward him. Instead of regular waves, not much different than a brain under the deep psych field, Helen's emotional lines were jagged and sharp. Almost as sharp as Myrtle's had been.

"Same thing on the other sensor," Luis said, glancing that way. "More points showing up as we speak."

"Something is wrong with me," Helen said, her voice trembling now. "My throat is hot and swelling up. My face, too. I have a fever."

"I don't think it's a fever," Luis said. "Nothing is wrong. But something is different. Did you do anything unusual last night or this morning? Outside of what you normally do?"

She shook her head again, this time causing the net to shift to the side. Luis adjusted it, watching the readings jump again.

"Nothing different. All I've done different is coming in here," she said, her voice rising. "Letting you look at my brain. Is this all because of your deep psych?"

Luis blinked, opening, then closing his mouth.

"I don't think...I don't know. We've never done this kind of testing on the Becalmed before. Not on anyone on Bitanthra, actually. The testing itself should be neutral, but something is changing. That could be it. Are you willing to continue?"

She stared at him, chin quivering.

"Is this going to go away? When the tests stop?"

"Do you want it to, Helen?" Tegwin said, standing on the other side of the bed. Luis saw several more bright red points appear inside the translucent skull.

"I don't like whatever is happening to me. I said I would help you, though, find out what's happening with the babies. I didn't say I wanted you to change me."

"We don't have to keep going," Luis said. He wanted to jump in and figure this out, badly, and right now. But he couldn't stand the frightened look in eyes and a face so clearly unused to such things. "All of this is voluntary, remember? Every bit of it is up to you."

Helen turned toward Drew, and Luis followed her gaze. The Becalmed man still seemed unfazed, not caught up in whatever was affecting Helen.

Drew didn't have his sensor net on yet, either.

"You can keep going," Helen said, drawing Luis's attention back. "As long as you promise me you'll try to fix this. Whatever is wrong with me."

"I don't know if I can, Helen. I can't promise that."

"But you'll try to, right? I want to help, but you have to promise you'll try."

Tears rolled down her cheeks, and she drew back, as if she could escape them. Luis felt his own eyes welling up.

"I will try, Helen. I promise."

"Go ahead, then. I'll do my best."

"We'll try just with Helen if that's okay with you, Drew." Luis waited for the Becalmed man to nod. "Then we'll focus on you."

Luis turned back to activate the deep psych field, hoping he hadn't made a promise to Helen that he couldn't keep.

"Activating field in three…two…one. Still doing okay, Helen?"

"I still don't feel good, but you go ahead."

"Now that you're under, let me ask you if you know what's changed today. What's different?"

Helen's smooth face wrinkled around her eyes and nose, the first time she'd reacted that way to anything.

"My belly is all stirred up and my back and neck hurt, and I feel like hot water is sloshing around in my chest. My throat, too. If this is what everyone else lives with, you can keep it. I'd rather stay Becalmed."

"I hope we can do that for you," Luis said. "Do you feel like some part of your mind is open now? Something you couldn't get to yesterday?"

"Only the part that's all agitated and shaky, not like part of me at all. Something outside of me, so far I can't reach it. But it can reach me."

Luis caught Tegwin's gaze. So close to what Myrtle said about the Becalmed and the poison. That it all came from far away.

"I won't keep you under too long today, Helen. I'll ask you a few more questions, then I'll let you relax. We'll talk to Drew."

Drew and his scans were nearly the same as Helen's. He got more anxious as soon as Luis slipped his sensor net into place, and the questions only made it worse. Luis decided to cut their sessions short rather than risk causing them too much upset.

He'd never worked with or even heard of humans with no emotional responses. He'd certainly never worked with humans who suddenly gained that ability as adults, with no preparation or warning.

Luis did not want to wade too deeply into that territory without a whole lot more preparation, for himself and the Becalmed. Especially with two people who had no interest in the changes being permanent.

"Tegwin, can you help me with his net for a second? We're just about finished."

When she leaned in, the number of red marks in Drew's sensor jumped up again. Luis froze, his hand on one side of the man's head, Tegwin's on the other.

"Wait," he said, not wanting to scare the Becalmed any more than they already were. "Tegwin, reach toward me. Toward my hand."

This time, the readings on the viewscreen spiked. Drew groaned, and sweat broke out on his face. Luis saw muscles tense up all over his body.

"Are you in pain, Drew?" Tegwin said. "Does some part of your body hurt?"

"Nothing hurts. Not like that. Not my arms or my legs. My chest hurts, my stomach. My head feels like it's going to fly apart!"

Luis and Tegwin both stepped back, eyes wide. Luis held his hands over the plastic skull emanating the deep psych field for Drew.

"Okay, Drew, I'm going to stop the field now. You'll feel better in just a second. Ending field in three…two…one."

As soon as Luis touched the sensor temples, Drew's drawn up body relaxed. He opened reddened, watering eyes and sighed.

"Same thing happened to me as Helen," he said, looking from Tegwin to Luis. "Same exact thing. What are you doing to us?"

The warm tingle in Luis's chest, his hint that he was onto something, flared up into a raging fire. He knew his face was as flushed as Drew's was, and he smelled his own sweat. He didn't feel like he could possibly reassure anyone at the moment, but he had to try.

"I'm sorry this happened," he said, grabbing Drew's arm to help him sit up. "What I told Helen is the truth. We've never worked with the Becalmed before. You're helping chart new territory here, and we appreciate it more than I can say."

Drew blotted his face with his shirt sleeve, staring at the damp spots. Luis saw faint lines on Drew's smooth flesh when he turned back.

"That's not what I thought I'd be doing when I woke up this morning. You people walk around feeling like this all the time? Is that what it is?"

"Not all the time, thank goodness," Tegwin said. She kept glancing at Luis, her face pale. "But that might be what's happening. If you've never had emotional responses before, it would probably be quite uncomfortable."

Helen hadn't moved or said a word. She sat watching on her own exam bed, and the tight set of her eyes and mouth made Luis think she wasn't quite back to her Becalmed self.

"Are you feeling better, Helen?" he said. "Now that you're out of the field?"

She stared at him for a few seconds, her eyes stony and cold. Luis was amazed how such a small difference changed her whole face.

"I feel better, sure. I don't like how upset Drew was just now. Has this whole thing been about trying to trick us? Fix us? Make us more like you?"

Luis closed his eyes, shaking his head. His internal fire died down, but it didn't quite go out.

"No, not at all. I've helped people work better with their emotions, but only if they wanted me to. I didn't expect this to happen."

She nodded, her eyes still cold.

"Want to call it off for today?" Luis said. "Let us do a little research, see if we can figure this out? Maybe once you two are away from here for a while, back to your normal routine, you'll feel more like yourselves."

"I hope so," Helen said. She stood and held out her hand to Drew. "I sure do hope so. We'll be back in the morning."

Drew took her hand and stood beside her, and they walked toward the door together.

Right before he stepped out, Drew turned back to Luis and smiled.

Chapter 11

Tegwin closed the door behind the Becalmed couple, then leaned against it. She took a deep breath before she spoke.

"What just happened, Luis? What did we do to them?"

Luis squeezed his temples, trying to slow his spinning thoughts.

"I don't think we did anything. But something changed. I have to get out of here. Walk with me?"

Neither spoke until they got to the path around downtown. The same one where Luis had walked with Ben in what felt like a different lifetime. The sky was the same deep blue where the heavy cloud cover broke, the trees and grass the same rich shades of green.

The same bunches of school kids sorted themselves into groups on the playground, one half laughing and playing. Luis couldn't drag his gaze away from the group walking in silent circles around the fence.

"Are we changing them, Luis? Is deep psych some kind of a cure?"

"I don't think it's the psych field." He held up his wrist, turning the bracelet so it caught the scattered sunlight. "I think it's this. And I don't believe Helen would call it a cure at all."

"Bitan? They've been around that their whole lives. Is there any in your sensory nets, or the field generator?"

"Not even a bit of dust. That's one of the few tech devices I know of that uses no Bitan at all. Put those two together, though, and we may have an entirely different field. Maybe a much stronger one. People don't usually move under deep psych, but they both did."

They walked in silence for several minutes. Luis brushed his fingers through the chest-high bush like Ben had, holding his hand up to breathe in the fresh apple scent. Forcing himself into physical reality, trying to slow his thoughts enough to catch them.

He lowered his hand, accidently touching Tegwin's. She brought him all the way out of his mind and into his body when she twined her warm fingers through his.

"What do we do now?" she said. "I'm not so sure Helen or Drew will be willing to work with us anymore after today. Do we try to find people willing to try it, knowing what might happen?"

"I think Drew will be back. Did you see his eyes when he left? You're probably right about Helen, but Drew liked what he felt. That doesn't mean we can just experiment on them, though."

"He gave consent, didn't he? We just explain how things have changed. I think he understands that better than we do, anyway. Then we could try. This could help all those kids, Luis. This could keep Bitanthra from collapsing, which it *will* in less than fifty years."

Luis looked down at his bracelet, where the tiny grain of Bitan was. He still hadn't seen any.

"Tegwin, you mentioned getting up to the mines, getting a look at Bitan and how they extract it. If that's what made the difference, the tiny bit in this bracelet, more deep psych alone may not be the answer even if Drew does agree. Is there someone on the surface who can authorize us getting more of it? Getting some larger pieces for the exam room?"

"See if it will amplify the effect, whatever it is." She pursed her lips. "Probably not anyone on the surface, since they're still meeting up on the *Bountyfield*. Almost everyone with authority on Bitanthra is there. A whole lot of people with TransGalactic authority, too."

"I probably shouldn't say this to my planetary liaison, but can we work with the Bitanthrans instead of TransG?"

She stopped, turning to face him.

"Why? What do you think they'll object to?"

Luis shrugged, holding up his free hand.

"I don't know, maybe nothing. Probably nothing. But this does concern everyone on this planet more than anyone else. It's their children, their way of life threatened."

"The whole galaxy is concerned with Bitan production, Luis. That's what this whole thing is about. Without it-"

"I know, I understand. That is why I'm here. You know how slow a big corporation can be. They control Bitan, but they send people through years of hypersleep for a meeting! We might be days or weeks waiting for approval. Maybe months. We might not get approval at all. I want to try to help these people. Figure this out. Why would TransGalactic care *how* if we solve their problem?"

Tegwin grabbed his other hand, squeezing her eyes closed for a moment before she stared into his.

"Okay, listen," she said. "Ben comes from a mining family, one of the first to settle on the planet. His father is on the management level that goes to these big meetings up on the *Bountyfield*, but he always stays to coordinate from here. I think he's actually in charge of planetary operations right now."

"No one knows what's going on better than Ben," Luis said. "He sees these families all the time, all year long."

"Let's go talk to him, then. See what he thinks. I can't promise any of this will work, but I'm willing to try."

Chapter 12

T HEY FOUND Ben back at the medical facility, sitting in the lobby with a young woman. She didn't look much out of her teen years, with skin nearly as dark as Ben's and an upward tilt to her eyes. She leaned forward with her elbows on her knees, sobbing.

Ben glanced up at Luis when he and Tegwin walked in, his own eyes red. He rubbed the woman's back but didn't say anything.

Another nurse opened the office window, waving Luis and Tegwin over.

"Is anything wrong? I saw Helen and Drew leave a while ago."

"We're fine," Tegwin said, keeping her voice low. "We need to speak to Ben whenever he's free. Can you let him know, please?"

The door beside the nurse's window opened, and a woman's voice called the younger woman. She scrubbed at her eyes, hugged Ben, and walked inside.

When the door closed, Ben let out a long, low sigh.

"More and more every day," he said, looking into Luis's eyes. "What can I help you two with?"

"Got a minute to come back to our exam room?" Luis said. "We may be getting closer to figuring this out."

When Luis closed the door, Ben spoke before anyone else could.

"What's going on with Helen and Drew? Neither one of them

looked happy when they left. Seeing normal expressions on their faces bothered me more than I thought it would."

"That's what we may need your help with," Luis said. "We used the deep field with them yesterday, no real result. Then today, they both responded. They'd calmed down a lot by the time you saw them."

"You mean they responded emotionally?"

"Not only responded." Tegwin pointed to the still-lit skulls displaying the Becalmed couple's brain maps. "Their brains mapped to new points. Strongly."

Luis held up his wrist. "We think the difference was this. I didn't get it until this morning. When Tegwin stepped close to help me with Drew, he got even more emotional."

Ben sat on one of the exam tables, tilting his head to the side.

"You think Bitan cures them? They've never lived anywhere but here."

"That's what I thought, too," Tegwin said. "Luis told me deep psych has never been used here, and the field doesn't use any Bitan. The two together may work differently. We don't know if it's a cure, but it's doing something."

"They didn't seem hurt in any way?" Ben said. "I've never seen any of the Becalmed as upset as they were, especially Helen."

"I don't think they were hurt," Luis said. "Not physically. Surprised for certain. Drew wasn't as upset as Helen. I think he'd be willing to try more."

"That young woman out there," Ben said, rubbing the back of his neck. "She just got engaged a few days ago. She was in here begging me to help her, to make sure she doesn't get pregnant. Begging me not to tell her family. Or her fiancé. If we can stop this from getting worse, I'll do whatever I can. Do you need more subjects to work with?"

"Maybe, but not yet." Luis sat on the exam table opposite Ben. "What we really need is more Bitan. Larger pieces of it. I don't think the deep psych field alone is doing this."

"I thought your father might be able to help us," Tegwin said. "We're hoping to see if it works before we involve TransGalactic directly. They might make us wait a long, long time before they make a decision."

Ben nodded once, then jumped to his feet.

"They have to spend a couple of years in hypersleep before they make any damn decision. Come on, close up here for the day. I'll take you on a field trip out to the mines. Time to see what makes Bitanthra and this whole galaxy run."

Chapter 13

Luis regretted his big breakfast before they even got off the ground.

They'd returned to the same transit zone where he and Tegwin arrived, but none of the big, smooth official shuttles waited for them. Ben walked toward a tiny model, with four cramped seats up front and an open, flat cargo bed in the back.

"How far is the mine?" Luis said, his jaws already aching. "Can we get there another way?"

"Not unless you want to hike for about three days up the mountain." Ben stood with his hand on the roof of the shuttle. He'd pulled on a black jacket, but he still wore his light blue uniform. "You can't be afraid of flying. How did you get out here?"

"He's not afraid," Tegwin said. She dug into her pocket and handed Luis a few plastic-wrapped disks, striped red and white. "Luis gets terrible motion sickness."

"Why didn't you tell me?" Ben started back toward town. "Wait here, I'll get you something."

"That's okay, Ben." Luis smiled at Tegwin, hoping he didn't look too green and sick already. "Nothing I've ever tried works. I think I've tried everything ever invented already."

Ben put his hands on his hips, shaking his head.

"You haven't tried everything, because you've never been to Bitanthra before. If you think you can make it, we'll go on now. But let me just see what I can do for you when we get back."

"You got it," Luis said. "I'm willing to try just about anything. Fly as smooth as you can, and I'll warn you before it's too late."

Ben did the best he could with the small craft, and he kept up a running narration the whole time to help Luis concentrate. The exploration of the planet and the discovery of Bitan. The story of his family's arrival on Bitanthra, getting the original mines set up and running. His own experience working in ore processing and sorting before he switched to medicine.

Luis focused on the landscape and Ben's voice, clenching and opening his fists. The shuttle climbed smoothly up wooded slopes covered with an unbroken canopy of soft-leaved trees. The forest shifted as they climbed higher, getting more steep and rugged.

Jagged grey outcrops broke through masses of deep green pine trees, the tallest Luis had ever seen. The trunks and branches were covered in mats of fluffy moss in every shade he could imagine. The shuttle passed through cloudbanks, covering the windscreens in mist and huge drops of water.

"How you doing, Luis?" Ben said. "We're about five minutes out."

"I'm okay," Luis lied. "Just keep talking."

He gripped the seat, clenching his teeth as the shuttle turned, a long, slow bank to the right.

"I'm sorry about that." Ben glanced at Luis. "We have to stay in approved flight paths once we get this high. See the ore shuttles up ahead?"

Luis popped another of the mints into his mouth, breathing in the sharp aroma. A line of slow-moving, massive versions of the craft he, Tegwin, and Ben were in ranged along the ridgeline.

All the transports moving to the left were full to the top of the precious Bitan, obviously green even from a few hundred meters out. The line heading to the right were all empty.

"They load up at the mouth of each mine," Ben said. "Then head back to the big storage areas in the valley. When it's been a while since a TransG freighter has been here, it looks like you could make another mountain out of the Bitan piled up there."

"So they may not miss a couple of pieces." Luis tried to smile.

"They'd miss it," Tegwin said. "Even with that much, the loads are weighed down to the milligram."

Ben brought the shuttle in low under the line of transports, heading to a flattened space on top of the mountain. A cluster of stone buildings in regular rows took up most of the space, surrounded by a ring of shuttles of various sizes and shapes.

"TransGalactic headquarters for this region," Ben said. "A few families live up here, and a bunch of the miners stay during their work shifts. We'll find Dad here while they're loading up the *Bounty- field*. Guaranteed."

Luis waited for several seconds after Ben landed, eyes closed, willing his stomach to behave. When a strong gust of wind swayed the blocky shuttle, he took his chances and climbed out.

Ben stepped between Luis and Tegwin, shoulders hunched against the hard breeze.

"It never stops blowing up here. Just stay close behind me. Everyone else should be out working right now, so we won't have to dodge folks going off-shift."

Luis stared up at the huge transports as they walked under them, marveling at how the gigantic craft could possibly be so quiet. He counted at least thirty strides to cross the shadow of one.

"This is really a short crew up here today," Ben said, raising his voice over the wind. "Most everyone is down in the valley loading."

"It takes over a month to load the *Bountyfield*?" Luis said. His belly finally felt calm, and the sweat was drying on his face.

"No big freighter had been out here for a couple of years," Tegwin said. "The next one is already inbound. An extended break in the Bitan supply chain would be a disaster for more than Trans-Galactic. All the AlliedSystems would be in trouble."

Ben stopped outside the first building at the edge of the field, a two-story stone house with edges so sharp Luis thought they might have been laser cut.

"Dad can be a little bit hyper-focused at the start of a big load.

Let me get him talking, get his attention. Then you can jump in. He really is a great guy away from all this."

Luis hummed to himself as soon as they stepped inside, trying to straighten his hair and clothes after that driving wind. Several desks were scattered around the quiet, dark-walled space, everyone focused on meter-wide plas-screens in front of them.

"Ben, what brings you up here?" A tiny woman, barely as tall as Ben's chest, walked from behind the desk closest to the front door. "You know Dad's impossible to talk to when this mess is going on."

"Don't I know it. We have a couple of visiting doctors from TransG here on assignment. I wanted to make sure they see what we do out here in the back end of nowhere. Luis, Tegwin, this is my sister Anna Lee."

"Glad to meet you." Anna Lee gripped Luis's hand harder than anyone else on Bitanthra had. "This will be the best thing for him, really. Make him focus on something else for a minute so he'll relax."

Luis laughed, making sure he didn't look at Tegwin. No matter how high up Ben's father might be in the chain of command, trying to convince anyone to let them wander off with a near-priceless chunk of Bitan wouldn't likely make them relax.

"We'll do our best, ma'am."

Anna Lee flashed a crooked smile, a perfect miniature version of Ben's. She knocked on the broad wooden door beside her desk and opened it before Luis could think of what he was going to say.

Chapter 14

THE OFFICE WAS MUCH SMALLER than Luis expected, less than half the size of the room they'd just walked through. There was barely space for a sleek, black desk, several shelves stuffed full of photo-screens and printed books, and a few leather chairs.

The man standing behind the desk was medium height, unlike his towering son or petite daughter. Mr. Essena had a slender comm unit in his hand, and a spherical holo-reader, much larger than the one Luis carried, floated above the desk. Luis caught a glimpse of multiple moving documents, each full of charts and numbers, before Mr. Essena killed the display.

"Ben! What a nice surprise," The two men hugged, thumping each other on the back and smiling. "Taking a break to visit your old dad in the middle of the day."

"I know, I know. It's been a while. Work actually has been busier than usual lately. This is Doctor Luis Ahmad and Liaison Tegwin Fairbrooke. They're here from TransG, looking into what's been going on with our children."

"Mike Essena," he said, shaking Luis and Tegwin's hands. "I'm glad they're finally taking our trouble here seriously. Without our families, nothing runs on Bitanthra. Without Bitan, the whole galaxy doesn't run. Please, have a seat."

"I know how busy you are right now, Dad, so I'll get right to the point. Luis works with deep psych-hypnosis, trying to figure out what's going on. This morning, they were able to get through to a couple of the Becalmed."

"Did you find out what's been causing this?" Mr. Essena said, leaning forward in his chair. "No one else has had any luck so far."

"We're still not sure, no," Luis said. "We got emotional responses they've never had before, responses that seem to affect the brain as well. We think the difference might be the Bitan in these bracelets."

Mr. Essena blinked and drew back.

"There's hardly any in those things."

"That's what I thought," Tegwin said. "But as soon as Luis put his on and started work, everything changed. Mine increased the effect. Their brain patterns and everything shifted. Even without that, we had no doubt they were upset."

"Upset, huh." Mr. Essena rubbed his smooth chin. "Two of my grandkids are Becalmed. Much as rowdy kids like Ben and Anna Lee can be a handful, it's heartbreaking to watch them pull away like that. You think you have a cure?"

"We're not sure yet," Luis said. He paused, trying to guess what the right words would be. "The next thing we need to try, that I'd like to try, is working with more Bitan. Larger pieces. I'm hoping that would amplify the field more than these bracelets do."

Mr. Essena smiled, but he was already shaking his head.

"You've never been here before, have you?" He tapped the holo-reader, and the moving documents popped up again. "See all this? These are tracking the big load going on right now, down in the valley."

He tapped the side of the sphere, bringing up another set of displays.

"These track the mining operations up here on the mountain. At all times. TransGalactic is a wonderful company to work for, treats us very well. But they track every gram and molecule of Bitan. I don't know what they think we could do with it, or why we'd want to. No one sells or installs it in tech but them. I doubt they think we'd do anything at all, to tell you the truth. Still, they don't take any chances. The stuff is too valuable."

"Sir, this could solve the problems you've been having here," Tegwin said. "Help get the colony stabilized and keep it that way. I'm quite sure TransGalactic would be nothing but grateful."

"And they told you this?" Mr. Essena said, shutting down the displays. "When you asked about the Bitan?"

Ben held out both hands, palms up.

"You know better than I do how long they take to do anything. If we asked for authorization through them, the *Bountyfield* would be long gone, and Dr. Ahmad with it, before they ever make up their minds."

Mr. Essena looked from Luis to Tegwin and back again, tapping his fingers on the desk. The comm unit buzzed, making Luis jump. Mr. Essena glanced at it, then frowned.

"I'm truly sorry to disappoint you, but this isn't possible. Certainly not right now, with the TransGalactic flagship over our heads. One thing Ben might not know is they don't just weigh or count Bitan. Not anymore. They track the molecular signature."

He stood, and the others stood a second later.

"Anyone planetside and everyone up on the *Bountyfield* knows the supply won't hold out forever," he said. "Nothing else works the same way. Without it, communication is impossible across systems. They're planning to bring in automated scouting shuttles in a couple of years to scour the mountainsides and the paths under those big loaders. TransGalactic needs every grain of Bitan, and they're going to find it. I'm afraid you'll have to work through them on this."

"Thank you for your time," Luis said.

He was already running through his schedule for the next few years, wondering what he could bump to stay or return to Bitanthra. With the hypersleep journeys arranged so far in advance, it could easily be several years.

He'd have to find someone else with deep psych experience, see if they could rearrange their schedules. Or see if TransGalactic would let him adjust his caseload instead.

Tegwin interrupted his gloomy train of thought.

"Yes, thank you," she said. "May I ask how many grandchildren you have, Mr. Essena?"

Ben's father smiled, his mood instantly shifting.

"Five so far. Three girls and a boy. Two more on the way, which will have to do until Ben here makes up his mind about that girl he's been dating."

Tegwin smiled, and reached out to shake Mr. Essena's hand.

"That's lovely, congratulations. I understand your position about the Bitan, sir, I do. But I have to tell you, the rate of children born Becalmed has increased since TransGalactic last released information. It's passed fifty percent now, and still climbing. I hope you can see your way clear to help us as soon as possible. May I reference you in my official request?"

Mr. Essena shook himself.

"Of course, please do. I'll do everything I can, Liaison Fairbrooke."

Chapter 15

No one spoke until they were nearly back to Ben's shuttle. Luis stared up at the transports over his head, so vast and slow they seemed to hanging still. He couldn't stop himself from watching the ground under his feet as they walked, hoping for one of Mr. Essena's stray chunks of Bitan.

"So you'll file your request with TransG," Luis said. "Then we'll see how long it takes? Any chance they could come through sooner?"

Tegwin shook her head. "We're not exaggerating how slow they are, Luis. They're locked into long-range thinking, which they have to be in a way. They started construction on the *Bountyfield* ten Earth years ago for this specific trip. It's booked for at least the next thirty-five years already. Probably more after these meetings."

"And if this colony collapses in the meantime?" Luis saw the school kids, walking in endless circles instead of playing. "That won't get them moving any faster?"

Tegwin glanced at Ben, and Luis was surprised to see he was smiling.

"Go right ahead, Tegwin," he said. "I have no illusions about how this place works."

"If the colony collapses, or before it does, really, TransGalactic would bring in other workers. They don't want to, we talked about this. Production costs would skyrocket with much higher salaries, and constant transport and training time thrown on top of that. But even with all that, Bitan will keep moving."

"Have they considered how fast the Becalmed population is growing?" Ben said. He wasn't smiling anymore, but he didn't look nearly as upset as Luis felt. "How fast it's really growing?"

The nurse leaned against the shuttle, and Tegwin stepped close to speak above the roaring wind.

"Are you telling me it's higher than fifty percent now? The numbers I updated just a few days ago?"

Ben crossed his arms.

"I'm telling you it's jumped fifteen percent in the last few months. If it goes on at this rate, we'll be at seventy-five before the end of this Earth year."

Tegwin's face paled, and she held one hand over her heart.

"Why haven't you-"

"Reported it to TransG? We have. When you took up orbit. Around the same time you got your update, right?" He waited for her to nod. "Now I don't know if this is just their normal glacial pace of operations, or if they've decided to let the colony fail instead. If I had to guess, I'd say they weren't expecting those numbers. Otherwise they wouldn't have bothered bringing Luis and his expensive equipment all this way."

"They rearranged my schedule," Luis said. "Bumped or reassigned several cases to get me here. I was just now trying to figure out how we could manage to do that again so I could stay."

"How often do they rearrange *any* schedule?" Ben said. "For any reason? They're wanting to save this place if they possibly can. I'll sign on to your request, Tegwin, and I know a few other people who will as well. Obstetricians, teachers, folks like that. We'll see if that gets their attention."

They all got settled in the shuttle, and Luis opened his last mint. He wasn't quite recovered from the ride up.

"Why did you ask my father about grandkids, Tegwin?"

"I thought...I hoped if I put it in those terms, he might be willing to help us. I think he wants to, don't you?"

"I know he wants to. He asks me about it a lot, that's why I suggested coming up here. What he didn't tell you is one of those babies is due in just a couple of weeks. No one on Bitanthra wants this figured out more than he does."

Luis managed to hold out until they arrived back in town, with the return ride much smoother and faster. But he had to detour into the brush before they walked back to the medical facility.

"Don't you leave here without letting me get something for you," Ben said. He still had a small smile, and he acted much less worried than either Luis or Tegwin. "You might be surprised at what all grows around here."

"Whatever you have, I'll try. Can I ask you something?"

"I told you, that's what I'm here for."

"Tegwin and I were talking about the temperaments of most Bitanthrans. How some of them might be a little more emotionally reactive than typical humans. Does that sound right to you?"

Ben snorted. "We deserve our reputation as a rowdy bunch if that's what you're asking."

"I know you've all been concerned about the Becalmed and that getting worse. Has the rest gotten worse too, more intense?"

Ben rubbed his chin, exactly the same way his father had.

"I'm not really old enough to remember, just in my late thirties Earth Standard. But there were stories when I was off-world doing my medical training. People talking about how Bitan made us a little crazy. I was just a kid and didn't pay much attention. I thought they were just picking on us because we're such a small, rural colony."

"Would there be any kind of records we could look at?" Tegwin said. "Medical or maybe school records?"

"You think this is related?" Ben said.

"I don't know how it could be," Luis said. "But we don't know what causes any of this yet. I don't want to rule anything out. No matter how TransGalactic handles our Bitan request, I'm here for a few more weeks at least. May as well use the time."

"I'll see what I can dig up. Do you have any data for that, Tegwin?"

"No, but I have been coming here for a long time. Longer than you'd believe with hypersleep. I think the population is changing, too."

Luis pulled out his small comm-screen. "I'll get started writing up the data we have so far for your request, Tegwin. I'll check my schedule for the next few years, then work out a testing protocol for Bitan. I'm not giving up until I have to."

Chapter 16

Luis nearly missed a step when they rounded the corner toward the medical center. Two people stood in front of the door, a woman and a man. Both had their arms crossed, and neither looked happy.

"Myrtle and Wills," Ben said. "I'm guessing they've spoken with Helen and Drew."

"And they're not going to want to speak with me," Luis said. "Or maybe they do, but I'm not going to like it."

"They didn't have any trouble with their testing, did they?" Ben glanced at Luis. "I can head them off, but it would help if I knew what I was walking into."

"They didn't get as upset as Helen did this morning," Tegwin said, slowing her pace. "I'd say Myrtle got a bit upset with her first psych field."

"I don't think she's happy about any of this," Luis said.

"They're scared," Ben said. "Like the rest of us. Let me see what's going on."

The two leaders stepped forward and uncrossed their arms, but neither of them were smiling.

"How are you two doing this afternoon?" Ben shook hands with both of them. "I was just showing our guests the Bitan operation in action."

"We're fine," Myrtle said. She never took her eyes off Luis. "I was hoping Luis and Tegwin would join us for lunch this afternoon. Fill us in on how their work is going."

"We'd be glad to," Tegwin said. "What time?"

Willis stepped forward. "We can have everything ready by the time you wash up and meet us at our house if that works for you."

"We'll be there," Luis said. He tried to be optimistic about the invitation. At least they hadn't yelled at him out here on the street. "Just give us about ten minutes."

"See you there." Myrtle inclined her head, then they both walked away.

"Should I be worried?" Luis said when Ben closed the medical center door.

"I don't think so," Ben said, with that same little smile. "Just be honest with them. That's all most people want, especially when it comes to their children. Tell them the truth and do the best you can for them."

"That I can promise."

The table wasn't quite as stuffed full as the first time Luis had eaten with Willis, barely an hour after leaving the *Bountyfield*. There was more than enough food for four people, but not enough for twice that many.

His solitary dinners from the food stores in his apartment had been filling, but not especially satisfying. He was thankful the conversation was light and pleasant enough so he could enjoy the meal after his stomach's rough morning.

The respite didn't quite last until the last plates were cleared.

"So tell us, Luis," Myrtle said, leaning back in her chair, "what have you learned so far with Helen and Drew?"

Be honest, Ben said. Might as well take that advice.

"We had a bit of a surprise this morning. When we activated the psych field, they both had emotional responses. Helen didn't seem to care for it, but I think Drew was curious."

Myrtle glanced at Willis, and they both nodded. First test passed, Luis hoped.

"Helen stopped by here after they finished up," Willis said. "She wasn't pleased, no. Is this some kind of cure? What do you think made the difference?"

"It's too soon to call it a cure." Luis thought of Helen's cold, stony eyes. "Helen has no desire to be like us. She made that quite clear."

"She told me the same thing," Myrtle said. Luis caught the faintest trace of a smile. "She said if we all walk around a mess inside like that, it's no wonder we're always fighting and crying and carrying on."

"She has a point," Tegwin said. "I had a brother and a sister, and our teenage years were nothing but drama."

"Why are you not calling it a cure?" Willis said. "For the ones that want it, or for the young children? Sounds like this would help them."

"It might," Luis said. "We don't know how long the effect will last, or if it would cause some other kind of problem. With the adults, I'm afraid of slamming them into emotions with no time to adapt. Both Helen and Drew had strong reactions, a bit above typical to be honest."

"Where were Willis and I on that range?" Myrtle said.

"A bit high a couple of times. When I asked you about what was causing the numbers of Becalmed to grow, for instance."

"That's going to set most of us off, I believe," Willis said. "I'm not surprised we're above normal, either. If you're thinking it *could* be a cure, what do you need to do next?"

Luis looked at Tegwin, and she shrugged. This was probably the place in the whole galaxy where Bitan was the least secret.

"We think these comm bracelets made the difference." Luis held up his wrist. "The ones TransG gives permanent staff like Tegwin, or people on assignment for them, like me. But the amount of Bitan inside is so small."

"We were trying to get a larger sample," Tegwin said. "Up by the main mine. They weren't able to help us, so we're going to make a request to the *Bountyfield*."

"They track every speck and scrap up by those mines now," Myrtle said. "Not like when we were younger."

Luis stared at her, afraid to speak. Tegwin did it for him.

"When you were younger? Are you saying someone in town might have larger pieces?"

"You expect me to answer that question from a TransG liaison?" Myrtle said, amusement clear in her voice. "We've heard how strict they are about it now, how they're gathering up all the stray pieces they can find."

"Doubt they'd pay what it's worth, anyway," Willis said. "Even to the ones who mined it for them."

"I can't pay anyone," Luis said, trying to keep his voice calm. "I don't have any local currency. Even if I could access all of my galactic credits, I don't have nearly enough for the speck of Bitan in this bracelet, much less what we'd need."

"What *do* you have, Luis?" Myrtle said. "What can you offer us?"

"I can offer to do my best to help your children. Adults too, if they want it. Anyone who lets me use Bitan for this, I can promise I'll give it back. There's no possible way I could sneak it onto the *Bountyfield*, anyway."

"How long do you think you'd be waiting for that official request to come through?" Willis said. "TransG wasn't exactly fast last time we tried to get anything changed here. We plan for months and expect years."

"They're the same," Tegwin said. She had her hands knotted tightly in her lap, obviously as anxious as Luis was. "Weeks would be a miracle."

"And you'll be gone by then." Myrtle nodded to herself. "Well, the best we can do is think about it, maybe talk to a few people. I can't make any promises. I doubt anyone I know actually has any. But you answered our questions, and that means a lot to us."

"That's all I can ask," Luis said. "If Helen or Drew are still willing to work with me, I'll do my best for them. You too, or anyone else who wants to help. I'll do my best."

Chapter 17

Luis rubbed his achy eyes, trying to get the numbers and data in front of him to stop blurring. He'd been in the exam room for hours working on the report for Tegwin. He normally had days to dig through, especially when writing up a treatment or experimental protocol.

He didn't want to delay this project by even one minute if he could help it.

The truth was he had more than enough to justify for a return trip to Bitanthra, probably with a few technicians and all the equipment he needed. The results from Myrtle and Willis's single deep psych field were almost as interesting as the Becalmed.

Older long-term memories stored the same as most humans. Average distribution throughout the brain, some stronger with more emotional ties than others. The more recent memories, though, within the last thirty Earth years, were anything but average.

The newer long-term memories for both were stronger, deeper. Nearly enough to reach traumatic levels for typical humans. Too many at that level for people living on a peaceful world.

Something was changing here, at least for Myrtle and Willis. Working with more subjects was no longer a nice idea Luis would pursue if he had more time or more sensors. He had to bring in more people, downloading and resetting the sensor nets daily if necessary.

The tiny grain of Bitan around his wrist might just have to do.

Luis was staring at the exam beds, wondering if he could risk a quick nap without falling asleep for hours, when someone knocked.

Ben opened the door when Luis called out, a huge grin on his face.

"What are you doing here so late?" Luis glanced at the time on his notescreen. "What are you doing *awake* so late?"

"Well, I had an urgent comm from my dad. Seems he's been in touch with some of his old friends down here, pretty much nonstop since we left. He still can't send us any Bitan from the mine, so don't get your hopes up about that."

"I've got plenty to study while I'm still here," Luis said. "Maybe with our three bracelets, we'll see a difference."

"Sure, we can do that. But you might want to come see what was out front waiting for me."

Luis stretched as he stood, groaning at the crackles in his back. He'd been sitting there way too long. His sluggish mind finally caught up with what Ben said by the time he got to the nurses' office. A shade was pulled in the window, blocking the view out to the lobby and the street.

"They sent Bitan?" Luis stared at the pile of packets and envelopes, even one gleaming wooden box bigger than his two hands. "Myrtle and Willis?"

"No idea, and that's the way they wanted it. Dad didn't tell me anyone's names. All they ask is we put all of it back in the same containers."

"How much is all of this worth?"

Luis picked up the box, marveling at the multi-colored inlays and intricate metalwork.

"I doubt we could price some of these in galactic credits," Ben said. "I've never seen this much outside of the mines. I'd imagine once TransG gets around to sweeping the town, all of these will be gone unless we can work out something with them. So everyone keeps them well hidden."

Inside the fabric-lined box were two pieces of Bitan, each as big as Luis's fists. He held one up, surprised at how heavy it was.

"They had enough to carve them. It's beautiful."

The dark, pine forest green surface was polished to a glasslike finish, forming a rounded cube. Grooves a few millimeters deep made swirls, lines, and spirals, each fiery with flashes of jewel tones as Luis turned the Bitan.

"No one was really sure what they had here," Ben said. He picked up the twin to the one Luis held. "Carved ones like this go back to the very first colonists to arrive, before TransGalactic got involved."

"I can't tell you how much this means to me, Ben."

"You can show me, Luis. Me and everyone else. I'll get you all the subjects you need, give you support staff if you need us. Help us figure out what's going on with our kids."

Luis nodded, not sure he could speak.

They carried the Bitan back to the exam room and unpacked it all, arranging the pieces in a row in front of their containers. The samples ranged from a few millimeters across to the two in the box, all carved or at least polished.

The treasured reminders of the first residents of Bitanthra might end up saving future generations.

"You're asleep on your feet, Dr. Ahmad," Ben said. "Everything is ready here, and it sounds to me like you have more than enough written up for Tegwin's official request. I'd guess she might appreciate a little company, too."

"Yeah, we probably should still do that request, huh? If they do come through, I can get these back to their owners a lot sooner. We need to start with these smallest pieces, I think."

Ben spoke from right behind Luis's ear.

"Luis! Put the screen down. Go back to your room and get some sleep. Better yet, go join your liaison and tell her I said the same goes for her."

The nurse was smiling, but Luis knew better than to ignore that tone of voice from anyone.

"I'm going, right now. You heading home?"

"I'll catch a few hours in one of the other guest rooms. I'll have a stimulant waiting for you in the morning. We're both going to need it."

Chapter 18

Luis had never been one to underestimate the comfort of sleeping beside another person, especially one so compatible with him. Tegwin had indeed still been awake and more than willing to take Ben's stern advice. The few hours Luis managed did more for him than an entire night on his own.

Ben was explaining to Tegwin how they ended up with enough Bitan to pay for their own *Bountyfield* by the time Luis staggered into the exam room the next morning. Both had already finished their own stimulant drinks, and Ben handed one to Luis without interrupting his story. The earthy, steaming hot beverage cleared his thinking as soon as he swallowed it.

"Taking these from the families would be a crime." Tegwin held a slender piece of Bitan as long as her hand, carved with symbols in a language Luis didn't recognize. "Just as much as from any of the indigenous populations back on Earth or anywhere else."

"We hope that's how TransG sees it someday," Ben said. "But for now, we keep these hidden. Most of us don't even know who has what. I sure didn't. Dad might tell me someday if he ever decides I'm grown up enough."

"I'd never even heard rumors about them," Tegwin said. "Not in all the times I've been here. I think you're right about submitting the official request anyway, Luis. You know I was up half the night working on it too, so we might as well."

"I have a basic testing protocol ready." Luis activated his screen and sent the documents to Tegwin and Ben. "If anyone shows up to let us test. We may have to take you up on your offer of more subjects."

"Dad said he was going to talk to a few people," Ben said, heading toward the door. "I think Myrtle and Willis will too, after all the conversations flying around town last night."

"Is this going to cause you problems?" Luis said after Ben left. "With TransGalactic?"

Tegwin stepped into Luis's arms, then turned to gaze at the row of Bitan, shaking her head.

"If they ever find out I knew about this and didn't tell them, maybe. I'm serious about these staying here. I don't have a lot of influence over cultural issues, but my brother worked with creating settlement procedures on a few colonies when he was first starting out. He might know how we could go about doing that here."

"You ready for this?" Luis brushed her red hair back from her face, resisting a strong urge to kiss her. "Assuming anyone shows up?"

"This is all new to me," she said, laying her head against his chest. "Deep psych field was only a theory when I finished my training. Are you ready?"

Luis broke away and walked in a circle around the exam beds, adjusting everything for at least the tenth time since the previous afternoon.

"This is outside anything I've ever done or read about. We could help save this colony, the culture they have here. Or, we could prove that it can't be saved. Most of the time I'm trying to help individuals, you know? Not save an entire colony."

Ben opened the door enough to peek through, his usual bright smile firmly in place.

"Your first four subjects are here."

"Four?" Luis turned to Tegwin. She shook her head. "Bring them back."

The door opened wide, and Helen and Drew walked in, followed by Myrtle and Willis.

"I didn't think…I'm so glad to see all of you!" Luis said, not sure if he was about to laugh or cry.

"We all had a good talk last night," Myrtle said. "What you're doing is the best chance we've had to figure out what's happening here for a long time. Since the trouble first started, really. We at least want to do our part."

"We can get started right now," Tegwin said. She held out her hand toward the exam table. "Unless any of you have questions."

Helen and Drew both nodded and stepped forward.

"Your promise still holds, Luis?" Helen said. "I know you might not be able to fix what already happened. But you'll try not to change me if you can help it?"

Luis took her hand, helping her onto the table.

"I promise. Thank you for your trust. How are you feeling, Drew?"

The Becalmed man smiled, the expression more natural than Luis would have believed two days ago.

"I admit I was scared yesterday. I know more what to expect now. I think I'd be fine if I get changed a little more."

"Perfect. A test and a control. Exactly what we need. Do you think you can get your sensor net on, Helen? That way we won't get too close to you with the Bitan bracelets."

She nodded, and she had herself set up and ready before Tegwin and Luis were finished connecting the net and the table's other diagnostic sensors for Drew.

"What we'll do is take a quick scan to see how your brains are looking today." Luis touched the skull-shaped sensors, waiting as maps of Helen and Drew's brains lit up the interiors. "You can watch these if you want, Myrtle and Willis. The scan will give us a basic idea whether the changes are lasting. Then if all goes well, we'll try Drew with the deep psych field."

Neither of the Becalmed's brain maps had changed overnight, which was what Luis expected. He had no idea what to expect with the next part of the test.

"Okay. Your brains look the same as they did yesterday. The effect is lasting so far, and it's not progressing on its own. If you're ready, I'll activate the deep psych field. Then we'll see how Bitan affects Drew."

Luis touched the sensor temples, then held his fingers over the top of each skull.

"Starting field in three…two…one." He tapped the top of each skull. "How are you feeling, Helen? Same as yesterday?"

"I'm the same. Still have a mixed up spot inside my head, but it's not as bad."

"Drew? How about you?"

The Becalmed man had his eyes closed just like Helen, but his face was more tense. His eyes were squeezed closed, his mouth drawn up.

"I feel about the same. The truth is I want you to try to change me. I liked what happened yesterday. I thought about it all night long."

Luis looked at Myrtle and Willis. When they both nodded, he waved Tegwin forward.

"We're going to try only the Bitan in these bracelets now. Not for you, Helen, only for Drew."

They held the silver bands on either side of Drew's head. He took a deep slow breath, but his body didn't draw up like it had before. Myrtle and Willis leaned down to peer through the skull sensors.

"I'm seeing a few changes in brain waves," Luis said. "No new points in the brain map yet. What do you feel, Drew?"

"Warm in my belly, churning around. I feel like I'm wide awake."

"Good." Luis picked up two of the smaller pieces of Bitan, giving one to Tegwin. "We're trying larger pieces now. You can tell me to stop anytime you want to. Remember that."

They held the ore around Drew's shoulders, then gradually moved closer. The movement of his brain waves intensified, making deeper peaks and valleys. His heart rate and respiration increased as well.

"Chest feels tight," Drew said, shifting his arms and legs. "Muscles, too."

"I'm seeing increased activity that may be anger," Luis said. "Try breathing deep like you did before, then blow out the tension with your breath."

When Drew's vital signs were closer to normal, Luis and Tegwin moved the Bitan to beside his temples.

"If you're comfortable, I'm going to ask you a few questions," Luis said. "Some of what we did yesterday." He waited for Drew to nod. "Do you know what makes you Becalmed, Drew?"

"Too much coming in. More than we can stand. Hurts too bad."

"Too much coming from people around you?"

"No. From far away. Another place. Bad things, bad people."

Luis looked up at Myrtle and Willis.

"Do you know what he's talking about?"

They both shook their heads, brows wrinkled.

"Helen, you can hear what Drew's saying," Luis said. "Does that sound right to you?"

"That's how it felt yesterday," she said. "When you changed my brain. Like something outside could get in where I didn't want it."

Myrtle pointed at the skull showing Drew's brain map. A few new red dots glowed, more scattered than the day before. They were almost as big and intense as Myrtle's strong long-term memories.

"We're going to try bigger pieces of Bitan now, Drew." Luis let Willis take the smaller bits of ore and give them larger ones. "I want you to keep thinking about that place far away. See if anything gets more clear."

Drew clenched his fists, and Luis saw his thigh muscles tighten.

"Is this going to hurt him?" Myrtle said. "Hurt his brain?"

"All these sensors have warnings built in," Luis said. "The brain does what it can to protect itself. One big way is drawing blood in from the limbs. If his hands or feet get cold, or his heart rate gets too high, we'll know we need to stop."

"I want to keep going," Drew said. His fists were still clenched, but he was smiling. "I like the way this feels."

"You're doing really well," Tegwin said. "Can you tell anything more about the far away place? I know the Becalmed don't dream all that often, but do you think it's somewhere you dreamed of?"

"Some kind of trouble. Secret. No one talks about it." He paused, his forehead and mouth wrinkling. "I don't think it's a dream. Doesn't feel like here. Doesn't feel like in my head. Don't dream much, though. I hope I dream more when I'm changed."

"Maybe you will," Luis said. "Rest for a minute, Drew. You too, Helen. We're not going anywhere, just taking a break."

He activated the white noise dome over the two of them and waved everyone else over.

"Is it possible the Bitan is doing more than amplifying their emotions?" he said. "I know this might sound irrational, but it does enable faster than light communications across all the known systems."

"You reminded me that we don't have any idea why they're Becalmed," Tegwin said. "They've lived their entire lives on a planet full of Bitan, with mountains of it moving around on the surface. I'm not ready to rule anything out."

"I've never heard of anything like this, though," Myrtle said. "Sending a voice or data with Bitan is one thing. But thoughts? Feelings?"

Luis stared at Myrtle, her first deep psych running through his mind. People didn't always remember what they said when they were under.

"Do you remember what you said about this, Myrtle? Under the field? Lots of times people can't. More often than not, really."

"You mean about poison? I do think that's what it is, without any kind of field."

Tegwin shook her head. "You said it felt like it didn't come from here. Like it came from far away."

Myrtle sighed and crossed her arms.

"No, I don't remember that. I suppose you have everything recorded like you told us, or else you wouldn't have said so."

"I do. I'm not trying to cause trouble or make you feel bad. But like Tegwin says, we can't rule anything out just yet."

"What does that mean?" Willis said. "If it is something like that, what could we do about it?"

"That's a whole bunch of steps ahead of me," Luis said. "I don't think I'd know where to begin, anyway. If this is some kind of broadcast, I hope Tegwin would know what to do."

Tegwin laughed, raising one eyebrow at Luis.

"I hope you're not serious. First thing I'd do is ask for help. How can you even begin to verify some kind of external broadcast?"

Luis stared at the row of Bitan along the wall without seeing it. Saying he was working beyond his training and experience didn't even come close.

So far, anyway, he was beyond his imagination.

"Well, right now we have two people who've said a problem, a poison, is coming from far away. Under deep psych hypnosis. No one has ever been able to lie when they're under the field. The first step in verification is recreation."

Myrtle squeezed her lips so tight that they disappeared.

"You want me or Willis to try it again. See what happens with Bitan this time. Right?"

Luis nodded. "It is voluntary. I don't mean volunteer or else, either. I'm not going to coerce you or make you feel guilty. I've love for both of you to try. And, if you don't want to, that's the end of the discussion."

"Is it going to change us?" Myrtle said. "Like it is Helen and Drew?"

"We haven't tried any typical Bitanthrans with Bitan yet," Luis said. "What I'd do is verify your scan from the first day, then we'd watch while you're under. I can stop if I see any changes, or I can ask what you want to do if it happens."

Willis held out his hand to Myrtle.

"Let us talk about this for a couple of minutes," he said. "You can ask Helen and Drew some more questions, right?"

"Absolutely." Luis grabbed his discarded comm badge from the work table. He'd been so excited when Tegwin gave him his official comm bracelet that he'd forgotten all about it. "You can use this to get into my room, or Ben can let you into another one."

"I think the hall will suit us just fine." Myrtle took Willis's hand and followed him out.

"A transmission," Tegwin said. She rubbed her upper arms. "That doesn't sound like a pleasant one to get."

"No. If it's true, we'll have more questions than answers. And no easy way to deal with any of it."

"Typical day around here, Dr. Ahmad. Let's see what else these two have to say in case Myrtle and Willis agree to let you tinker with their brains."

Luis stopped the white noise, then sat beside Helen.

"What's happening with you, Helen? Do you have any sense of trouble coming from far away?"

"I still feel like I can't reach it. Today I don't feel like it can reach me. That's safer. Better."

"Okay, good. We only have one more question for you today, since you're the control. You're one of the leaders of the Becalmed. Do you think many of you would want to be changed? If you could?"

"A lot of people want us to change. Our families sure do. But I don't think many of us want to. We don't want to leave our home, or cause everyone else to have to leave. But most of us like the way we are."

"I'll make sure everyone knows that. One last question for you, Drew. Do you mind if we try a little more Bitan?"

Tegwin handed Luis the long, slender piece he'd seen her with earlier that morning. She held its near-twin.

"Go ahead."

Luis and Tegwin moved the Bitan wands closer, watching Drew's vital signs. This time his brain activity increased, but his breathing and heart rate stayed normal.

"He's adapting so fast," Luis said under his breath. "Drew, I want you to think about that far away place. You'll still be safe here, but do you think you could feel more of it? Like opening a window?"

Drew was silent for a long moment.

"I think I could open the window and I'd know more. I'm afraid, though. Feels like a dream there, a bad one. The dreams that scare regular kids."

"A nightmare." Tegwin shivered. "Adults have those, too."

"It might be a nightmare," Luis said. "I want to ask Myrtle and Willis about this first, since they've had nightmares before. Then we may ask you again."

"Will you let me try, too?" Drew said. His heart rate increased a little, and his cheeks flushed. "Let me look through the window? I want to see a new place even if I never leave home."

"Of course, Drew." Luis glanced over as Myrtle and Willis came back in. "You can open it as wide as you want to. We'll make sure you're safe. Okay, I'm bringing both of you out of the field in three...two...one. Helen opened her eyes in a calm face, as if she'd just woken up from a nap. Drew was smiling again, his eyes bright and merry.

Luis no longer recognized the Becalmed man he met a few days ago. He hoped Drew understood others in his community may not, either.

Chapter 19

Myrtle left no doubt about who was in charge as soon as Helen and Drew got to their feet.

"We'll help you, Luis, or at least I will. From what you tell me, I got a stronger sense of something coming from outside of Bitanthra than Willis did. Mine was more like Drew." She looked at Willis, and he nodded. "I'd feel better if Willis stayed awake. I know that sounds like I don't trust you, but I wouldn't be here if I didn't."

"Of course, we can do that," Luis said, trying to keep up. "We'll do whatever makes you the most comfortable."

She turned to Helen and Drew.

"I know you two are leaders of your community, and all of this affects you directly. But I need you to leave while we're doing this. I'll feel a lot more comfortable."

Drew shook his head and started to speak.

"No, Drew," Myrtle said. "Don't forget I'm older than you. This is medical treatment, right?"

This time Tegwin gathered her wits in time to respond.

"We do classify it that way, yes."

"Then I have every right to privacy." Myrtle touched Drew's shoulder. "We're not trying to hide anything from you. I have a feeling this isn't going to be easy is all."

Drew scowled, but he let Helen take his arm and walk him out of the room. Myrtle sat on one of the exam tables.

"Now let's see what you can figure out."

Luis returned Tegwin's half smile as they both jumped to do Myrtle's bidding. He sat beside her when the sensor net and monitors were all in place.

"We'll get the field established, then start with the smaller pieces of Bitan. I know you have a lifetime of experience with emotions, Myrtle. But if this gets too strong or feeling out of control, you can tell me to stop. Promise me you will?"

She stared at him, gaze steady but eyes narrowed in fear.

"I promise, Luis. If it is too bad, you can treat me for trauma or something like that, right?"

"I can. I don't want to get to that point, though. Your brain activity is normal, so we're ready. Starting field in three…two…one."

Luis and Tegwin each held the smallest pieces of Bitan close to Myrtle's head. The intensity of her brain waves increased, but her vital signs stayed level.

"Focus on what you felt before," Luis said. "The sense of poison from outside Bitanthra."

"Feels like a light shining," Myrtle said. "Or music from a long way off."

They switched to larger pieces of ore.

"That's louder. Stronger." She shifted her back and shoulders. "No one knew this could happen. But no one can figure out how to make it stop."

Tegwin pointed toward Myrtle's skull sensor display. Luis didn't see any new dots, but some in the amygdala were glowing brighter to match her increasing brain activity.

Fear. And anger.

"Drew talked about opening a window," Luis said, taking one of the Bitan wands from Tegwin. "Do you feel like you can do that, Myrtle? Or maybe pull the feelings closer to you?"

Myrtle took a long, slow breath, but her heart rate increased.

"Hidden away. No one knows they exist. No one wants to know."

"Do you have any sense of what kind of place it is?" Luis said. "A planet, a moon? A ship, maybe?"

He and Tegwin held the Bitan wands alongside Myrtle's head, nearly touching her temple and jaw. She shifted her legs, then spread her fingers wide. Movement she shouldn't have been able to manage under the field. Just like Drew.

"I feel trapped, deep under the ground. Cold, dark. Not like I'm supposed to be. So many there. So many…"

Tears rolled down Myrtle's cheeks, cutting through the sweat.

"You're starting to show signs of physical distress," Luis said, watching her breathing and heartbeat. Both were getting faster. "We can pull you back now, take a break."

She shook her head, squeezing her eyes tight.

"No break. Not yet. Lost and terrified. I don't want to leave them there."

She held out her hand, and Willis took it in both of his. Luis saw tendons stand out on her wrist, her fingers sinking into Willis's flesh.

The fear levels in her brain waves were near the top of normal ranges, but her breathing and heart rate slowed. Luis's own heart jumped at the concentration of red around Myrtle's fear centers.

"Can you find anything about them, Myrtle? Any bits of language? We can't normally read thoughts with deep psych, but we've never gotten emotions from another mind, either."

"The outsiders bury them, put them away. Like they're not real at all. If anyone finds out, they would have to leave."

Luis's stomach turned over even though he was sitting perfectly still. He knew the horror stories from early colonization days. Everyone who worked for TransGalactic did. It seemed humans didn't behave much differently when they moved to new planets as when they'd moved to new continents on Earth centuries before.

"Do they feel human to you, Myrtle? Can you get any sense of that?"

Her whole face crumpled and she turned her head away. Her voice was strained, forced through a tight throat.

"Monsters. Humans are monsters. Kill us instead. Kill us all."

"Can you try to send to them?" Luis said. "Whoever you're in contact with? Try to let them know we're going to help them, to hang on?"

Myrtle's body tensed, and Luis heard the first pinging alarm from the bed's monitors. Her hands and feet were getting colder.

"I can't find them. We can't help them if I can't find them."

"Listen to me." Luis held his hand over the skull sensor, getting ready to stop the field. "We know you can contact them, at least two of you can. I think they must have Bitan, so they have to be a wealthy colony. We *will* find them, Myrtle."

She shivered, and Luis heard her teeth chatter. Myrtle drew in a huge, great breath. As she let it out, her brain activity peaked, then started to decline.

"Hang on," she whispered. "We'll find you. We'll find you."

Myrtle opened her eyes as soon as Luis ended the field.

"Did I just lie to them? You said we *couldn't* lie under the field. We can't possibly find them when we don't even know where to start."

Luis turned to get a blanket, but Tegwin already had one. They tucked it around Myrtle as closely as they could, but her temperature was already coming back up.

"Something as valuable as Bitan will be tracked, Myrtle." Luis hoped it was the truth. "Anyone who can afford it can't stay hidden forever."

Chapter 20

Luis closed the door to his apartment and leaned against it, rubbing his temples. The same spot that primed the deep psych field on the skull sensors. He wished he could instantly activate the same focus and calm inside his own stormy brain.

Ben and Tegwin had helped get Myrtle and Willis settled in to another of the guest quarters, then checked on Helen and Drew in theirs. All the Bitanthrans were fine as far as Luis could tell. Vital signs normal, resting comfortably. They were all understandably wary of doing more, but hopeful that they could help figure out whatever was going on.

Underneath all that, Luis could see Drew was trying to hide his growing excitement. For a man who'd never dealt with emotions at all, much less how to hide them, Luis thought he was handling the rapid adjustment quite well.

Luis didn't feel like he was doing well himself. Not at all. He'd had the door closed for all of five minutes, and he was already regretting his own suggestion that he and Tegwin take a break. Alone. Maybe sleep for a little while, let their minds sort through and figure out what to do next.

His mind was only spinning faster and faster, his heart and gut joining in the chaotic motion and distress.

He walked into the kitchen and held his hand over the drinks spigot, with no clue what he should dispense. A light sedative, enough to let him relax but not quite sleep? A stronger one to knock him out for a few hours and settle his whirling thoughts? Or the strongest stimulant in the kitchen's programming, one that would overpower his late night and send him careening into another?

Luis settled for apple juice instead, grown and pressed in sprawling orchards not far outside of town. The fruit was as crisp and tart as any Earth apple he'd ever tasted.

Cold glass full of amber liquid in hand, he abruptly decided staying in his apartment when he couldn't sit still for more than a few minutes didn't make sense. At least he could get outside, walk around in the cool, foggy air.

He nearly dropped the glass when he opened the door to see Tegwin raising her hand to knock.

"You too?" she said, smiling. "I'm going to lose my mind if I try to sleep. You didn't sound like you wanted company, but maybe you want to with me?"

"I was just heading outside, and I very much want your company. I haven't really taken advantage of having the planetary liaison for the Bitan homeworld by my side. I might ask you a bunch of questions."

"I'll be driving you nuts asking how we can combine Bitan and deep psych for people who aren't from Bitanthra soon enough. If it amplifies the field for everyone, we may solve more than one problem on this visit."

Luis swallowed the last of his juice, managing to set the glass on the counter without breaking it.

That was what his mind had been endlessly circling, just out of his reach.

"Maybe we can try that out right now," he said. "If you're willing."

Tegwin leaned against the kitchen wall with her arms crossed. Luis was relieved to see her eyes held more challenge than caution.

"You want one of us to try it. Going under the field."

"It's a logical next step. At least while everyone else is resting.

We'll know a hell of a lot more about how this works, how much effect the Bitan has for people from anywhere but here. We might even be able to locate where the signal's coming from."

Tegwin shook her head slowly.

"We don't even know what we're looking for. What kind of life it is. We may be able to see if Bitan changes things, sure, but how could we locate anything?"

Drew spoke from just inside the open door.

"I'll help. I want to. I'm not going to sleep any time soon, either."

The spark in Luis's chest, his clear hint he was about to zero in on the solution, flared hot.

"We can try," he said. "But do you have any idea how to direct me? Where it came from?"

"No." Drew stepped into the apartment, his eyes bright and excited. "I know how it felt, though. Can't we both go under the field together or something? Maybe Myrtle can help us since she's used to emotions."

Luis rubbed at his face.

"That's not…No one does that outside of training. And only then, after all subjects have a good idea of what they're doing. It can be dangerous, Drew."

"Dangerous how?" Drew said. "More than changing my mind into something new? Or dangerous to you?"

"Well, to both of us, really," Luis said. His mind was already running through calibrations and setup, getting two mapped brains into the same field. Three if Myrtle was willing. "We don't have an instructor here to monitor us, for one thing. One or the other of us could get into trouble. Any of us. Mental or physical, if the field gets out of balance."

"I can monitor you," Tegwin said. "I've been in on how many sessions now? You keep talking about how advanced and automated the systems here are, Luis."

Luis wished he'd gotten out the door for that walk before the conversation went this far. And he wanted to try Drew's idea.

Right now.

"I just want to help them," Drew said, his voice soft. "Whoever they are. Whatever they are. If we just find out *where* they are, maybe we can. Maybe TransGalactic can."

"If it means saving this colony," Tegwin said, "TransGalactic will do whatever it takes. Come on, Luis. What do I need to know that the diagnostic systems here don't already monitor? That you don't know yourself?"

Luis leaned against the counter, tapping his fingernails against the cold stone. She had a good point. Once TransGalactic finally saw a clear reason to get involved, to throw all their resources behind a problem, they finally did move quickly.

That could be the best, fastest way to save Bitanthra and whoever was sending the signal.

"Okay, we'll try it," he said, walking toward the door. "We'll see if Myrtle is willing to help us, that's a good idea. But I'm setting parameters on the monitors and on the bed's diagnostics. This whole thing stops if any of us get into any trouble."

Tegwin bowed her head and waved her arm.

"Lead the way, Dr. Ahmad."

Chapter 21

THE SETUP WAS FINISHED LONG before Luis was ready, or at least before his nervousness overcame his excitement. It was a simple matter of adjusting the connections, the communications, between three of the sensor skulls and nets. Instead of connecting one to one, all sets now worked in parallel. The fourth stood ready to display the combined data as needed.

Tegwin, Drew, and Myrtle watched every change he made. They all asked questions, and Tegwin made notes the whole time. Luis didn't mind the attention, knowing explaining as he went would act as a backup. If he could teach it, he could do it correctly.

Ben sat between the exam beds with three of the oval data pods in front of him. He'd hesitated, but only long enough to work out the safety protocols with Luis. He was nearly finished changing the settings.

Helen sat beside Willis in front of the row of Bitan. Neither had tried to argue with Drew or anyone else, but they'd insisted on watching.

"Pay attention to how this is going to work," Ben said, waving everyone over. "The alert levels are higher, or lower in some cases. The big difference is instead of just an audible and visual alarm, these are connected to the deep field emulator now. If you hit more dangerous levels, the panels will cut the field."

"What if we don't want that?" Drew said, scowling. The expression still looked strange on the man's youthful face. "I wanted to keep going after the alert, and you told me Myrtle did too. I don't want that machine to cut me off if I almost know where they are."

Ben glanced at Luis. Myrtle nodded, but she didn't look as distressed as Drew.

"We have to be careful, Drew," Luis said. "This is a first-rate medical facility, one of the best I've ever worked in. I'm including my training days in that. But one reason is so you can have less staff here, right, Ben?"

"He's right. We're so remote it can take weeks to get specialized help. Years in the case of someone like Luis. They handle the most serious injuries to the miners on the orbital med station. So we have as much automated down here as we possibly can."

Luis nodded. "That helps us, and Ben is an excellent nurse. If we run into real trouble, though, we'll be on our own. We can call out for assistance, sure. But we can't take too many risks, Drew."

The Becalmed man put his fists on his hips and stared at the ground. His cheeks were red, and his voice trembled when he spoke.

"I just don't like everything automatic like that. Can't you fix it so Tegwin can override it, or you, Ben?"

Tegwin touched Drew's shoulder. He twitched, but didn't move away.

"I'm going to tell you something I'm really not supposed to. I'm pretty sure you already know, though. The reason the Becalmed don't work in the mines or any other dangerous operation is because you don't seem to have fear. Without that, you can get into a life-threatening situation that you wouldn't otherwise. Or put other people into danger even when you don't mean to."

"We do know that," Helen said, her voice barely above a whisper. "We don't want to hurt anyone."

Drew looked up at Tegwin. He dropped his hands to his sides.

"We could get you under the field to ask you this," Tegwin said, "but I'm hoping you'll just tell me the truth. Do you think you've changed enough to be afraid for your life, Drew? Afraid for your mind?"

The Becalmed man sat heavily on an exam table, holding his head in his hands. Luis watched his shoulders rise and fall slowly, but he could hear those breaths. He would have bet a year's salary what Drew was going to say.

Luis would have won that bet.

"That's the part I don't like out of all of this," Drew said. "I'm scared to *death* most of the time. Every shadow makes me jump at night, every breeze and noise. My chest stays tight and my muscles hurt. I keep thinking about bad things that could happen to Helen and Myrtle and Willis, and to all of you. I'm afraid this part will keep getting worse. I'll be too fearful to even leave my house."

"I think a lot of that will get better," Luis said, standing in front of Drew. "Lighter, easier to deal with over time. You might not remember this, but when you were under the field, I asked you to take in a deep breath and blow out, like you were letting some of the anger pass through you. Can you try that?"

Drew breathed in, his chest hitching a few times, then breathed out in a loud hiss. He looked up at Luis with tears standing in his eyes.

"I feel a little bit better. How'd you know to do that?"

"Our bodies are every bit as involved with emotion as our brains are. You have to learn how to work with the physical responses to help with the emotional ones. And, I knew because I have decades of practice. That's all."

Luis sat on an exam bed, taking his own deep breaths.

"Can you please put in an override, Ben? So you or Tegwin will have to make the choice to stop the field?"

Tegwin stared into Luis's eyes, then Drew's and Myrtle's. Myrtle sat on the third bed, nodding again.

Tegwin shrugged and turned to Ben.

"Go ahead. They all look scared to death to me. That's probably right where they should be."

She helped with their sensor nets, then helped Ben activate the monitoring on all the beds. Luis had already explained everything that was different about the dual field, but he couldn't stop himself from going through it again.

He knew he'd be eternally grateful to Tegwin and Ben for listening instead of telling him to shut up.

"This will take both of you. Start the brain mapping for each of us. Once that's done, start the fourth sensor. Then you can activate the deep field. The fourth sensor will coordinate and show you what's happening, what's matching up among us."

"Will do," Tegwin said. "We'll keep watch over all of you. If you get into trouble, I'll use that override without hesitation."

Drew rolled his eyes, but he smiled at Luis. Humor added in now. They couldn't properly call him Becalmed, not any more.

"Starting the mapping," Ben said.

Luis tried to relax against the exam bed, which was every bit as comfortable as he'd imagined. Every part of his body felt cradled, weightless.

He wished his mind felt the same way.

"Baseline established." Tegwin turned the monitor so Luis could see it. "Drew's brainwaves aren't that different from yours now, and Myrtle's are a little higher. Any last advice?"

Luis tried to laugh, but his throat was too dry. He wanted to help the mysterious source of the signal, and he wanted to help the Becalmed. Even if that meant leaving most of them as they were and preventing more from being born to save the colony.

He wasn't sure he wanted to experience the nightmare that led more than a generation of Bitanthrans to block their emotions as some kind of self defense.

"Remind me that Drew and Myrtle are taking the lead at first," Luis said. "Then remind them to let me be in charge once in a while, too. Don't get too close to us, either. People usually don't move under deep psych, but that's another rule out the window."

She nodded, a half smile on her face. Luis's belly filled with heat far beyond a simple mission pairing. If he came through this deep psych with his mind intact, his heart was going to be in trouble.

"Safe journey, all of you," Tegwin said. "Starting field in three… two…one."

Chapter 22

THE PHYSICAL SENSATIONS of Luis's body faded away, one after the other. His back against the soft exam bed. The chilly air against his hands and face. Clothing, from his shirt and pants all the way down to the weight of his shoes. He knew he'd struggle to move his body right now if he tried, even though the Bitanthrans had managed.

His sense of smell increased, bringing in Tegwin's familiar scent, a lingering wood fire from Ben, and some kind of pipe Willis probably smoked at least an hour ago. His hearing did the same, picking up everyone's breathing and the smallest movements. His eyes were already closed.

He knew most of that would fade away just like his body's feelings had. The only thing that lingered by design brought Tegwin's voice.

"All of your readings look good. I'm entering the sequence to bring Luis and Myrtle into the field together. Then we'll add Drew if all goes well."

Luis focused on opening his brain, as if he could physically pull down the barrier of his skull. The feeling increased until a tingling sensation moved throughout his mind, spreading slowly through his body.

He forced himself to breathe deeply through increased fear, and greatly increased anger. If these were normal levels for Myrtle and the other typical Bitanthrans, it was no wonder they had such a fierce reputation.

"Both of you still with me?" Tegwin said.

"Still here." Luis heard Myrtle say something along the same lines.

"Your emotional readings are up, Luis, but not at critical levels. Be ready in case Drew brings in a whole lot more. He's coming online now."

Luis gasped before he could stop himself. This time it wasn't just fear and anger that jumped, though those spiked white hot into his head and chest. Joy, dread, impatience, amusement, even lust surged through him. He hadn't been such a hurricane of emotion since he was a young teenager back on Earth.

"Everything just jumped," Tegwin said. Luis tried to control a burst of desire for her, hoping his body didn't respond without his permission. "How you doing, Luis?"

"I'm fine. Trying to hang on. We'll have a lot more training and adjustment with Drew once we're done here."

Luis thought he heard Myrtle mutter something like good before all of his attention turned to something new. Something alien.

"Picking up a new reading," Luis said. "Maybe our signal."

"Myrtle, can you focus on what you felt before?" Tegwin said. "Drew, can you do the same?"

The faint sensation, like a whisper in another room, turned up loud and clear. Luis couldn't find one clear feeling, one clear being, to hold on to. His mind plunged into a million shifting bits of sand.

"So many," Luis said. "All at once. Is that what you're feeling?"

"Too many to count." Myrtle's voice was soft and airy. "Nothing to grab hold of."

"Can you bring Luis closer?" Tegwin said. "Show him more?"

The *many* sensation intensified, prickling all over Luis's flesh. He thought his arms and legs shifted, but it was too distant to catch.

"Can't get closer," Drew said. His disappointment raged through Luis, nearly bringing him to tears. "Not like before."

"We're going to try Bitan in a second," Tegwin said. "Take a few breaths for me first. Try to calm that response before we go deeper."

Luis realized he was breathing hard and fast, and he was sure his fists were clenched. A giant pit of agonizing heat tore through his middle. Certainty that they'd never succeed, no matter how hard they tried.

He heard Drew and Myrtle breathe when he did. One, two, three times.

"You're doing great, Drew," Luis said, trying to convince himself. "You too, Myrtle."

"You all are," Tegwin said. "Bringing the Bitan toward you now."

Luis's mind *jumped*, propelled at unknowable velocity and distance. The many feeling resolved, turning from sand into countless tiny bubbles. The abrasive scratching disappeared, but now he was drowning in terror and fury.

"What…what are you?" he whispered, pushing the words out through his mind. "What happened to you?"

Whispering, like rain in a forest or the white noise field, filled his head. Luis couldn't find a single word or thought to hold out of billions.

"More Bitan," he said, not sure if his voice was loud enough to cut through the whispering. "Need a stronger field."

"Going up one size." He recognized Tegwin's voice, but she sounded underwater. "Watching your brain levels, though. Getting close to red."

Luis sucked in air as he was pushed forward again, and this time he knew Myrtle and Drew were with him. He could feel them, the color and shape of their thoughts.

One whisper grew louder than the rest, and he realized he could hear thoughts.

But not from Drew or Myrtle. These didn't feel remotely human.

Each word, each syllable came from a different consciousness. Luis felt his brain struggling to translate raw emotions into words.

Trapped. Terrified. Dark. Forgotten. Buried.

"Who are you?" Tears rolled down his cheeks. "How can we help you?"

Bury us more and more. Don't even know we're alive. Invisible. Unseen. Draining our life away.

Luis's chest and stomach felt crushed, pressed in from all sides. The bubbles he'd sensed earlier boiled now, abrading him worse than the sand ever could have.

"Help me reach toward them," he said in a rough voice. "Find something we can recognize."

"Find the anger." Myrtle's voice boiled the same as Luis's flesh. "The fury. This way."

The pressure and scraping intensified into heat, heat that felt like Myrtle and finally like Drew. Luis slipped into the raging current, leaving all of his training and experience and civility and humanity behind.

He was all fire and rage and velocity, compression and suffocation and darkness.

A piercing noise jerked a sliver of his awareness back. The brain activity alerts he'd insisted Ben set.

"That's it, all three of you are in the red." Tegwin's voice spiraled and twisted, touching Luis and floating away. "Dropping the field in-"

"No!" Three throats, one voice, one mind. "Almost there!"

A low, grinding ping, repetitive and harsh, joined the singing alarm.

"Okay, that's my monitors." Ben. Warped and fluttery, nearly impossible to grasp. "Body temperature dropping, along with heart rate and respiration. Time to cut it."

"More Bitan, please," Luis said, begging Myrtle and Drew to help raise his voice. "One more push. Let us find them. They're running out of time!"

Luis had no sense of time to tell how long Tegwin delayed. Anywhere from a nanosecond to millennia were the same to him. He and Myrtle and Drew within still sang with relief when she spoke.

"Turn up the heat in the room, Ben. On the beds, too. You have one minute, Luis. Less if I hear one more alarm. Make it count."

Luis wasn't sure if he spoke with his throat or only inside his mind.

"Drew, you have to lead us. Don't be afraid, don't hesitate like we would. Throw us. Throw us as hard as you can."

The clammy, shadowed cloud of fear shrank down to nothing, replaced with a glowing blue shower of pure joy and enthusiasm. Luis felt himself contract along with Drew and Myrtle, shrinking far past where their bodies could have fit, beyond where their conscious thoughts could exist.

The three of them slipped into a stream of that darkening blue, shading into green, pressure behind them building with explosive force.

Beyond wind.

Beyond water.

Beyond the speed of anything but light.

They shattered into a consciousness as many as the stars, as the atoms in the galaxy, the universe.

Branching out together, linking through the land and sea and stone. Making up the solid ground, the earth that sustains an entire world.

They weren't on that soil, or even in it.

They *were* that soil, every particle and molecule.

"Tell us how to help you. How to find you."

Stop them crushing us. Forcing us to suffocate and die. Draining the life away from us, drop by drop.

"Extraction. Water. Something. Destroying life they don't even know is there."

The fury Myrtle led them to shifted, changed, faster than Luis could react. Shock to fear, faintest hope to brightest exultation.

The touch of Myrtle and Drew dissolved into a multitude, amplified into the frantic grasp of recognition.

You see. You feel. You are here.

Luis's voice, his thoughts, echoed and rebounded far more than he and Myrtle and Drew could have ever imagined.

"We can find you. We'll stop them hurting you. We have to go now."

The answering shriek sent Luis recoiling, slipped the tiniest strand of nerves back to his body.

He heard the last alarm braying impossibly far away.

"If we die back there, no one will ever find you. Remember my voice, all our voices. Let us go so we can help you."

Desperate pulling, wanting to shred them away from their fading bodies. Resistance Luis could not fight holding all of them. Drowning them beside the billions they'd finally found.

Myrtle screamed forward, her rage and joy magnificent as it was terrifying. Luis leapt into her.

Taking the rage as his own.

Following the blinding path she blazed.

He could only hope Drew followed.

Chapter 23

Luis heaved and gasped, trying to remember how flesh and bones and lungs worked after an eternity away. He squeezed his eyes shut against the glaring lights, tried to draw away from the overheated air on his drenched skin.

"Luis! Cut the field, Tegwin, now!"

Someone touched his forehead, hands cool and soft against his flesh.

"The sensors cut it a few seconds ago," Tegwin said. "See how Myrtle and Drew are doing. Luis? Back with me?"

"Almost. Can't work out how to breathe yet."

"Same way you always have." She touched his chest and his stomach. "In and out. Sounds like you found something."

Luis concentrated on the gentle pressure of her hands, pushing down, relaxing. He heard Willis talking to Myrtle, and Ben and Helen talking to Drew.

"Something, yeah. No idea what."

"Tell me before you forget." Tegwin cupped his cheeks with her palms. She spoke over her shoulder, reminding the others to ask the same question. "The recording is still going, and I'm not letting you or anyone else go through that again."

Luis did the best he could, talking even as the surreal experience faded from his mind and body.

"Extraction," Tegwin said. "Water, or something like petrol, maybe?"

"I'm not sure about that part. They felt like, well, like they were part of the planet. Part of the earth, the soil. Anything on the surface or under it could feel like extraction to them. I know this whole thing sounds nuts, and I'm afraid it doesn't help us much with finding them."

Tegwin smiled, looking sideways at Luis, the glance that melted his heart right before he went under. She handed him a warm mug, instantly taking possession of the rest of him.

"What part of this whole mission hasn't been at least out of the ordinary? You happen to know someone with access to TransGalactic's records. Planetary liaison and all. I'd say we need to start about thirty years ago, from when the first Becalmed were born."

Luis swallowed all the stimulant at once, groaning as it drove the last chills from his fingers and toes.

"This place could have been colonized for decades before that. There have to be dozens of new colonies in all that time. Hundreds."

"I'm sure there are. But we know exactly when every one of them went online with Bitan. That's an instantaneous connection, remember? And an expensive one, not available to a small or failing colony, especially so long ago. That cuts the numbers considerably."

Drew stood, holding on to Helen for a second before he walked to Luis's bed. He looked far more stable than Luis felt.

"I think we'd recognize them," he said. "Don't you? The way they feel, what they say."

"Maybe. Only if we talk to a person planetside, though. I don't want to do that again."

"When can you have the list of colonies?" Myrtle said. She was still on the exam bed, Willis sitting with his arm around her. "So we can get started?"

"I'll start the search in the morning," Tegwin said. "Ben, you told us anyone in town would be happy to feed us. If you can find someone to handle this whole group, we'd certainly appreciate it. No arguments. Nothing else happens until everyone gets a good night's sleep."

Chapter 24

Tegwin's low voice dragged Luis out of a dreamless sleep, deep enough that his stiff arms and legs told him he hadn't turned over all night. Not since he and Tegwin had finally fallen asleep, at least.

The trouble he'd sensed had bloomed full force throughout his heart and mind as soon as he held Tegwin's warm body to his own. Weeks away from the end of this mission, and Luis was already dreading the separation. He hadn't made the mistake of getting overly attached since his first couple of pairings decades ago.

Light from the wrong side of the bed confused him for a moment. Everything was reversed in the tiny space. Seating area, kitchen, front door. He didn't remember going into Tegwin's apartment rather than his own, but the pile of TransGalactic blue bags rather than his black ones confirmed it.

She sat by the small round kitchen table by the windows, holo display activated in front of her, note tablet in hand. Instead of talking to someone on the comm like he'd thought, she was muttering to herself.

The scent of fresh coffee coming from the huge mug on the table brought Luis all the way into consciousness.

"Good morning." He sat up, stretching his back. "How long was I out?"

"About ten sweeps, same as the rest of us. Want coffee?"

Rather than answer, Luis grabbed his robe from the foot of the bed and walked into the kitchen. He poured a mug for himself with equal parts coffee and Ben's stimulant drink, then refilled Tegwin's cup.

"Find anything?"

She turned the tablet toward him as she took a long drink.

"Fifty-seven colonies came online with Bitan within our time-frame," she said. "Several were lifeless worlds, no more than rock with a rudimentary atmosphere. I've pulled out thirty-three as likely targets for our signal."

Luis scrolled through the list, wondering if some kind of new sense would alert him to the right one. If it was, he was missing the signal.

"I'd guess there will be some kind of biomass," he said. "Existing long before any colonists arrived. A form we may not recognize as sentient."

"From what all three of you said, I expect it will be diffuse. A hive intelligence, even more so than Earth ants or honeybees."

Luis sighed, rubbing his arms.

"That's still a lot to try to sort through without throwing ourselves out there again."

Tegwin grinned, then walked to the food prep pod. Less than thirty seconds later, she sat a plate in front of Luis. Light brown toast, applesauce, and the delicious scrambled chicken eggs he couldn't get enough of, all at the perfect temperature.

"There are a few more secrets planetary liaisons keep from the general public. You know how the larger pieces of Bitan amplified your deep psych field? They work the same way with communications. Most ships, comm units, and colonies hold the smallest amount needed to get them onto the network. A flagship like the *Bountyfield* holds considerably more."

"That can't make the signal faster," Luis said. "It's already instan-taneous."

"No, not faster. Stronger, though, able to carry a much heavier signal with more information. Multiple channels in simultaneous use. You never notice the limitations until you operate through one of the bigger arrays. I suspect we can adjust that signal, make it diffuse enough to target an entire colony instead of the comm links."

Luis took both of her hands in his.

"And you have the authority to make that adjustment, my dear Liaison Fairbrooke?"

She squeezed his hands and shrugged.

"Not directly, no. I was just finishing an emergency addendum to our official request. Between that and the recordings from last night, I'm hoping TransG responds a lot more quickly than usual."

"Everyone else gave permission? Myrtle and Drew did?"

"Last thing last night, right after you crashed. Ben sent the notice over before I had a chance to ask."

Before Luis finished his breakfast, Tegwin's comm chimed through. She switched the external sound on before answering.

"Everyone appropriate in there?" Ben said, and Luis could hear the smile in his voice.

"Appropriate and mostly alert," Tegwin said. "Everyone else good this morning?"

"We're great here. In fact, we'd appreciate it if you'd join us in the nurses' station. We've had some developments this morning that you might be interested in."

Luis thought about crossing the hall to his apartment for a change of clothes, but something in Ben's voice kept him from taking that much time. The last time the nurse had summoned Luis, it had been for a room full of Bitan worth more than most planetary incomes.

Ben waited with Myrtle and Willis, Helen and Drew. If anyone noticed his robe, no one said a word. A video comm was displayed on the large central screen, with the TransGalactic logo front and center.

"We're ready here, *Bountyfield*," Ben said, speaking toward the screen. "Please replay the command message for Dr. Ahmad and Liaison Fairbrooke, then we'll stand by."

The blue and gold logo dissolved, revealing Ben's father and a woman Luis didn't recognize. She wore a TransGalactic command uniform, like Tegwin's but decorated with various symbols and several gleaming metallic insignia. Her age was impossible to guess as part of a hypersleep fleet, but her short hair was more silver than black.

"Commander Holbruck," Tegwin whispered. "Chief of the Deep Space Fleet."

"Good morning," Commander Holbruck said with a nod. "I've been briefed on the progress of your mission, Liaison Fairbrooke and Dr. Ahmad, including your official request. Director of Mine Operations Essena joined us today with most interesting recordings from a recent group psych-hypnosis session."

She turned to Ben's father.

"I believe these recordings will allow us to better understand and address the risks to ongoing Bitan operations," he said, "and more importantly, to the stability of our colony. All of us on Bitanthra and throughout the AlliedSystems express our gratitude for your efforts so far, and our hopes of moving forward."

"After careful consideration," the commander said, "I'm directing TransGalactic to put all necessary resources at your immediate disposal. We await your response."

After several seconds of silence, Luis laughed out loud and caught Tegwin in a hug. Everyone else joined in, with Drew louder and more boisterous than the rest.

Only Helen stood to the side, a tiny smile on her face.

"You did it," Luis said. "We all did it! How did you get your father to go up there, Ben?"

"We had a chat last night is all. He's up half the night whenever a freighter's loading anyway. Once he heard the recordings, he asked for those and all our other data. I didn't know he was going topside until this came through a few minutes ago."

"Speaking of topside," Tegwin said, jerking her chin at the screen. "Commander Holbruck, ma'am. Director Essena. Thank you for your attention and quick response."

Luis fought the urge to run back to his apartment, settling for pulling his robe closer to hide more of his sleep shirt. His spiky, messy hair would just have to do.

"The possibility of a decades-long violation of a sentient species is too serious to send through normal corporate channels," the commander said. "Whether the settlers are aware of the problem or not. What do you propose, Liaison?"

Tegwin pulled her comm tablet out and touched the screen.

"Sending our emergency addendum now, ma'am. I've gathered a list of possible colonies, all coming online within the required time-frame. I propose adjusting the Bitan array on the *Bountyfield* to a diffuse target of the entire planet, and transmitting while subjects here are under the deep psych field."

"Not the same field as last night?" Ben's father said. "Sounded to me like you were in physical distress."

Tegwin turned to Luis, eyebrows raised.

"No, sir," he said. "With the assistance of the larger array, we should be able to employ a normal field. Assuming our subjects here agree?"

Drew grinned, stepping forward beside Luis. He bounced on his feet, like he was struggling not to jump toward the screen.

"Yes sir and yes ma'am. I'll do anything I can to help Dr. Ahmad."

Myrtle smiled and nodded, and Willis did the same at her side.

"Helen?" Ben said, holding his hand out to the Becalmed woman.

She waited against the wall for a long moment, staring at the screen. She finally stepped between Ben and Drew, but she was shaking her head.

"I'm sorry. I can't. I want to help, I do. But I don't want to change any more than I already have. I want to stay Becalmed."

"We won't force any of you," Commander Holbruck said. "Every citizen of Bitanthra will make their own choices in this delicate matter. We all thank you for your efforts to save your colony."

Helen nodded and slipped into the background again.

"I'll review your proposal, Liaison Fairbrooke," the commander said. "And bring the Bitan array chief and crew in to consult immediately. Everything sounds reasonable at the moment. We will have to operate within a tight schedule with our array offline, at the chief's discretion. Please be prepared to act quickly during that timeline."

"Yes, ma'am," Tegwin said. "Thank you both."

When the screen went blank, she turned to Luis. Her kiss fired his chest and every other part of him into full, vibrant life.

"Ready to work up another protocol, Dr. Ahmad?"

"As fast as I can write it."

Chapter 25

For the first time in his life, Luis went through planetary deceleration without a trace of complaint from his normally unruly stomach.

The passenger transport vessel *Zortea* was nowhere near as vast or as new as the *Bountyfield*. But as the passenger flagship for Trans-Galactic, the *Zortea's* accommodations were more comfortable and luxurious.

Rather than huddling in the lowliest crew quarters, Luis relaxed in one of the spacious VIP recovery suites. The bedroom was larger than his apartment back on Bitanthra, with a warm air suspension bed and fragrant thermal baths and shower.

He'd been unable to resist combining earthy patchouli with sharp pine in his bath, trying to recapture the air of the Bitan homeworld. Much to his surprise, he enjoyed the results enough to record the recipe for future use.

Part of Luis resisted all the decadence, thinking back to the rock-hard bunks and solid metal walls that had seen him through countless queasy re-entries over the decades. He didn't actually need plas-screen walls set to preview each environmental zone of the destination planet, scenes from a distant homeworld, or anything else the occupant desired.

The foggy mountains of Bitanthra surrounded him at the moment.

He could certainly get by without mood-sensing crystalline lighting from Outer Rigia, or ambient music tuned to his waking bio-rhythms.

Luis also knew better than to argue with TransGalactic when they insisted on providing such posh accommodations. And he had to admit he'd miss them on future missions now that he was able to enjoy the experience. He had at least a few years before he had to worry about that.

He'd left the polished wooden door open, so he heard movement in the dining area beyond. After a lifetime of hypersleep travel, Luis and his growling stomach were looking forward to his first expertly prepared recovery meal from the best chefs in any fleet in the galaxy.

The scent of coffee mixed with Ben's stimulant brew finally got Luis moving. He savored the way his toes sank into the thick Tafeya-fiber rugs, how the lighting shifted from warm reds to brighter blues as he moved.

The suite's airlock door was just closing as Luis entered the dining room, and his heart leapt at the sight of Tegwin waiting for him. She sat on the far side of a huge round table laden with dishes and bowls all covered with copper, gold, and silver domes.

She wore a green version of his purple Kayren silk robe, the color setting off the red tones in her hair perfectly. Luis felt like he hadn't seen her in far longer than the six years of hypersleep.

"Good to see you, Director Ahmad."

Luis caught her in a long hug and a peppermint-flavored kiss. The intense, fiery connection forged between them in the last weeks on Bitanthra hadn't waned at all from his perspective.

"Good to see you, Director Fairbrooke. Do your duties as head of diplomatic relations for the Gosijune System still include briefing a lowly psych officer on changes while we were in transit?"

"Only for the head of tele-psych operations. Everyone else will have to find an overworked and underappreciated planetary liaison."

"If they've assigned any yet," Luis said, sitting beside her. "Have the colonists agreed to resettlement terms?"

"Everyone who wanted to leave has already gone. All ground-based infrastructure has been removed, restoring the ground cover and bio-mass to their original states."

She bit into an orange fruit with pink flesh held in one hand while changing the dining room's plas-screens with the other. A lush, tropical world replaced Bitanthra's rocky landscapes. Thick beds of blue moss surrounded lower, flatter areas taking on paler shades of the same coloration. In the distance, towering black and purple plants ringed the open space.

"The Gosijunes are recovering," she said. "Slowly but surely. A few of those trees are sprouting in the more temperate zones. The polar ice caps are receding too, getting back to their original size. As far as we can tell, that's still the only area on the whole planet where their colony organism hasn't penetrated."

"How did TransGalactic set up landing ports?"

"Turns out as long as our hover platforms move enough to allow the entire surface to get sunlight, the Gosijunes do just fine. We have a system of twenty landing ports and thirty residential bases so far. The orbital facilities bring the total accommodations up to nearly five thousand."

"And Bitanthra?"

She smiled and laughed under her breath. Luis hoped they'd have a little time alone before it was time for the drop to the surface. Once they'd finished eating, of course.

"Drew is bursting with wanting to talk to you. He's been in nearly constant contact with the Gosijunes. His emotional training went wonderfully. Ben says he'll always be exuberant and sometimes a bit moody, but he's handling all of the changes himself now. He's actually expecting his second child with a typical Bitanthran woman. Ben's expecting his third."

Luis shook his head, trying to imagine Drew staying calm while keeping up with toddlers and later teenagers.

"They'll both make wonderful fathers. Sounds like the birth rate is recovering."

"Back to normal levels. Before the Becalmed."

"How's Helen doing? Still their liaison?"

Tegwin paused long enough to finish her stimulant-coffee mix and pour herself another.

"This is wonderful stuff. I'll have to put in for a bonus for Ben. Helen is still the Becalmed liaison, yes. To tell you the truth, I think she's a little sad that no more were born once we made contact with the Gosijunes. Sad as she can be, anyway. She's doing a great job coordinating the ones who want deep psych treatment."

Luis helped himself to a second serving of loretfish lox, the perfect balance of spicy and sweet too good to resist.

"Double that bonus for Ben with my authorization. Thanks to him and his magic herbal brew, I finally understand why people eat so much after hypersleep. How many of the Becalmed are seeking treatment now?"

"Looks like it will stabilize at around thirty percent for any level of treatment. About a quarter of that stops at the mild adjustment Helen has. Seventy percent end up in the middle ranges. Only five percent go as far as Drew and full emotional restoration. He's convinced more will return for higher levels once they get to know him better."

"He's probably right." Luis watched the plas-screen shifting to an arid region covered with fuzzy mats of brilliant yellow growth. He was afraid of the answer to his next question. "How long will your assignment here be, Tegwin?"

She stared into her bowl of steaming tri-grain porridge for several seconds.

"Setting up a new diplomatic outpost is quite different from a run of the mill liaison mission. This won't be a typical outpost either, not with the coordination of Gosijune telepathy and the Bitan network. We'll be assisting with your tele-psych training program, too, scaling that up once you develop the protocols."

She ducked her head and looked sideways at Luis, melting his heart all over again.

"How does four years sound?"

"Like we're about to land in paradise."

ABOUT KARI

A science fiction fan from the first time she caught a grainy black and white rerun of *Lost in Space*, Kari Kilgore's wanderlust and imagination lead her all over the world on grand adventures. Her heart and family bring her home to her native Appalachian Mountains of Virginia. From that solid base, she and her husband Jason A. Adams bring those adventures to life in fiction.

Kari writes science fiction, fantasy, romance, and contemporary fiction, and she's happiest when she surprises herself. She lives at the end of a long dirt road in the middle of the woods with Jason, various house critters, and wildlife they're better off not knowing more about.

The Confidential Adventure Club

For Kari's exclusive free After The End stories and deleted scenes, discounts, early pre-sale releases, adorable pet photos, and a whole lot more not available anywhere else, pay a visit to The Confidential Adventure Club at www.smarturl.it/c-a-club.

Hope to see you there!

www.karikilgore.com
www.spiralpublishing.net

ALSO BY KARI KILGORE

I hope you enjoyed *Dispatches from the Galaxy* as much as I enjoyed writing it. For more space opera and galactic empire stories, be sure to keep an eye out for Dispatches from the Galaxy at www.dispatchesfromthegalaxy.com.

For more science fiction from both me and Jason A. Adams, visit Spiral Publishing's Science Fiction page at www.spiralpublishing.net/book-tag/science-fiction.

Be the first to know about release dates and check out more of my fiction across almost every genre at www.karikilgore.com.

The Confidential Adventure Club

Want more fiction from Kari, including stories, discounts, and box sets not available anywhere else? Want to hear about locations, research, and other cool things that inspired this story and beyond? Want all that and adorable pet photos, too?

Join The Confidential Adventure Club and get a thank you gift of a free short story and a whole lot more at www.smarturl.it/c-a-club.

Hope to see you there!

Dispatches from the Galaxy Stories:

Restricted Species

The Becalmed

The Garbage Belt

Plurapod Pathogen

The Changes Cascade

The Storms of Future Past Series:

Dreaming the Storm

Joining the Storm

Into the Storm

Fighting the Storm

Sensing the Storm: A Storms of Future Past Prequel Story

Storms of the Heart: A Storms of Future Past Romance

Storms of Future Past Books One through Four Collection

The Voices through Time Series:

Songs in the Mountain

Secrets in the Land

Walking the Ghosts: A Voices through Time Novella

Terminalia Short Stories:

Terminalia

Little Five

Novels:

Until Death

The Dream Thief

Hand Me Downs

Novellas:

Legacy of the Land

In the Pines

DNA Never Lies

Collections:

Fantastic Women: A Dark Fantasy Novella Trio

Fantastic Shorts: Volume 1

Near Future Forward (with Jason A. Adams)

Fantastic Shorts: Volume 2

Partners in Romance (with Jason A. Adams)

www.ingramcontent.com/pod-product-compliance
Lightning Source LLC
Chambersburg PA
CBHW051843180726
48284CB00007BA/2027